I0692060

Point of View

by

Suzanne Rossi

Point of View

Cover Art by *Kim Mendoza*

The Wild Rose Press, Inc.
PO Box 708
Adams Basin, NY 14410-0708
Visit us at www.thewildrosepress.com

Publishing History
First Crimson Rose Edition, 2017
Print ISBN 978-1-5092-1746-5
Digital ISBN 978-1-5092-1747-2

Published in the United States of America

I kept my eyes glued on the sketch, refusing to look at the others, afraid of what I might give away.

"Is that better?" Charlie asked.

I gazed at a woman in her late twenties or early thirties with a kittenish face. Mischief glowed from her eyes, and the smile said she enjoyed life. I wanted to cry. That love of life would be extinguished if we didn't find the killer first.

"The hair's a little fuller."

He made a few swift strokes with his pencil. "How about now?"

"Yes. That's the woman."

Charlie handed the sketchpad to Reed who studied it for a few seconds before handing it to Bobby Jack.

"Nice looking lady." He passed it on to Mike.

"I can see why the killer would choose her." The sketch made its way to Jill.

She held it in both hands. Her facial expression changed from curious to horrified and her eyes widened in disbelief. She gasped, her fingers tightening on the pad.

"Jill? What is it?" Mike demanded.

"I—I know her."

"What? Who is it?"

"It's Lisa."

"Lisa who?" Mike demanded.

"Lisa Parker. My sister."

**Other Suzanne Rossi titles
available from The Wild Rose Press, Inc.:**

*ALONG CAME QUINN
ALL IN THE FAMILY
A TANGLED WEB
NEARLY DEPARTED
HEAR NO EVIL
THE REUNION
DEADLY INHERITANCE
DEATH IS THE PITS
THROUGH MY EYES
A NOVEL DEATH
RENDEZVOUS WITH DEATH
THE GOOD TWIN* (2016 Maggie Award Winner)
*THE ASSASSIN
KILLER CONFERENCE
THE MURDER OF GRACE BRYANT*

Dedication

I never envisioned a sequel to *Through My Eyes*, but when a reviewer said she wanted to see more of Sasha and Reed, it sounded like a good idea. Even though the end of the book had the two of them on the road to happily ever after, I could see conflict in having them split up. I also saw a chance for upping the emotional ante of everyone involved. Plus, I did leave Linnie and Bill's relationship hanging. And so *Point of View* was born. And just to take this a bit farther down the road—what if Reed and Sasha opened a private investigation agency? Hmmm, a psychic PI. Interesting. A possible series? Perhaps. Thank you to Cindy O for giving me the glimmer of an idea or two.

Chapter One

I awoke panting and sweating from the nightmare, my fist pressed against my pounding heart, the beats echoing in my ears.

Not again. Oh, please God, not another one.

Like praying would help. It never did. The nightmares still arrived with sickening regularity.

I tossed back the covers and hurried to the bathroom on wobbly legs, then waited for my stomach to cramp like always. It didn't take long. I threw up and when I had myself under control again, staggered down the hall toward my office. The soft glow from the computer screen welcomed me as though it knew I'd be coming.

I pulled up my nightmare diary, entering the new information while it was still fresh in my mind. Fresh in my mind. What a silly phrase. The hideous dreams stayed vivid until the bodies were found, and then horrific reality replaced the mental images. Who was I kidding? I remembered every detail from every murder, clear and in living color. They never faded.

First, I had to decide if the nightmare was a possession-type where I viewed the events in real time through the eyes of the victim, or if it was one of the precognition dreams which gave us a week, maybe ten days, before the murder occurred. Since I had seen three separate locations, I deduced we had time to stop a tragedy.

I finished and reached for the phone. Bobby Jack needed to know another one was coming his way. It didn't matter that the clock read three o'clock in the morning. He'd know the instant he heard my voice that trouble laid ahead.

"'Lo?" he mumbled after the fourth ring.

"Bobby Jack, it's Sasha."

"Sasha?" He was silent for a moment, and then I heard the sheets rustle. "Please, tell me you're just lonely."

"I wish I could, but you know I'm not."

"Damn. Meet me at the station as soon as you can. I'll call Charlie. Are you all right?"

"Yeah, I guess so."

We hung up. I showered, dressed in the first clothing I found: a tattered pair of jeans, an Ole Miss sweatshirt, and cowboy boots. I grabbed my coat, car keys, and hit the road, driving through the dark Mississippi night as fast as I dared.

A stiff wind blew from the north. Cold rain fell. The rhythmic slap of my windshield wipers had a hypnotic effect, making me long to close my eyes. I turned on the radio and ignored the whoosh-whoosh, concentrating instead on what I'd tell the police.

Robert Jackson "Bobby Jack" Beauregard was a homicide detective with the Memphis Police Department. I'd known and worked with him for close to three years.

For years, I'd kept the secret of my psychic abilities between my psychiatrist and myself, but when I envisioned the murder of a young woman through the victim's eyes, I could no longer maintain the status quo.

It had been a frightening time. My powers had skyrocketed from simple ESP to full blown psychic prediction and beyond—some of which were still new. I had a hard time dealing with them.

Bobby Jack and I had been paired together shortly after the death of Jeff Hammond, a former cop and serial killer. I reported dreams and visions and he investigated. Sometimes we caught the bad guys, sometimes we didn't. We currently chafed at our inability to solve the last two murders.

Now, racing through the cold, blustery night, I wondered what tonight's vision would bring. Would we win or lose?

****

At five in the morning, I had no problem finding a parking space. Taking a deep breath, I entered the police station, rode the elevator to the second floor, then walked down a short hallway to the conference room and stepped inside.

"Morning, Miss Bellwood, wish I could say I'm glad to see you."

"Hi, Charlie. Me, too."

Charlie Kendall was a sculptor who volunteered as a police sketch artist. He had a great touch. The Memphis police used an excellent computer program for putting together the right hair, eyes, noses, and mouths of suspects, but Charlie's hand-drawn sketches added something extra, something that made the face more human—more identifiable. I'd worked with him four times in the last two years. Tall and thin, he often referred to himself as the poster boy for the starving artist, even though he made a decent living.

"How about some coffee?" he asked.

3

"Sounds great, one sugar, lots of cream. Where's Bobby Jack?"

"Checking missing persons."

"I hope it's too early for that."

"You know Bobby Jack, he likes to be proactive. He had a couple of new people in his office. Maybe you'll get some help this time. I'll be right back with the coffee."

Help? I didn't like the thought of new people being brought in. A rolling sense of discomfort surged through my psyche. Something was up.

I pulled out a chair from the table in the conference room, but was too antsy to sit. Instead, I walked over to the window and shivered, then let my gaze wander over the rain-slicked street two stories below.

Early February in Memphis usually had a split personality. One day the temperature would hover near sixty, and the next it would plunge into the lower forties. The last weather report had predicted possible sleet by noon with snow to follow.

Memphis drivers and snow just didn't get along.

Charlie reentered with my coffee. I turned from the bleak scene outside and flopped in the chair, warming my hands over the rising steam from the Styrofoam cup.

"Cold?"

"I'm always cold, especially after a nightmare."

I rubbed my hands together, and then picked up the cup, blew on the nearly boiling liquid, and took a cautious sip risking a scalded mouth. It was over-brewed and tasted of cardboard. I didn't care. At least it was hot.

The conference room door opened and Bobby Jack

walked in followed by a man and a woman, each carrying a similar Styrofoam container.

"Hi, Sasha. Really sorry to see you." He leaned over, kissing my cheek.

"Yeah, I know. How're Cindy and the kids?"

"Fine."

His brusque reply was strange, but I put it down to concern about why we were here.

Bobby Jack traced his lineage to the Civil War general, P.G.T. Beauregard, and in keeping with fine Southern tradition, had been christened after two other Confederate generals, Robert E. Lee and Stonewall Jackson.

He pulled out the chair across from me and set his cup along with several file folders in front of him. Bobby Jack looked like a man in the throes of sleep deprivation. Lines cut from his nose to the corners of his mouth and across his forehead as if hewn into granite. A slight redness in the whites of his eyes told me he either suffered from a chronic lack of shut-eye or was hitting the bourbon again. I decided on the former. Cindy wouldn't let him backslide. She understood being a cop had its ups and downs, but she'd kept him on an even keel for over seven years.

"Sasha, this is Mike Young and his partner Jill Conway. They're both new to this precinct. I've told them some about you, but would you like to fill in the gaps?"

I shook hands with the newcomers as they each took a seat, sensing hesitancy on her part and extreme reserve on his, as if he didn't quite know how to react to dealing with a psychic.

"And this is our sketch artist, Charlie Kendall,"

Bobby Jack continued.

Everybody nodded and repeated the greetings before turning their attention back to me.

"What kind of gaps do I need to fill in?"

"Bobby Jack said you're a psychic with precognitive powers," Jill said with a smile.

Petite, she looked no more than thirty-five years old with light brown hair and blue eyes. Her steady gaze was warm, inviting confidences.

I'll bet she's terrific during interrogations. I had the feeling I'd seen her in the station before, but wasn't sure. I rubbed a hand across my eyes. *Think about it later. There's too much going on at the moment.*

"He told us you have dreams that come true," Mike added. His voice had a neutral tone.

He didn't smile, and I immediately sensed skepticism. I judged his age at forty, maybe more, and his height somewhere between six feet and six-two. His dark brown hair showed a touch of gray at the temples. Chocolate brown eyes stared at me with a measuring expression.

"No, Detective Young, I have *nightmares* that come true." I tore my gaze away and sipped my coffee.

"How long have you had this ability?" Jill asked.

"I've had psychic abilities all my life. The nightmares are fairly new."

"How long have you been helping the police?" Mike said with a raised eyebrow.

"A little over three years."

I shot a glance at Bobby Jack who doodled on the cover of one of the folders. He didn't meet my eyes. My first instincts were right. Something was going on I didn't understand. Sweat dampened my palms. I closed my eyes, breathed in, and then exhaled slowly, opening my mind.

Turmoil bubbled within Bobby Jack. His emotions swirled, ebbing and flowing between anger, frustration, and resignation. I opened my eyes and our gazes met. Then, he closed his mental door.

"Miss Bellwood, are you all right?" Mike inquired in a low voice. "Are you in some kind of trance?"

Realizing he'd asked a question, I pulled out of Bobby Jack's head, and into his. Skepticism and outright hostility crowded his mind. The skepticism I understood, but the hostility pissed me off.

"No, Detective Young. I'm tired and a little dizzy. Low blood sugar. This is a police station. Aren't there any donuts around?"

Charlie laughed. "I'll go scrounge some up." He left the room.

"What did you ask?" I sipped more coffee. It had done its job. The bone-chilling cold I'd felt earlier was gone. I shrugged out of my coat and tossed it on the table.

"I asked why it took you so long to bring your abilities to the attention of the police."

"Because I didn't want to be labeled as a freak. I wanted friends. I wanted to go on dates and to the prom without the nickname 'Carrie' tattooed on my forehead."

"She worked with us on the Jeff Hammond case," Bobby Jack told him, not looking up from his drawing. "It's all in the files."

"I'm sure we can bring ourselves up to date later," Jill commented. "Tell us about this nightmare that's got me out of bed at such an outlandish hour." She drank some of her coffee and grinned.

She was good—damned good—at inviting trust. Her partner was another story. At the moment, however, I needed to forget my misgivings and give them a heads-up on what might soon happen. It wasn't about me. I gulped more coffee.

"First of all, you need to understand that I dream through the eyes of others. I see things from their point of view. Sometimes it's the victim, sometimes the killer. This time I saw things through his—the killer's—eyes."

"Or hers," Bobby Jack interjected.

"Or hers," I acknowledged, remembering Roberta Wilson who had murdered her husband. "This one begins with a woman on a jogging path."

"Can you identify where?" Mike said.

"No, it's in a park of some sort, and please don't interrupt. It destroys my train of thought. The woman is medium height with blonde hair worn in a ponytail. It swings back and forth through the opening in the back of the baseball cap she's wearing. At first, she's maybe fifty yards ahead of the killer, but gradually he closes the gap. He comes close but doesn't pass her."

I finished my coffee and set the cup aside. Young and Conway took notes.

"The scene changes to a mall parking lot. The woman is heading for her car, juggling several shopping bags. The killer is slowly walking toward the entrance. He watches, pays attention to her actions, and then strolls past her going in the opposite direction. The image is darkened as though he's wearing sunglasses and the view is partially obstructed with the bill of a cap."

"As if he knows her or is afraid she might recognize him," Bobby Jack murmured.

"Possibly. The scene shifts again to a sidewalk. I'm not sure where, but it's nighttime. The victim emerges from a building and walks to her car parked around the corner. Now, he strikes. He comes up from behind and grabs her around the neck. I...I see a flash of light like something reflecting off a shiny surface. I knife maybe. There's a street light on the corner, so most of what I see is in shadow. The scene ends. That's all."

"In other words, he escalates from stalking to violent action," Jill said with a frown. "Does he know her or is it a random thing?"

"I'm not sure."

"Do you see his face at any time?" Mike asked.

"I misspoke. I don't know if it's a man."

"All right, do you see the perp's face?"

I resented his ultra patient tone and answered with sarcasm. "Since there are no mirrors around, the answer is no."

"Does the woman put up a fight in this last scene?"

"No, she's too scared."

"How do you know that?" Jill wondered.

Damn, I hadn't meant to reveal that much. I folded my hands on the table in front of me.

"From the look on her face." I thought it sounded convincing.

Bobby Jack knew my powers included a lot more than visions and precognition, but not even he knew everything, and I sure as hell didn't want to clue in these new people until I trusted them.

Mike looked at me with a raised eyebrow. "How can you see the look on her face if you're viewing this through the perp's eyes? He's behind her, right?"

I ran a hand through my hair. "Okay, from her actions then. Look, can we just get on with this before I lose the images?"

"What about the locations? Does anything look familiar? When the victim's jogging, what's she wearing?" he asked.

"Gray sweatpants and a bright blue sweatshirt."

"Can you ID the mall? Is it Wolf Chase?" Jill inquired, naming the biggest mall in Memphis.

"Possibly. There's a lot of traffic and it's crowded."

Charlie returned carrying a box of donuts. I'd forgotten about his mission.

"Here you go. I finally found one with more than two donuts in it on the fourth floor. Eat fast before Burglary discovers they've been robbed."

Jill and Bobby Jack laughed as they grabbed for the goodies. I didn't. Neither did Mike. He sat back in his chair and hit me with a sharp gaze.

Before he could speak, Charlie said, "I need another cup of coffee. Can I get anyone else a refill?"

"I'll take one," Bobby Jack said.

The rest of us shook our heads. One cup of this awful brew was enough.

When he left, Young continued the interrogation. "The sidewalk where she's abducted—you said it was nighttime—any idea of where she's coming from?"

I met his gaze, reached for the box, grabbed a donut, and took a bite of a slightly stale glazed yeast before answering.

"No. It's just a building."

"How about an office? Do you see the building at

all?"

"It's two, maybe three stories, but I don't sense a lot of other people around, yet the parking spots on the street are full or nearly so."

"Sasha, where does the killer get the knife?" Bobby Jack asked, brushing powdered sugar from his shirt.

"Out of his coat pocket."

"Which side?"

"The right—he's right handed."

"Do you see his arm when he puts the knife to her throat? What color is the jacket?" Bobby Jack insisted.

"Brown distressed leather."

"Like a bomber jacket?" Mike suggested.

I nodded. "Yes, that might be it. The sleeve has a knit cuff and there's a small tear near the right elbow."

"Let's concentrate on the victim for a moment," Bobby Jack said. "Does she do anything unusual either before or during the attack?"

"Not really. She's wearing sunglasses while jogging, but doesn't turn her head to view her fellow runners."

"How about at the mall?" Jill asked.

"No, no awareness of anything other than getting her purchases into the trunk of the car. Her purse is sitting on the bumper, and she never looks up when the guy walks by."

"So she's committing the cardinal sin of not being on the look out for possible problems in a parking lot. Damn it, what is it with women who don't pay attention?" Mike snapped.

"Men aren't always so alert to their surroundings either," Jill told him in a frosty voice.

"Yeah, but when was the last time you heard of a

man being abducted from the mall?"

I crammed the remains of the donut into my mouth and massaged the area between my eyes. A small throb signaled the beginnings of a headache. Charlie returned with the coffee. I glanced at him, and then Bobby Jack.

"Sasha's getting tired," Bobby Jack commented. "She can only sustain this for a few hours. Why don't we get on with putting Charlie to work?"

"Good idea," I seconded.

Charlie gathered his sketchpad and pencils.

"Why don't you use the computer program for sketches?" Mike asked.

"Charlie is the best," I claimed. "I always do better with him than through the cyber world."

"How come?" Jill wanted to know.

"Charlie puts life into his drawings," Bobby Jack answered. "Sometimes, I wouldn't recognize my own wife from those computer generated images."

"Thank you for the glowing commendations," Charlie said with a smile as he sharpened a pencil. "Are you ready to begin?"

I nodded and scooted my chair closer to his side.

"What shape face?"

"Oval," I replied. A few quick stokes produced the outline of a face.

"Eyes?"

"Kind of slanted, and blue or gray, I think."

"You dream in color?" Jill asked.

"Most of the time. The more horrific the murder, the brighter the colors."

"And how bright were the colors tonight?" her partner asked.

"Not very. In fact, just the clothing came through

in what I'd call vivid hues." I spoke slowly. I had no idea why the nightmare had gray tones.

"Then how do you know the color of the woman's eyes?" Young challenged.

My patience with this guy was running thin. "I don't know for sure. It's simply an impression. Can we get on with this? I want to be as accurate a possible."

We worked our way through the nose, mouth, and eyebrows before stopping to review.

"The chin is more squared," I said. Charlie erased, and then filled in again. "Yes, that's better. But the eyes are too close together."

We all sat silently as Charlie worked. Slowly, the eyes widened.

"Ears?" he asked.

"Average, I guess. There wasn't anything remarkable about them. I mean, they didn't stick out."

Charlie sketched, and then said, "What about the hair? You said it was in a pony tail?"

"Only in the park. It was loose the other times."

"How long?"

"Long—past her shoulders with the ends curly."

"Any part in the hair?"

"Yes." I closed my eyes for a moment to remember before opening them again. "On the left. The locks tend to fall into her right eye. She's constantly brushing them back."

Jill shifted in her seat and frowned.

"Color?" he asked.

"Blonde." I shot Young a glance. "Maybe that's why I assumed the woman had light colored eyes."

He didn't respond.

Charlie worked for the next ten minutes, adding

facial expressions at my direction. Still something was missing, some spark that would bring the portrait to life.

"It's her eyes," I finally told him. "The emotion isn't quite there."

"Which emotion?" he questioned.

"I'm not sure."

"If you're seeing this through the killer's eyes, I'd think the emotion would be fear," Mike said.

The flat tone had me glancing at his face once again. He skewered me with narrowed eyes. I'd let myself slip. I shouldn't have any knowledge of the woman's emotions the killer hadn't seen.

"Yes, of course there's fear, but that won't help us. We need to know how she looks at any given moment. I'm trying to draw on the mall scene. There isn't much to go on," I explained hastily.

Bobby Jack cut me a look, and then opening one of the folders in front of him, pulled his gaze away. Mike caught it. A gleam of speculation showed in his eyes. Jill scrutinized all of us.

I squirmed in my chair, and glanced at the clock on the wall. It was after six o'clock, and I was dog-tired.

Too tired—I'm making mistakes.

Mike Young already suspected I wasn't telling all I knew, and I think the light had dawned on Jill Conway, too.

Suddenly, the door to the room opened and Detective Reed McIntyre, my ex-fiancé, entered. Stunned, my gaze locked on his craggy face. A familiar surge of heat coiled in my belly. Even after two and a half years, his mere entrance into a room sent my heart rate up.

"I'm sorry, this is a private consultation. You'll have to leave," Young said in a sharp voice, a scowl on his face.

Reed stared back with an impassive expression and hard blue eyes, but said nothing.

Bobby Jack waved his hand. "That's all right." He introduced Reed to the new detectives. "Reed works with cold cases. I called him."

"Why? This isn't a cold case," Young said.

"He's worked with Sasha before. I thought he might be of help on this one."

I tore my gaze from Reed. Something was definitely going on. I'd only worked with Reed once, and it had almost gotten him, my psychiatrist, Linnie Anderson, and me killed.

While I had no problem reading Reed's emotions—concern for me and irritation with Young—Bobby Jack's mind remained closed.

"Bobby Jack, why would you call Reed? What's going on?" I demanded as Reed pulled out a chair and sat next to me.

Bobby Jack cleared his throat. "Sasha, I didn't tell you earlier, but you won't be working with me on this one. Mike and Jill are taking over for a while." His eyes finally met mine.

"Why?"

"Departmental changes."

"What departmental changes?"

"I'll explain later," Mike said.

I faced him. "Explain now."

"The captain thinks you and Bobby Jack are becoming too close to be objective," Mike told me in blunt terms.

"What?" I jerked my head toward Bobby Jack who shrugged. "That's nuts. We work very well together."

"The point is, the last two times this happened, you didn't find the killer. The Captain thinks new blood, two pairs of fresh eyes, might bring a different perspective to the situation," Jill said. "I have to admit, this psychic thing is new to me. I've never actually dealt with someone with your abilities, but I'm not necessarily a skeptic either."

I shot a glance at her partner. "What about you? I sense a lot of hostility."

"You seem to sense a lot of things, Miss Bellwood."

I didn't like the sarcastic tone, but refrained from saying anything.

"However, in answer to your question—yes, I'm a skeptic, but then I tend to look at everything with a skeptical eye. I automatically think people are liars."

"Are you suggesting Sasha's lying?" Reed asked in a smooth tone.

"I just think there's more to her than meets the eye," Mike replied.

Jill jumped in. "Take it easy, Mike. Reluctance to talk about things is natural at a time like this. She doesn't know us."

I swept a hand through my hair. It cascaded between my fingers and settled back onto my shoulders. I tucked the strands behind my ears. I wasn't getting the whole story. My shoulders slumped. God, I was tired.

"I take it Reed is supposed to form some kind of liaison," I said to Bobby Jack.

"I thought it might make the transition smoother."

Reed shifted in his chair. "Admit it. You don't

react well to change."

"You're not so hot at it either," I snapped.

"I see everything is still my fault," he murmured.

I heaved a deep breath to control the anger working its way up through my chest.

"I never said everything was your fault."

"No, but you thought it."

"Oh, are *you* the psychic now?"

"Look, I don't know what you two are talking about, but I suggest you save this argument for later," Young said, turning his gaze onto my former fiancé. "And I don't think your expertise will be needed, Mr. McIntyre."

"Yes, it is, Detective. You don't understand Sasha or her abilities. I do. You could, of course, try this on your own, but I wouldn't guarantee the results. Her dreams are frighteningly real and accurate."

"Mike, I don't think we should turn down any help that's offered," Jill said. "After all, this is new to us, and I'm willing to work with Sasha and Mr. McIntyre."

"Detective McIntyre," Reed corrected.

She's willing to work with Reed and me? Bully for her. I wasn't so sure working with any of them made my list.

"Here, how's this?"

Charlie's voice pulled me out of my worries. I turned my attention to the portrait.

"Almost—make her smile a little, just an upturning at the corners."

I kept my eyes glued on the sketch, refusing to look at the others, afraid of what I might give away.

"Is that better?" Charlie asked.

I gazed at a woman in her late twenties or early

thirties with a kittenish face. Mischief glowed from her eyes, and the smile said she enjoyed life. I wanted to cry. That love of life would be extinguished if we didn't find the killer first.

"The hair's a little fuller."

He made a few swift strokes with his pencil. "How about now?"

"Yes. That's the woman."

Charlie handed the sketchpad to Reed who studied it for a few seconds before handing it to Bobby Jack.

"Nice looking lady." He passed it on to Mike.

"I can see why the killer would choose her." The sketch made its way to Jill.

She held it in both hands. Her facial expression changed from curious to horrified and her eyes widened in disbelief. She gasped, her fingers tightening on the pad.

"Jill? What is it?" Mike demanded.

"I—I know her."

"What? Who is it?"

"It's Lisa."

"Lisa who?" Mike demanded.

"Lisa Parker. My sister."

Chapter Two

I studied the faces of the people around me after Jill's remarkable declaration, and then tapped into their emotions. Bobby Jack's eyebrows rose and his eyes narrowed. Internally, I read his hope that maybe this would be an easy case for a change.

Reed's expression remained impassive, but his inner turmoil raised his blood pressure. His concern was for me, but I removed myself from his mind before delving any deeper. My situation wasn't important.

Charlie looked satisfied and his emotions mildly curious. His mental fingers were busy molding clay.

Mike scowled while exasperation flowed through his mind and body.

Jill's emotions bordered on panic. I hadn't expected a seasoned cop to let feelings rule. She dropped the sketchpad.

"Your sister? Come on, Jill, knock it off. You've either had too much or need more caffeine." Skepticism dripped from Mike's voice.

She fumbled in her purse withdrawing a wallet. Mike took it from her shaking fingers and flipped it open.

"There. That's Lisa," Jill said, pointing to a picture in a plastic sleeve.

Mike scrutinized it for a second. "There's a vague resemblance, that's all. Get a grip."

"Don't patronize me. This man has just drawn my sister."

Bobby Jack reached for the wallet. "Does kinda look like her. Does she live in Memphis?"

Jill ran a hand through her hair. "No, St. Louis."

I drew in a deep breath. "No wonder the park didn't look familiar. I've never been to St. Louis."

"To my knowledge you haven't been in many Memphis parks, either," Reed said in a dry tone as he glanced at the photo.

I shot him an irritated glance, not needing his sarcasm at the moment. His mind still held concern, but he'd shut down anything else readable. It was a skill learned in the six months we'd been together.

Charlie didn't bother with the picture. He reclaimed the drawing.

"Damn, I'm good," he murmured. "If this is anywhere close to what your sister looks like, I'd love to have her model for me. Her face is remarkable."

I stared at him. He'd just drawn the face of a potential victim and his only thought was having her model for him?

Jill yanked her cell from the purse. "I've got to warn her."

Mike grabbed it from her hand. "And say what? That some flake down in Memphis had a dream about her? I still say this whole thing is nuts."

I took offense to the word flake, but Reed beat me to a response.

"Detective, I'll only say this once. Don't ever use that terminology again. Sasha is no flake. She sees and feels things the rest of us can't. Believe me when I tell you it is not a pleasant experience. She doesn't have to tell us about any of it."

Young almost, but didn't quite, curl his lip. "And I suppose you have first hand knowledge of this?"

"Yes."

The two men stared at each other. Reed's face was set in combative lines. I tapped into both of their emotions. Mike seethed with resentment, but whether it was aimed at Reed or me, I couldn't tell. Reed was just plain pissed, and while I appreciated his defense of my abilities, I could take care of myself.

"Mike, you owe Sasha an apology," Bobby Jack said. "Without her, several cases would have gone unsolved and landed on Reed's desk. Her dreams are for real."

"You're also being rude," Jill snapped. She heaved a deep breath. "Okay, I'm calmer now. Let me see that drawing again."

Charlie handed it over. While she inspected it closer, I stared Mr. Skeptic in the eyes.

"Detective Young, it may help you to know that for years I kept these visions to myself. I didn't like being laughed at or dismissed as a carnival huckster. I came forward because of one vision that changed the direction of my abilities and my life. I don't want recognition or accolades. I want to prevent an innocent person from being killed."

He ran a hand over his face, but his emotions were still unsettled.

"All right, I apologize, but this whole psychic thing flies against common sense and science."

I could tell his apology was not heartfelt, but played along anyway. "I understand. Reed had the same disbelief when we first met."

"I can see now that this woman's eyes are slightly tilted where Lisa's aren't," Jill said from across the table. "And my sister has a dimple in her left cheek, plus the cheeks in the drawing are fuller, but damn it's close."

I ran a hand through my hair and massaged my scalp. Tiredness flowed from head to toe. So many emotions sapped my energy. I was ready to go home.

"If y'all will excuse me, I'm out of here," I said, rising and gathering my coat and purse.

"I think that's a good idea, but before you go, is this dream pre or retro cognitive?" Bobby Jack asked.

"I'm not sure."

"What's that mean?" Jill wondered.

"Precognitive would mean it's going to occur. Retro means it's already happened. Occasionally, the dream or vision is a mixture."

"In other words, some of your dream could have already occurred, but the ending might still be up for grabs?" Young asked.

"It's possible." I stifled a yawn with my hand. "Guys, I've got to get home. I'll check in this afternoon."

Bobby Jack rose and put a hand on my arm as the others filed from the room. Reed paused at the door, and then left.

"Sasha, I need to tell you why Jill and Mike are taking over."

"It's not because we drew a blank the last couple of times, is it? What happened?"

He shifted from foot to foot, refusing to look me in the eye. "The last couple of months have been rough, both here and at home. I...I started drinking again.

Cindy threatened to leave unless I got help. As soon as I can get you, Mike, Jill, and Reed caught up and comfortable with each other, I'm going into rehab. I told the brass two days ago."

I laid my hand on his arm. "I'm so sorry. Is there anything I can do?"

"No," he said with a smile. "I was due to enter the facility next Monday, but your phone call tonight pushed it back."

Guilt squirmed its way into my chest. He patted my hand.

"It's not your fault. So things are delayed for a few days. I'll be too busy to get loaded."

"I haven't talked to Cindy in a while. What...I mean, how..."

"How did I fall off the wagon?" He massaged the back of his neck. "It started when we couldn't solve the Margie Hollis murder. The night we were officially told we were off the case, I stopped at a bar on my way home. Cindy was out of town with the kids. Then, the Rafe Quillen case tanked, too. Things spiraled. Came to a head last week when I walked in the front door drunk."

"I don't know what to say." Internally, I sensed his anger, self-disgust, and the fear he might not be able to shake his demons.

"Don't worry. Things have a way of working out." He turned and walked out of the door.

I sat abruptly in a chair. Poor Bobby Jack. Poor Cindy. I made a mental note to call her later in the day. She was a nice woman who loved her husband and family. Bobby Jack's slippage must have been devastating.

The door opened and Reed came in.

"I take it Bobby Jack's told you the whole story," he said, perching on the corner of the table.

I nodded. "You know?"

"Yeah, he told me when he phoned earlier."

"This is going to be a rough one. I'm used to dealing with Bobby Jack. Jill seems all right, but Mike Young is a pain in the ass. I'm not sure I want either of them knowing the full extent of my abilities."

"I think that shrink of yours is enhancing your *perception* of your abilities."

"Leave Dr. Schenk out of this. You never liked Dr. Silberstein either."

"Silberstein was all right, but I thought Schenk was rushing you into new territory."

"You were jealous."

"I was worried."

"Yeah, so worried you threw me out of the house."

"I did not throw you out. I simply suggested that maybe we needed breathing space."

"In the two months I lived with Linnie, you called exactly twice—once to ask if I'd accidentally taken your Toby Keith CD, and once to say you'd found it. That's not breathing space, that's dumping. You dumped me because you couldn't deal with my growing abilities. How do you think that made me feel?"

He pushed away from the table and paced toward the door before turning around, his hands gripping the doorjamb, the knuckles white.

"What I couldn't deal with was being shut out. How do you think I felt? My stomach tightened every time you woke up screaming from a nightmare. Then you'd go into the bathroom, puke, and get on the phone

24

to Silberstein, or Schenk, or Bobby Jack. You never discussed what happened with me. Never asked my advice. Didn't even want my comfort."

My chest constricted. It was true, but I didn't like hearing it. I sensed his hurt and anger. It was killing me.

"Dr. Silberstein *was* and Dr. Schenk *is* my parapsychologist. I worked with Bobby Jack. Did you ever think I might have been trying to spare you some of the anguish I felt at seeing people murdered?"

"And did you ever think that your actions hurt? That's what partners are for, Sasha—to support each other through good and bad. We were engaged for six months. After two, I knew we were in trouble."

I folded my arms over my chest and lowered my head. "The sad part is, I knew it, too. I dealt with horrible emotions from my dream victims and questions from Silberstein, then Schenk, and Bobby Jack. I couldn't deal with them from you."

He said nothing, and for once I didn't tap into his head. I couldn't, not now. I was physically and mentally exhausted, and my emotions were in the worst turmoil since three years ago when we first met.

Reed reached down and cupped my elbow, helping me to my feet.

"You're beat. Can you drive home?"

"Yes. What time is it?"

"Almost seven. Are you sure you can drive?"

I pulled the keys from my purse. "I'm fine, really, just tired."

He ran his hand through his hair, a habit I still found charming.

"If you need anything, call. Can we work together without letting our past get in the way?"

"I don't know, but Young could be a problem. He's a digger. He'll keep at it until he finds out everything."

"Deflect him to me if you can. I'll run interference."

"Thanks, Reed. I appreciate it."

I gazed into his face. He'd aged in the last couple of years. Gray hairs now threaded their way through the dark brown in a random pattern. The lines around his eyes and from nose to mouth, always deeply etched, had grown deeper. The furrow never seemed to leave his forehead even when he didn't frown.

He still maintained his trim body. I wanted to hold him and feel those strong arms close around me. The urge was so compelling I swayed in his direction, and then stopped the motion.

Don't give in to impulse. Not now. Get some rest and deal with the murder that's about to happen.

Reed nodded and walked from the room with a quick stride. I followed more slowly. After two and a half years, I still loved him. I couldn't live with him, but I loved him beyond belief.

It was enough to break my heart.

****

I made it as far as the station lobby before Mike Young accosted me.

"Miss Bellwood, is there someplace where we can talk privately?"

"Detective, I'm beat. I want to go home, go to bed, and sleep for the rest of the day. Tomorrow is soon enough." I tried to step around him.

He moved with me, blocking my path. "This won't take long. If you're right, then someone is about to commit murder. I need more information about the

26

details."

I sidestepped again. "Later."

I headed toward the front doors, my feet barely lifting from the shiny terrazzo floor.

"What are you hiding, Miss Bellwood?"

The question stopped me dead in my tracks. Slowly, I pivoted to face him and gazed into hard brown eyes.

"It's more than just dreams, isn't it? If we're going to work together, I need to know."

"Why should I tell you anything? You just called me a flake to my face and have exuded nothing but hostility from the moment you walked into the conference room. I can't and won't put my trust in someone like that."

"I can't apologize for how I feel until you show me I'm wrong." He scratched his eyebrow. "I just need something to go on besides a dream image."

"Even a dream image that happens to look like Detective Conway's sister?" I couldn't keep the taunting tone under control.

"Jill is a woman and tends to be emotional. The drawing was similar, not the same."

I refrained from shaking my head at his words. "What? Emotions aren't allowed in police work?"

"Emotions get in the way of logic, and I'm not here to talk about Jill. I need to know more about you." He cupped my elbow with his hand and steered me toward a hallway.

Emotions get in the way of logic? Who is this guy— Spock?

I didn't want to go, but had no choice. Halfway down the corridor, he opened a door and guided me through before releasing my arm. We stood in an empty office. He flipped on the light, and then turned to face me.

"Do you always see through the killer's eyes?"

"No. Occasionally, I see things from the victim's point of view, and sometimes, a third party."

"But this was definitely from the killer's?"

"Yes." I saw no reason to expand. Let him ask the questions.

"You do more than see, don't you? Several times you commented on the victim's feelings. Even McIntyre made a comment about you feeling things. Exactly, what kind of abilities do you have?"

Maybe if I gave him the shortened version, he'd leave me alone. God, I was so tired.

"I also have empathic abilities. I feel the emotions of others. For instance, right now you're frustrated, skeptical, and resentful as hell. Why?" Turning the tables never hurt.

He licked his lips and heaved a sigh. "Jill and I were working a homicide when we were pulled off to come here. I don't like leaving cases half undone to start new ones in a different locale."

"That's why you're frustrated. Skeptical I can handle, but it's the resentment that worries me."

"You're mistaken."

I closed my eyes and inhaled a deep cleansing breath, then tapped into his emotions and his mind. He didn't know how to block my advances. Within a few seconds, I had the answer.

Re-opening my eyes, I said, "You consider this a demotion. You believe Bobby Jack and I have been coasting on some kind of psychic con. And you resent being partnered with a woman because deep down, you think we're weak."

He gaped, his jaw unhinged, his eyes widening. Then he regained control, straightened, and wiped his expression clean.

"You're mistaken, Miss Bellwood."

I moved toward the door. "No, I'm not. You know it, and so do I. This discussion is over. If I were you, I'd talk to Bobby Jack and get the lowdown on how my premonitions are handled. I'll see you tomorrow."

With renewed energy, I stalked down the hallway and out of the police station. I didn't trust Mike Young and liked him even less. The professional relationship might be doomed before it even started.

****

I tossed my purse and car keys onto the kitchen counter and eyed the coffee pot. Dead tired, I craved sleep—dreamless sleep—but put it off a while longer.

Instead, I grabbed a bottle of water from the fridge, marched back to my office, fired up the computer, and opened a folder labeled Subject Emotions. It was a private file containing my observations on the emotions of others during an investigation. Today would see new additions, including mine.

I started with myself, typing in my reactions to Bobby Jack's announcements, Jill Conway's fear the victim was her sister, and Mike Young's obvious problems. I tried to keep my comments unbiased, but found it hard when it came to Young. I then tackled everyone's emotional reactions, keeping my observations to the basics. Tomorrow, I would delve deeper into all of them.

I left Reed for last, not because I was avoiding it, I

hastily told myself, but because I was unsure of whether he even belonged in this report. If he were a liaison, then I'd have to include him.

Finished, I chugged a large portion of my water. It was almost noon. If I went to sleep now, I'd be wide-awake tonight. Maybe an early dinner and in bed by nine would be better.

In the kitchen, I fixed a ham and Swiss sandwich and replayed the morning in my mind. Reed's appearance had surprised me, but I had to admit, his presence felt so right after all this time. I'd missed him, and for a moment, let my imagination wonder if we could take up again.

Unfortunately, his last words from the day he asked me to leave his home still rattled in my head.

"Sasha, I think it's better if we break this off now. Neither of us can handle the changes that never seem to stop. Your life is moving in a different direction. I can't keep up."

It had been typical Reed, blunt and to the point. I'd been deeply hurt, but knew he was right. Having sold my house in Midtown, I'd called Linnie asking to bunk in with her for a while. She'd agreed.

Although no longer my psychiatrist, she was still willing to listen. Occasionally, Bill, Reed's brother and Linnie's soon-to-be husband, sat in on my venting.

"That's why it's called an engagement," Linnie said. *"A busted engagement is better than a busted marriage."*

"Divorce is not fun," Bill had added. *"I have first-hand knowledge of that."*

I brought my mind out of the past. Picking at old wounds never solved anything.

When finished with lunch, I called Bobby Jack's wife, Cindy.

"Cindy, I'm so sorry about Bobby Jack."

She sniffed as if she'd been crying. "I know, but I have to admit when the phone rang last night, I knew his rehab would be delayed. For a split instant, I really hated you."

I winced inwardly, the old guilt at not being able to help everyone rising.

"Since the only times I see him are when we're on a case, I had no idea there was a problem until this morning. I swear it."

"I know and I don't mean it, but he was all set to enter the facility in the next couple of days."

"There are new people involved, so maybe he can still make it. He called Reed in as a liaison. What happened?"

"I discovered he was drinking again just after his last case went cold. A couple of drinks are no problem, but he can't stop there. He keeps going until the bottle's empty or he passes out. And he's not a happy drunk."

Her words unsettled me. "He's not abusive, is he?"

"Not in the sense he takes things out on me or the kids. If that were the case, I'd have scrammed long ago. No, he gets depressed." She paused. "He knew he was being replaced last week. It set him off. He directed all his anger and resentment toward Lieutenant Sims, then toward others at the station. I finally put my foot down and told him if he didn't get help, I was taking the kids and leaving. He agreed to enter a police-approved facility. You'd be surprised at how many cops are patients."

Actually, it didn't surprise me at all. People,

especially policemen, dealt with stress in all sorts of manners, many of which were not healthy alternatives.

"Cindy, if there's anything I can do, let me know."

"Make a smooth transition to the new team, so Bobby Jack can get his life back together."

I hung up. She was frustrated, sad, desperately afraid her marriage was over, and unsure of how to raise three children under the age of six on her own.

I shook my head and needing to keep busy, I piddled away the rest of the afternoon. Around five o'clock, I slapped a frozen dinner into the microwave and ate the fish concoction without really tasting it. Finished, I wandered into the living room, sat on the sofa, and closed my eyes.

Is now the time to try this? Or am I too drained from the past eighteen hours? Can I pull it off again?

"It" was a fresh wrinkle in my psychic abilities. The phenomenon had occurred two nights ago, and while new additions no longer frightened me, they did surprise.

For instance, I remember the first time I'd actually read a person's mind. It was Reed shortly after he'd asked me to marry him. Bobby Jack followed a couple of months later. One of our first successes involved me homing in on the thoughts of a killer. I heard, but couldn't actually communicate with anyone. Yet.

Then, the precognition thing reared its head. My clairvoyance and clairaudience abilities had sharpened, too. Sometimes the changes had come so rapidly, I didn't have time to be scared. Now, I just accepted them.

Still, the event a few nights ago had stunned me. Tired from an all-day housecleaning session, I'd plunked my butt on the sofa ready to watch some mindless reality show when I realized the remote was across the room on the entertainment center.

In a gesture meant to be exasperated, I'd held out my hand and said, "Come."

It obeyed, floating across the twelve feet separating us only to drop into my lap. Astonished, I'd tried again to levitate the damned thing, but failed. I'd immediately gone online to study the subject of telekinesis.

It was a fascinating ability, but to make sure I could do it again before telling my shrink, Dr. Schenk, I needed time to digest what I'd done. Stopping to think for a day or so helped with my acceptance of new powers.

I leaned my head back and closed my eyes, meditating into a calm, relaxed state of mind, no small feat considering the events of the day.

When ready, I opened my eyes and gazed at a book on the coffee table. Concentrating, I poured my energy onto the object, willing it to rise, pulling upward with my mind. The book trembled. I concentrated harder. The paperback moved slightly to the left, but didn't lift.

I closed my eyes again to refocus, then opened them and tried again. This time, the top half of the book rose as if to stand on edge. I bore down, and the bottom half joined in the fun.

The thriller now hovered a half an inch above the glass. My God, I'd done it. My glee was short lived. The book wobbled, and then fell back with a small thud.

Exhausted, I gave up for now. But I had moved an inanimate object with just the power of my mind. It was scary, exhilarating, and exciting all at once. Now, I needed to practice until I could show Dr. Schenk. I assumed I would become more proficient the more I did it. That's the way things had always worked before.

I had a new skill. *What on earth am I going to do with it, and what will Reed say?*

Chapter Three

An incessant ringing drilled into my sleep-fogged brain. Like an onion, the layers of unconsciousness peeled away until my eyes opened. Sunlight slanted through the narrow slats of the window blinds. The promised sleet and snow of yesterday had never materialized. I squinted at the clock and saw it read seven forty-five. The ringing had ceased, so I punched my pillow into a more inviting shape and prepared to snooze again.

No such luck. The ringing resumed, only now I recognized it as my landline telephone located in the living room. I let it ring, waiting for the answering machine to pick up.

"Hello, you've reached 555-1947. I'm unable to take your call at this time, so leave your name, number, and a brief message. I'll get back with you as soon as possible. Thanks and have a nice day."

Whoever had called hung up without leaving a message. I pulled the covers up under my chin and prepared to catch a few more zees when the damned ringing began again. Obviously, I was not meant to sleep any longer.

Cursing, I tossed the comforter and sheet aside and stomped from the bedroom. In full irritation mode, I picked up the phone and snapped, "Hello."

"About time. I've been calling for the last fifteen

minutes."

"Who is this?"

"Mike Young. Are you coming into the station today? I don't know what time you start work, but I've been here since six."

"I come in whenever I damn well feel like it."

A long pause followed my snarky statement.

"I see. Let me rephrase that—when will you grace us with your presence?"

"It's a good thing I'm forty miles away because right now I want to smack you. I'll be there when I get there." Then a thought occurred, and my irritation diminished. "Why? Do you need me? Has something happened?"

"You tell me. You're the psychic."

"Young, I'm hanging up and unplugging the phone."

"No, wait." He paused again and I heard him heave a couple of deep breaths. "After you left yesterday, Detective Beauregard contacted the St. Louis police to see if they had any unsolved murders using the scenes you reported. I just thought maybe you should be here to read them when they start coming in. After all, it was your dream."

"Detective Young, I need coffee and breakfast. I should be there by ten-thirty." I hung up with more force than necessary.

A shower helped my irritation level recede. The coffee gave me energy, and the cereal with sliced bananas and milk tasted good.

I glanced out my kitchen window while spooning the cereal into my mouth. Not wanting to be a burden to Linnie, I'd moved to Holly Springs, Mississippi almost eighteen months ago. The break-up with Reed had still been a fresh wound and I needed to put as much space between us as possible.

The house sat on the outskirts of the town, and had once been the guesthouse on a large plot of land owned by a mid-nineteenth century cotton farmer. Magnolia Hall, as the main house was named, had been the family's town home. My little portion of the estate was a cute cottage with two bedrooms, a living room, dining room, and a surprisingly large kitchen. The house suited me, the rent was reasonable, and my landlord, a descendent of the original owner, supplemented his Social Security with my monthly cash contribution.

I finished breakfast, and deciding to irritate Young further, dressed in jeans and an Elvis T-shirt along with my cowboy boots. He probably expected something more professional. Yesterday, I'd noticed Jill had dressed in nice slacks, a sweater, and a blazer in spite of the ungodly hour she'd been summoned to work.

With rush hour over, I zipped up US 78 into Memphis, making the downtown area in an amazing forty-seven minutes. I congratulated myself on being fifteen minutes early.

At the station, I grabbed another cup of coffee from outside the conference room, and rooted around seeking a stale donut. Finding none, I entered the room. Jill Conway was the lone occupant. She sat reading an open file folder. I noted her neat beige slacks and lightweight powder blue sweater. The blazer from yesterday was draped over the back of her chair.

She looked up and smiled. "Hi, Sasha. Did you sleep well?"

"I had a great night's sleep. I could have slept

longer if it wasn't for your partner. Called me at quarter to eight."

She laughed. "That's Mike. When he's ready to work, he expects everyone else to be just as ready."

"Where is everybody?"

"In Detective Beauregard's office waiting for those files to come in via e-mail. He, Mike, and Detective McIntyre wanted to read them."

"So Reed's here, too?" I asked casually. In spite of my pretended indifference, I looked forward to seeing him.

Jill sent me a penetrating glance. "Yes, he came in about eight o'clock. I have the feeling there's history between the two of you."

"You could say that," I replied, pulling out a chair and removing my coat. I sipped some of the forgotten coffee from the mug. "We were engaged."

"I'm sorry. I didn't mean to open old wounds."

I shrugged. "You didn't. It was a couple of years ago. We're still friendly."

I didn't tell her I hadn't seen Reed in over a year nor did I want to discuss him or our relationship.

"Did you have a good night's sleep?"

Jill shook her head. "Awful. I kept thinking about the drawing and how much it looked like Lisa."

She twirled a pencil between her fingers and I sensed her deep concern. Some of the fear had dissipated, but the worry remained. I sipped my coffee knowing she had more to say.

"I…I called Lisa this morning."

Startled, I jerked, splashing some of the liquid on the table. I quickly wiped it up with a tissue from my purse.

"You warned her?" I asked, sincerely hoping that was not the case.

"No, no, nothing like that. I just called to say hello and chat." She refused to meet my eyes.

"And how is she?"

"Oh, she's fine. Everything is going well."

I didn't even attempt to be subtle, but rammed my mind into hers for a closer look. She flinched, almost as if she felt me enter.

I'd been wrong about the fear fading. It remained overpowering even though she tried to mask it. Jill felt a strong protective instinct toward her younger sister. The uncertainty was distracting her from the task at hand.

"Tell me about you and your sister," I said, trying to calm her ragged nerves.

She dropped the pencil and leaned back with a smile. "Lisa is thirty, beautiful, talented beyond belief, and always sees the best in people. It's the last trait that bothers me. She has lousy judgment in men. Always manages to latch onto the worst liars and leeches. I tried to convince her to join me when I moved here seven years ago. She refused, saying she didn't need a mother hen clucking over her."

I had no problem visualizing a hovering Jill. "How is she talented? What does she do to pay the rent?"

"Lisa is the original free spirit. She's an actress. Pretty good, too. Does a lot of theater in St. Louis."

"Is that where you're from? St. Louis?"

"Sort of. We were born and raised across the river in Belleville, Illinois. Our parents died in an automobile accident when Lisa was seventeen. For the next few years, it was just the two of us."

"Have you always been a cop?"

Jill nodded. "It's the only thing I ever wanted to do. I moved here because the opportunity for advancement was better than in St. Louis." She paused and bit her lip. "I just wish Lisa had come with me, but I couldn't convince her. She loves St. Louis."

I leaned forward and placed my hand on her arm. "Try not to worry, Jill. There are a lot of blonde-haired women in the world. The chances of me dreaming about your sister are astronomical. The woman of my vision is probably right here in Memphis."

She inhaled a deep breath. "I sure hope you're right. I know I'm not being logical, but I can't help it."

The door to the room opened. Bobby Jack, Young, and Reed entered. Bobby Jack tossed several file folders on the table. He looked awful. His bloodshot eyes and trembling hands told me his night had not been the best—he was hung-over as hell. I wondered how Cindy had handled it and made a mental note to call later.

I shifted my gaze to Reed. His expression rarely varied from the stone-carved image, yet I read concern in his eyes. In his mind, the concern was not for Bobby Jack, but for me. He glanced at me and shut his mental door.

Young pulled out a chair and sat. "Glad you could finally make it, Miss Bellwood."

Reed's irritation re-opened the door. He wanted to smack the detective in the mouth. I suppressed a chuckle. His reaction was the same as mine when Young had called earlier.

Ignoring the sarcastic Mike, I asked Bobby Jack, "I understand you made contact with the St. Louis police.

Hear anything from them yet?"

"No, but I pulled several old files here to see if what you dreamed and the MOs matched. Why don't you and Jill take a gander?"

"According to Miss Bellwood, there are three separate scenes. This is all you could find?" Young asked, fingering the files.

"For the moment," Bobby Jack answered in a sharp tone. "I'm still checking. Chances are this isn't the first time the perpetrator has stalked or killed. If an MO can be found, it might give us a head start."

Young turned his gaze onto me. "And you didn't see this guy's face at all?"

I bit back hot words and answered in a civil tone. "No. I viewed things through his eyes."

"You said you sometimes viewed things through the victim's eyes or like a fly on the wall. Can you be hypnotized to view a scene that way?"

"No, Detective Young, I doubt that would work."

"Call me Mike, and why not? Have you ever tried it?"

"No, but…"

"So why not do it?"

"Because, hypnotism is exhausting and can impair Sasha's powers for hours," Reed cut in.

Young waved a dismissive hand in Reed's direction. "I don't think I need any liaison for this, McIntyre. Why don't you go back to your cold case files?"

A slow flush crept up Reed's neck to his cheeks. I didn't need psychic powers to read his fury.

Before I could defuse the situation, he said through gritted teeth, "You need me all right. Sasha is very

41

sensitive to negative vibrations. They screw with her visions. I'm the only one who can keep her calm. And from the look on her face right now, I'd say she'd love to belt you a good one. Your attitude stinks, Young. All that hostility and skepticism will block anything positive."

The detective's eyebrows rose. "Really? You work with her on one case and that makes you an expert?"

"Yes!"

"Seems to me Detective Beauregard would be of more use since the two of them worked together for the last three years. What makes you so special?"

"Mike, knock it off. Detective McIntyre must have good insight or Detective Beauregard wouldn't have suggested his joining us. You're being rude and obstructive. I want to see this solved quickly," Jill said with a frown.

"Jill, you're still thinking like a sister instead of a cop. Called your sister yet to ask if she's okay?"

Jill bit her lip. "Yes, I did. She's fine and so am I."

The emotions swirling around the room were intense. Anger poured from Reed. Bobby Jack simmered with resentment. Jill's fear for her sister had not withered one iota. And Michael Young? I sensed hostility, but something else—something deeper, darker—lurking below the surface. It took a moment for me to identify hatred, but of whom or what, I had no clue.

I'd never worked under such conditions, not even that first time when Reed was so skeptical of my abilities and frustrated by his *inability* to capture a serial killer. I saw disaster looming.

I took a deep breath to clear my head. "Look you

guys, this isn't going to work unless we're all on the same page. Reed is right; negative energy fogs my channels. I may see things as skewed or interpret what I see wrong. It's happened before. Mike, you and Reed need to bury this animosity. He's also right about me not opening to you. Trust has to form first. And at this moment, I don't trust you enough to tell you my secrets."

"What secrets?" he replied with a raised eyebrow.

"If she told you, it wouldn't be a secret now, would it?" Bobby Jack said. "For instance, how would you react if Sasha suddenly went into a trance?"

"A trance?" Jill asked, a startled expression on her face.

"It happens," I told her. "Usually when I view in real time through the eyes of the victim. I can't do anything about it."

"That's where I can help," Reed said. "I know how to keep her grounded to where she's at."

I breathed a sigh of relief. The internal tensions of everyone in the room lessened.

"All right," Mike said, turning his gaze toward me. "Explain to us how this dream or vision thing works."

"The dreams are dreams. I guess nightmares better describes it. But when I go into a trance, my peripheral vision darkens, and my hearing mutes. Then I'm filled with the presence of another. Like water from a pitcher into a glass. I see whatever I see, and then come out of it."

"Have you always had this ability?" Jill asked.

"I think so, but I wasn't aware of it until I was six." I sighed. "It was all so easy then. I'd see a lost item as though in a still photo and locate it by the surrounding

43

environment. That doesn't happen too often anymore."

"Why?" Mike questioned.

"The other abilities took over."

"What other abilities?" he persisted.

I held his gaze with mine. I had no intention of telling him or Jill the full scope of what I could do.

"The dreams, the visions."

"In other words, in a vision, you become the victim, but in a nightmare, you're the killer?" Jill asked.

"Pretty much."

"All right, you see. Do you also hear?" Mike said, doodling with a pen on the front of a file folder.

I clasped my hands together on the table and suppressed a shudder, remembering my first nightmare. I not only heard Kathy Watson's killer, I felt every thrust of the knife he used to murder her. The pain, the warmth of the blood flowing down her side. I had experienced what she did, including the terror.

Reed covered my hands with his. He opened his mind and I read his concern. He didn't need psychic abilities to know what I was thinking. It was Kathy's murder that had brought us together.

"Well?" Mike said in an impatient tone.

"Sometimes."

I wasn't ready to tell him or Jill any more. If the usual pattern followed, I'd either have a vision or another nightmare before too long. The door opened and a policewoman entered the room with an armful of files. She set them on the table and left without word.

Taking a long, deep breath, I lifted my chin. "Why don't we get to reading these files? The sooner we find a pattern, the faster we find the killer—hopefully before he strikes."

"Good idea," Bobby Jack said, rising to distribute the folders.

Reed, sitting next to me, leaned over and whispered, "Can I buy you lunch?"

Suddenly, I wanted very much to be with him. "I'd love it. Where?"

"Close by. I have to get back to my office this afternoon. How about the Riverfront Deli?"

I nodded. "Sounds good."

We both picked up folders and read, seeking a prospective killer.

****

The Riverfront Deli is a Memphis institution serving up the best sandwiches in the Mid-South. The tuna salad and BLT concoctions are to die for. A small bronze plaque outside the door announced its claim to fame in a two-minute scene from the movie, *The Firm*.

Reed and I squeezed our way past departing customers and snagged a table. I had barely taken off my coat when a waiter appeared. I honed my negotiation skills on Reed.

"I'll order the BLT if you order the tuna. I'll trade you half of mine for half of yours."

"Deal," he said with a grin.

We ordered the sandwiches and sweet tea, a Southern staple.

"So how are things over in cold cases?"

He frowned and shrugged. "Okay, I guess. I was fully reinstated in the department about a year ago, but kept in cold cases. Cold cases bore me. The action's already happened—a long time ago. I'd rather be in the thick of things again. I keep putting in for a transfer back to homicide, and keep getting turned down on a regular basis."

I suspected his life-threatening injuries sustained in the line of duty several years before might have had something to do with the rejections.

"You mean the cold cases bore you because you don't have a personal interest in them like you did while chasing down a serial killer?"

"I suppose," he replied, taking a deep breath. "Once that case was solved, I had a problem filling the void. My sense of purpose wasn't as strong. I want to do things again. I want to feel worthwhile."

"But you bring closure to all those families when you solve a cold case."

"I know, but sometimes it's years after the incident. I want to help them immediately—to ease the burden of pain they feel."

This confession didn't surprise me. Reed had always had a dedication deeper than the average person or cop. That was one of the things I loved about him.

The waiter brought our tea and promised the sandwiches in a few minutes.

"What's your take on Mike Young?" he asked when we were alone.

"He's angry, resentful, doesn't like you, thinks I'm full of shit, and I don't want to spoil my lunch by talking about him."

"Your relationship with him reminds me of ours when we first met. I'm jealous." The corner of his mouth lifted in a half-smile, making him look both wistful and vulnerable.

A surge of warmth glowed in the pit of my stomach. He still had the power to make me weak in the knees.

"Why do you dislike him so much?"

"He's rude, arrogant, and…" He paused, a furrow deepening on his forehead. "I don't know, there's something else I can't put my finger on. What did you sense? And don't try to tell me you weren't trespassing in his mind."

I took a sip of my tea before answering. "He's resentful at being involved with this and is a bit of a male chauvinist pig. Thinks women get a pass on requirements for jobs that have always been male dominated, like law enforcement and firefighting." I hesitated, not sure if I should bring up everything, then decided I trusted Reed more than any of the people on this case. "I also sensed hatred."

Reed's eyebrows rose. "Hatred? Of what?"

"I don't know. In fact, now I'm not sure if the hatred was his or someone else's. There were a lot of emotions bombarding that room this morning, but I sensed the hate when I was in his mind."

"You think it was coming from someone else?"

"Possibly. That bastard, Jeff Hammond, crowded my thoughts a lot on that first case. Wasn't until after the fact that I realized it. With all that intensity today, the same thing could have happened." I shook my head and slid my hands up and down the glass, the condensation chilling my fingers. I didn't want to talk about present or past cases. "Let's talk about something else. How's Linnie?"

Reed grinned. "Eight months pregnant and according to Bill, bitching about it day and night."

"Wait until she gives birth. She'll talk to God and blame your brother for everything. I've heard that often happens. Is she still working with the Gladden County counseling center?"

"She's on maternity leave at the moment."

He reached across the table to clasp my restless hands, his fingers stroking along the veins. Little rivulets of pleasure zipped up my arms and settled somewhere south of my tummy.

"Sasha, why don't you talk to Linnie? She may no longer have a private practice, but she'd make time for you."

I pulled my hands away. "I have a psychiatrist."

Reed leaned back. "I know, I know, but he's a…"

"Don't say it," I interrupted. "Dr. Schenk is bringing out all my abilities."

"I don't trust him—never did. Silberstein was all right, but Schenk raises red flags for me."

I inhaled a shaky breath. "Reed, I don't want to argue about my shrinks. We're going to work together again. Let's not have any of those negative vibes you talked about earlier. It's not productive."

He ran his hand through his hair, a sure sign he was going to capitulate to my wishes, but wasn't happy about it.

"All right, but please don't shut me out. Okay?"

"I won't. I promise."

Our food arrived. He placed half of his tuna salad sandwich on my plate and snatched half of my BLT. He smiled and winked as if all were right in the world.

I took a bite of the huge sandwich, my teeth crunching through the lettuce, tomato, and crispy bacon. My taste buds exploded. How did they take a simple sandwich to the gourmet level?

As I ate, I sneaked a peek into Reed's head. He'd learned how to block some of his thoughts from me, but not all. I read worry and sadness along with an odd sense of loss. He was lonely and hurting. Shocked, I realized he still loved me as much as I loved him.

It was hopeless, of course. I wanted to cry.

****

"If I promise not to discuss this case or psychiatrists will you have dinner with me tonight?" Reed asked as he dropped me off at the police station.

Remembering his loneliness, how could I refuse? "Of course, I will. Where?"

"How about Wonderly's at seven? It's on your way home to Holly Springs and not far from my house."

A horn honked behind us, the impatient driver glaring at us through his windshield.

"Wonderly's at seven. No problem."

I opened the car door and scrambled out, waving as Reed blended back into traffic. He no longer worked out of this station. The cold cases had been transferred to another precinct about a year ago.

Jill was in the conference room reading a file when I entered.

"Hi, have a nice lunch?" she asked, looking up with a smile.

"Great. Can't go wrong with The Riverfront Deli. How's it going here?"

"Slow. So far, I haven't seen anything that ties in with what you dreamed."

I pulled out a chair and grabbed a file. "Where's your partner?"

"He had to finish up some paper work on a case at our old precinct." She chewed on the end of her pen, and then glanced at me. I sensed she wasn't telling me the whole truth. "How did you get hooked up with

Detective Beauregard?"

"A few months after the Jeff Hammond case, I had a dream about a man being murdered. I viewed it through the killer's eyes this time." I shuddered.

"Must have been awful. I can't imagine dreaming about someone getting killed and knowing it could all be true."

"Not only was it scary, but I knew the victim."

Her eyes opened wide. "Oh, my God. Who was it? A friend?"

"Worse, a former boss. His name was Dr. Clarke Pennington and he was the head of the Paranormal Psychology Department at the University of Memphis."

"Geez, did it come true?"

"Yeah. By the time I had the dream he was already dead."

"So you went to the police?"

I nodded. "After Jeff, I'd made a promise to help, so I called them saying I had information."

"I'll bet Detective Beauregard was happy to see you."

"He was like everyone, skeptical and suspicious at first. I gave him the details. Then the call came in. Pennington's receptionist came to work and found the body in his office. His death matched pretty much what I told him."

"So how long did it take to find the killer?"

"Longer than it should have."

"Why?"

"Because Bobby Jack arrested me for the murder."

Jill's jaw dropped, and then she laughed. "Oh, no."

"I can see it from his point of view now. I had details only available to the police, knew the victim, and my departure from his employ was less than amicable. Pennington was an asshole who used people to further his career."

"How long were you in jail?"

"Not long. A few hours. Reed straightened everything out. Bobby Jack was embarrassed, but we finally solved the case. Pennington was killed by one of the people who came to him for help, but whose story he used in his last book. The woman was furious, stormed into his office after the secretary left for the day, and clocked him with a paperweight from the desk."

Jill laughed again. "Let's hope Mike doesn't make the same mistake."

"Let's hope there's no body to find."

Her mirth stopped, and I felt the fear return. Somewhere a killer waited and watched.

Chapter Four

We worked across the table from each other for several minutes until curiosity got the better of me.

I rose and poured a cup of coffee from the carafe on the credenza before resuming my seat. I blew on and then sipped the long-standing bitter brew.

"So tell me. Why is Mike Young such an ass?"

Jill grimaced. "He's not really an ass. Oh, he has his moments, but he's intense while on a case, always thinking about angles and asking what if. Sometimes it comes across as rude."

I rested my elbows on the table, cupped my chin in my hand and entered her mind. She was only lying a little. "Sometimes? How the hell did you ever get partnered with him?"

"About three years ago, his partner died in the line of duty—a shootout with a suspect. My lieutenant knew I'd been looking for a chance to work homicide, so offered me the job. Mike was less than thrilled, but made the most of it."

"Probably thought you got the job through some kind of equal-opportunity thing rather than your own merit."

"At first. I soon proved I knew what I was doing. He finally gave me a grudging respect."

She was deluding herself. From what I'd read in his mind, he held little respect for his partner.

Her eyes held a dreamy expression, and I couldn't help asking, "Mike's a good-looking man and you're very attractive. I've heard that some opposite-sex partners end up together. The two of you ever date?"

"No. Mike is too macho and has to be in control. The control thing got to be a hassle. I had to smack him down a few times." Jill rose, poured a cup of coffee, tasted it, and then made a face. "Tastes like crap."

"I know. I assume Mike's not from here."

"Born in Minneapolis and raised by an aunt and uncle in some tiny farming town near the Upper Peninsula. He hated farming. He said while still in high school, he began bugging the local sheriff for a job and eventually became a deputy at the age of eighteen."

"Awfully young. I thought you had to be twenty-one."

She shrugged. "It was a small town. When the deputy quit, the sheriff bent the rules for a kid who really wanted the job."

"How did he get to Memphis?"

"He eventually drifted to the Minneapolis police force, and then came down here about ten years ago."

The parallels to Jeff Hammond's life flashed in front of my eyes. Mike Young's professional background wasn't all that different. The similarities left me with a cold feeling as I remembered the hatred from earlier in the day. I opened my mouth to warn Jill, and then closed it again.

What could I say? I had no reason to suspect her partner of anything other than being an ass. I picked up another file.

"Guess I'd better get back to work."

I read, but didn't comprehend. Jeff Hammond's

teasing, laughing eyes, handsome face, and deadly personality—the complete antithesis from Mike Young—kept intruding. I shook my head to clear it. I didn't need a man dead for the past three years clogging my mental system. I had another killer to find—before it was too late.

****

I packed it in at three o'clock, telling Jill I had a doctor's appointment. She didn't need to know the doctor was my psychiatrist. Nor had I bothered to tell Reed.

Jill yawned. "I'm about to call it quits, too. Thought I had something a while ago, but the guy's still locked up."

We had covered the unsolved cases and now worked on the solved. For all I knew, the killer had served his time and was now free.

I pulled into the parking lot in Dr. Schenk's East Memphis office and rode the elevator up to the seventh floor. His receptionist smiled from behind her mahogany desk as I walked in. The entire atmosphere oozed opulence. Dr. Schenk did not come cheap.

"Good afternoon, Miss Bellwood. Please have a seat. The doctor will be free soon. May I get you something to drink? Coffee? Tea? Water?"

"No, thank you. What have you been up to lately?"

She made a face. "Typing up his research notes on Salem and witchcraft. I think that's the topic of his next book."

"Sounds interesting."

She leaned forward and lowered her voice. "You ever read one of his books? So boring, I thought I'd die."

I laughed. "How long will he be?"

"Ten minutes, give or take."

I nodded and took a seat in one of the leather club chairs in the waiting area, then picked up the latest gossip magazine. I had to hand it to my shrink; he didn't leave old magazines lying around. I was just into the juiciest Kardashian rumors when the inner door opened. Schenk stood on the threshold, a smile on his face.

"Sasha, good to see you. Come in."

I hustled through the door and settled myself on a leather sofa. My psychiatrist was about as nondescript as a person could get—medium height, slender, brown hair, blue eyes, and not one single distinguishing feature. In a room full of people, he'd blend into the carpet. I grinned inwardly remembering the receptionist's opinion of his writing. Apparently, personality and appearance meshed.

"How have things been going?" he asked, taking a seat in a chair opposite me.

I took a deep breath ready to tell him about my last twenty-four hours. "Not good."

"Tell me."

I launched into my story of the nightmare and its aftermath. Usually, discussing my paranormal abilities lifted the heavy burden of what I knew. Today, however, it remained settled on my shoulders. I felt uncomfortable as if my skin were a size too small for my body. I was about to ask Schenk why when he changed the course of the session.

"Well, I hope you and the detectives can find the killer before he strikes."

His tone was dismissive as though the situation

were unimportant. The attitude irritated me.

He shifted in his chair. "I'd like to explore something we discussed last time we met. Have you practiced any of the relaxation exercises I taught you?"

"Some."

"Did they help? Were you able to leave your conscious body and project your psyche to another location?"

I bit my lip. "No. I wasn't able to bring it off."

"How often did you try?"

"Two or three times."

"I see. I'm very interested in the idea of dual consciousness in connection with your particular abilities. Think how you could help others by being in two places at once." He stroked his chin. "Perhaps I should hypnotize you and leave a post-hypnotic suggestion about relaxation."

"I don't think that would be a good idea, Dr. Schenk. Hypnosis blurs my mind. I'm officially on a case at the moment. I need a clear head."

"Of course, of course, I understand, but this is very important. Let's talk about the chakras and how they may be affected by your latest dream. We'll leave astral projection for another time."

He droned on asking probing questions while I answered in brief sentences. For a psychiatrist, he had an unusual interest in New Age dogma. Reed's comments during lunch had me wary. I was exasperated with myself and with Reed for sowing the seeds of doubt in my mind.

The session took forever to end, and I could tell by Dr. Schenk's expression that he suspected my mind had wandered.

"Sasha, I sense your attention span is not its usual self. Care to talk about it?"

I heaved a breath and shook my head. "There are a lot of tensions with this case."

I told him about the changes and the reactions to them.

He pursed his lips and frowned. "Perhaps, you should withdraw from this particular case, if it upsets you so much. I'm sure they have enough to investigate. That would release you to concentrate on increasing your abilities."

Dr. Schenk's single mindedness reminded me of the late, unlamented Clarke Pennington. The whole atmosphere between doctor and patient had subtly changed. A chill ran down my spine, and then I mentally slapped myself for the suspicion.

Damn Reed anyway.

"No, I can't do that. I've given my word and intend to keep it. The expansion of my abilities will have to go to the back burner for a while." I decided the telekinesis thing would remain my secret for the time being, at least until my doubts receded or were realized. I'd deal with it later.

His frown deepened. "Very well, but I don't agree with your decision. Please continue to practice the relaxation exercises and the dual consciousness attempts." He glanced at his watch. "Time's almost up. Is there anything else you'd like to discuss?"

The emotions of my co-workers flitted through my mind, and that chill slithered down my spine again. I refrained from saying anything.

"Not today, thank you," I replied, standing.

He also rose, smiled, and walked me to a door

leading directly to the hallway. I slipped into his mind. He was not a happy camper. He didn't like that I refused to do as he suggested. He reminded me more and more of Pennington. Why hadn't I seen that ages ago? Reed certainly had. I was irritated Reed was right.

"Just remember, if you need me, don't hesitate to call."

I murmured a brief goodbye, leaving with an uneasy feeling something was about to happen—and it wouldn't be good.

****

I pulled into Wonderly's at six-thirty, which made me way too early. While I was at Dr. Schenk's, Reed had left a message in my voicemail saying he was stuck at the station, postponing our dinner until eight o'clock and requesting I meet him there.

Not wanting to return to the police station and those files, I'd killed a couple of hours at the Wolf Chase Mall. The lure of the unique shops in the two-story edifice was only part of the trip. I also cruised the parking lot to see if any of the areas matched my dream vision, but came away none the wiser. A parking lot is a parking lot and they all looked the same.

Wonderly's was a combination sports bar and steakhouse located in East Memphis. The beer drinkers sat at the bar, their interests focused on the dozen or so big-screen TVs encircling the room. Wine and martini drinkers preferred the more sedate dining room. I had no idea what kind of a mood Reed was in, but his voice had sounded tired and frustrated. I sidled into the bar and peered around for a free booth, finally spotting one halfway down the right-hand wall.

As I settled into the seat my eyes adjusted to the

dim lighting and I looked around. On the opposite side of the horseshoe-shaped bar my gaze fell on a familiar face. It was Bobby Jack and he looked awful.

I eased out of my seat and walked over where I slid onto the stool next to him. He didn't acknowledge my presence, instead lifting a glass filled with a reddish-brown liquid to his lips and gulping half. The scent of bourbon tickled my nose.

"Hey, there," I said, not liking the looks of this. "What's up?"

He lowered the glass and turned slightly unfocused, bleary eyes toward me.

"At the moment, my glass." He finished the drink and signaled the bartender. "Get me another bourbon and not so much water this time around. Okay?"

"How long have you been here?"

"What's it to you?"

I'd never seen Bobby Jack belligerent, and for a moment backed away. Maybe I should leave him alone and call Cindy.

"I'm sorry, I didn't mean to intrude. I was just surprised to see you here, that's all."

"I could ask the same of you. Are you following me?"

"Good Lord, no. Reed and I are meeting here for dinner. Would you care to join us?"

"Why? So you can bitch at me for getting drunk? I got an earful of that from my precious wife this morning."

I remembered how hung-over he'd looked and was upset at the tone he'd taken when mentioning Cindy. I didn't know how to answer. The bartender arrived with another drink and turned to me.

"Can I get you something, ma'am?"

"Yeah, white wine, Chardonnay, I guess."

"House or something else?"

"House is fine." I turned back to Bobby Jack. Already half of the new drink had been downed. "Come on, talk to me. What set you off tonight?"

He stared down at the wooden counter, breathing heavily through his nose, his lips set in a hard, thin line.

"Why the hell should you care? No one else does."

"That's not true. Cindy cares. Reed cares. We all care about you. I'm your friend. We've worked together for three years. I'd like to think I could come to you with a problem. Sometimes talking can help."

He laughed, but I detected no mirth.

"You're good. I guess you've been to enough shrinks to know the lingo. 'Talk to me. I can help you, Bobby' sounds bogus to me."

For a moment, a dart of anger burned in my chest, and then vanished. This was Bobby Jack and he was in deep trouble. I entered his mind, but the booze had fogged any perceptions I might glean. He raised the glass again.

I placed my hand on his arm, stilling the motion. "All right, maybe I can't help, but I can listen."

He lowered his hand and stared at me, then banged his fist on the bar.

"I'm being cast aside, Sasha. Like an old shoe. Two unsolved murders and they bring in new people to replace me."

"I thought Mike and Jill were contacted after you requested leave."

"They were, but I was told by my captain a month ago a change was in the works."

"What? You've known about this that long? What did he say?"

He finished the drink and signaled for yet another one. "Only that he was worried about my mental attitude and felt the time had come for me to move on to another type of law enforcement."

"I don't understand. What other type of law enforcement?"

His words didn't make sense, but then I wasn't officially a cop and frankly, didn't keep abreast of all the various branches of the department.

"I'm going to be working non-violent crimes for a while when I get back from re-hab. If I bother to go at all."

I wondered if someone had tipped off his captain about his drinking. This morning was the first time I'd ever seen Bobby Jack hung-over on the job. Had he been under the influence at work, too? Cindy mentioned the drinking had begun a few months ago.

The bartender brought my wine and a bourbon replacement. I sipped while he drank and ranted.

"And to send in Young! What the hell was he thinking? The guy's a certified hard ass. A skeptic who'll be a royal pain in *your* backside. Jill's all right and has good instincts, but Young? Know the first words he said to me yesterday? 'Guess you're out, huh? Can't believe I've been assigned to this nonsense. Working with a psychic? Like working with Bela Lugosi or some other horror show freak.'

"When I tried to explain what we did, he cut me off and said, 'Guess you didn't do such a bang-up job, did you?' Honest to God, Sasha, I wanted to kill the son of a bitch. I wanted to ram his head into the wall over and over again."

He raised his glass with a shaking hand. The liquid dribbled down his chin. Bobby Jack wiped it away, and then smoothed his wet hand down the leg of his slacks. Without missing a beat, he went on to rant about everyone he knew, including his wife.

I had no problem entering his mind again, although the thoughts were still too jumbled to make much sense. He was furiously angry at the world, but most of all at himself. The professional failures of the last year had allowed personal failure to ease through the cracks. He knew he was wrecking his life and was terrified he couldn't regain control.

I pulled out of the ugliness of his thoughts and sipped my wine, glancing at my watch. It was almost seven. Reed wouldn't be here for another hour. Bobby Jack sagged against me, almost spilling his drink. I needed to get him out of here before he passed out. Luckily, his home was only ten or so blocks away. I could drive him there and help Cindy deal with him, and then return in time to meet Reed.

I signaled the bartender. "Let me have the bill."

"No! I want another drink," he muttered, his words so slurred I could barely understand them.

"You've had enough." I took charge. "I'll pay the tab and drive you home."

"You will not. No home." He slammed the last of his drink down and raised the glass. "I want another."

"Sorry, sir, but policy is we don't serve another to anyone who has obviously had too much to drink," the bartender said, placing the bill in front of me.

I slapped three tens on the tray and slid it toward him, thinking he should have told Bobby Jack that sooner. "Keep the change. I'll be back in a little while."

"I said I want another drink, goddammit!"

Other patrons stared. The bartender glared.

"Look, if you don't leave now, someone will call the cops. You don't want that, do you?"

He laughed. "Tha's a good one. Cops. Cops already 'ere." His laughter turned into a strangled sob.

I slid from the stool and tugged on his arm. "Come on. I'll drive you home."

He pulled away. "No. Call a cab."

I glanced at the bartender who nodded and reached for the phone under the counter. While he dialed, I tried to listen to my friend's incoherent ramblings. The names of Mike, Jill, his captain, and several other officers in the precinct spilled out accompanied with expletives.

With the bartender's help, I got him into the cab and gave the driver my last twenty with instructions on making sure his passenger got into the house.

"If you don't mine, I can di...direct, I still know my own addresh," Bobby Jack said in an irritated tone and finishing with a belch.

He slammed the door and leaned forward, speaking with the cabbie. A moment later, the driver pulled away.

I sighed, and reached for my cell to give Cindy a heads-up. I doubted she'd be happy.

"Hello, Cindy? It's Sasha."

"Oh, hi, Sasha." Her voice held a defeated, slightly thick tone, as if tears had been shed.

"Look, I hate to add to your worries, but I just sent your husband home in a cab. He's a little worse for wear."

She was silent for a moment, and then sniffed. "I'm not surprised. He came home wasted last night and this morning yelled at me when I tried to discuss it. I told him to leave. I can't take any more. He called around five to tell me he's at the Sleep Tight Inn on Poplar."

Oh, God, no wonder he'd been sloshed to the gills.

"Cindy, I'm so sorry. Is there anything I can do?"

"No. Where was he?"

"At Wonderly's. I'm meeting Reed here for dinner and arrived early. He never mentioned you two had split."

"It's for the best. I don't want the kids to see him like that. Donnie's only six, but asked me today why Daddy talked funny and ran into the furniture. God, Sasha, it was all I could do not to burst into tears. I did as soon as he was on the school bus."

I sucked at this kind of thing. I never knew what to say, and didn't consider Cindy a close enough friend to ask intimate questions.

"I feel responsible. If I hadn't had that damned nightmare, he would be in rehab and you…"

"It's not your fault. Bobby Jack's been a bundle of stress for over a year. The job's getting to him. I begged him to request a switch in departments. I even called his captain when he started drinking again, hoping it would help. It didn't. Bobby found out, and well, the conversation degenerated from angry to downright verbally abusive."

So Cindy had been the one to alert his boss. I could see where he'd consider her actions a betrayal. So many undercurrents, so much sadness.

"Well, look at it this way. With new people working with me, he can go into rehab and get himself

64

under control again. He told me he'd been reassigned to lighter, less stressful duty."

"Trouble is, Bobby doesn't want to let go. His job is more important than his family."

Cindy sobbed on the last word. My heart crimped at the misery in her voice.

"Don't believe that for a moment," I admonished. "He loves you and the kids. I know he's been on the force for a long time. Maybe when rehab is over, he'll have a new perspective on things. Retirement can't be too far down the road for him. And he's still young enough to venture into a new career."

I sounded like a cheerleader. Bobby Jack Beauregard retired? Out of law enforcement? He was like Reed. Too dedicated to the job to even consider the option. They'd both view the dreaded "r" word as a death sentence.

Cindy sighed heavily into the phone. "I guess we'll have to take things one step at a time. All I know is right now, he's depressed and angry. I hope this transition to a slower pace at the station helps." A child cried in the background. "I have to go, Sasha. I'll talk to you later."

I hung up knowing she wouldn't call back for a long time and feeling awful for both of them.

Wandering back into the restaurant, I reclaimed the booth from earlier, ordered another glass of wine, and tried to put Bobby Jack's problems out of my mind. I needed to have a talk with Mike Young. In spite of our differences, we had to put the animosity behind us and present at least a semblance of harmony. For Cindy's sake if nothing else. The sooner her husband got into rehab, the sooner she could put her family back together.

But we needed to cooperate for another reason, too. Almost forty-eight hours had passed since my nightmare. Somewhere, lurking in the shadows, a killer was poised, waiting to strike.

Chapter Five

"So Cindy asked him to leave. Can't say that I'm surprised," Reed said when I told him. "And Bobby Jack was drunk when he left here?"

"Totaled. Why aren't you surprised? Did you know how far downhill he'd gone?"

"I suspected. This morning, he made little attempt to conceal he was hung over as hell. Young saw it. Jill saw it. Anyone within a ten-foot radius saw it."

"Not only was he hung over, but also homeless. No wonder he was sucking down the bourbon." I sipped my wine and fiddled with the silverware. "He lied to me."

"Who?"

"Bobby Jack. Yesterday he said he'd just informed his supervisor about the rehab, but tonight he admitted the captain had told him new blood was being brought in a month ago. And according to Cindy, the rehab thing has been in the works for a couple of weeks."

"The rumors are the entire psychic program is headed for the scrap heap. Money's tight. Even the police are scaling down their budgets."

"But my compensation was expenses only. I never profited from my work." Having inherited a bundle from my grandmother, I didn't need a regular nine-to-five job to pay the rent.

"But every dollar saved is a dollar that can go to

other departments."

Stunned, all I could do was stare. Why hadn't I sensed this upheaval? Because of Dr. Schenk's demands? I pushed the thought from my mind.

"I can't believe I didn't know."

"If you'd been around the station on a regular basis, you would have," Reed said.

"And Bobby Jack knew this? Why didn't he tell me?"

"You'll have to ask him. The Hollis case was heavy news for a while. Not only was the public pissed at not finding the killer, but a lot of homicide detectives thought they'd been shut out of the investigation by..." Reed stopped to gulp a large portion of his beer.

"A flake," I finished for him.

He lowered his eyes and nodded.

Margie Hollis, a suburban housewife and the mother of a toddler, had been found beaten to death in the kitchen of her home. Her year-old son sat crying next to her body. The floor was covered with blood, as was the baby. He'd crawled through it.

My participation was after the fact. I'd zoned out and seen the murder take place. She'd come home from the grocery, set the baby on the floor and the bags on the counter only to surprise a burglar. Panicked, he'd broken her skull with a bottle of wine. The killer had worn a ski mask, which blocked my view. He was still at large.

"I wasn't happy about not solving the crime either. And Bobby Jack begged for more time."

"Months with no new leads, no more visions, and other murders to investigate landed it on my desk." He hesitated. I sensed he had more information to impart.

"I also did a quick check on Mike Young."

"And?"

"He's a good cop. Lots of citations and commendations. Also had his fair share of reprimands. And one of the detectives at the Fourteenth Precinct tells me Jill Conway asked for a transfer last month. Seems she and Young had a public disagreement regarding some of his comments about women on the force."

"That doesn't surprise me. I read his emotions and they weren't flattering. Wonder why Jill didn't mention the transfer to me. We talked about Mike this afternoon."

"Apparently, her lieutenant talked her out of it, at least for a while." He picked up the menu. "What have you been doing lately?"

"You mean besides having nightmares? I do volunteer work at the local animal shelter, garden when the weather sees fit, read, watch TV. It's very boring."

"Other than the animal shelter thing, it sounds downright stupefying. How long has it been since you've seen Linnie?"

"Too long. Close to six months," I answered with a sigh.

"Why don't you go down and see her? She'd be happy to show you all the baby stuff. The woman could open a store."

"I may."

I picked up the menu and pretended to read, instead trying to slip into Reed's mind. Being with him again had erased the past couple of years. I felt comfortable, happy and admitted to curiosity. Was he thinking along the same lines?

He wasn't in the least bit happy. He was worried, concerned, and scared.

"You know, it's polite to knock before entering. Get out of my mind, Sasha."

I laughed. "Sorry. Old habits die hard. I understand the worry and the concern, but what's scaring you?"

The waiter stopped next to our table, preventing him from answering. He slammed his mental door by focusing on ordering.

"Made up your mind yet?" Reed asked.

"I'll have the Southwestern Chicken Salad and another glass of Chardonnay," I replied, disgruntled that he had shut me out so effectively.

"You can bring me another beer along with the Wonderly Whopper, medium rare, fries, and coleslaw."

The waiter left and for a moment I contemplated renewing my question about what scared him. Conversation that wouldn't start an argument was rapidly drying up.

Instead, I let my mind wander to the files I had read this morning. So far, nothing had jumped out and grabbed my attention. Several had been flagged as destined for Reed's desk soon. *Cold cases must frustrate the hell out of...*

Outside emotions slammed into me with a suddenness that took my breath away. Anger—no rage—along with fear and resentment washed through my psyche, leaving me gasping. I had no idea from whom or where they emanated.

"Sasha?" Reed asked, concern filling his eyes.

I couldn't answer. The room dimmed and the sounds of the bar became muted. My breathing slowed and I couldn't move. The emotions receded and were replaced with a vision. Pictures flashed before my eyes like a slide show.

"Sasha?" Reed asked again. "Oh, God."

His hands covered mine, grounding me to reality. I had no concept of time, but gradually the room returned to normal.

"Oh, shit," I said, gulping the rest of my wine. "How long was I out?"

"A minute or two, no more."

I now had no problem understanding what scared Reed. He was too slow closing the door. His fear was for me.

"What was it? What did you see?"

"Photos. I saw photos of the woman Charlie drew. They flipped by so fast they took on a motion of their own."

"What kind of photos? Was it real time or precognition?" he asked in an urgent voice.

"I don't know."

"Is she all right?"

I nodded. "She is if the pictures are precognitive." I took a moment to gather myself. "She was in some kind of a classroom talking with other people. Then she left and I saw her kidnapping."

"Does this mean she's a teacher? Can you identify the type of classroom? High school? College?"

"I don't know. She's frowning as if mad about something, not having a clue about what's to come."

"What about the people around her? Are they young? Old? Carrying books? What?"

"I don't know." My voice rose at the urgency in his. Luckily, the noisy bar crowd masked my agitation. I needed to calm down. Taking a deep breath, I lowered my tone. "The photos flipped by too fast. I also caught rage and fear."

Reed frowned. "I don't like this. The rage, the fear reminds me of Jeff. I'm worried how you'll handle everything with new partners."

I placed my hand over his. Instant warmth seeped into my frozen fingers. "I'll have you there to watch my back, and I won't be as unsuspecting as three years ago."

"Don't go back to Holly Springs tonight. Come stay with me. The guest room is made up. I even have a new toothbrush in the cabinet," he said with a smile.

"I'm not sure that's a good idea."

Before he could answer, our meal arrived. We ate in silence, and for once I made no attempt to read his thoughts or emotions. I had too many of my own floating around.

The thought of returning to the house in Germantown caused my heartbeats to quicken. Even though we'd be in separate rooms, I wanted to go. I needed his quiet strength. He calmed and understood me better than anyone with the exception of Linnie.

I ate silently, shifting my thoughts and trying to analyze my vision. If the woman in question was a teacher, then that meant Jill's sister was not the target. I'd tell her tomorrow. It would be one worry off her mind.

I concentrated on slowing the slide show. Was the victim carrying books? She looked too old to be a student, but then a lot of women returned to an interrupted college education. Maybe I should focus on the other people in the room. It was an eclectic group. Men, women, some young, some older. The scene wasn't clear. Could the killer be one of them? A classroom setting would make stalking easy.

"How's the salad?" Reed asked, chomping on a fry.

I was so deep into my thoughts I never tasted it. Now three-quarters gone, I speared another piece of spiced chicken and popped it into my mouth.

"It's fine. How's the burger?"

"Okay." He sighed. "I guess what I'm really asking is how are *you*? You haven't said a word in the last fifteen minutes."

"I was thinking about the vision." I told him my take on what I'd seen, including the information that Lisa was an actress. "Jill will be relieved."

"Assuming her sister wasn't a special speaker or something. For all you know, the scene could have been an acting class. That might explain the diversity of ages."

I stopped eating and stared. "I never thought of that. But what about the emotions I felt before the vision?"

Reed shrugged. "We're in a bar. You could have picked up on anyone here. That in turn might have triggered the vision."

From my seat, I slowly looked around the room. All the stools at the bar were occupied. Reed could be right. The middle-aged guy across from me had a scowl on his face. Another younger man sat a few seats away from him peeling the label on his beer bottle. He didn't look in a good frame of mind either. I slipped in for a closer inspection. Yep. Girl trouble. The older dude was pissed about not getting a promotion at work.

I heaved a sigh and pushed my plate away. I was

upset and needed an anchor.

"Reed, is the invitation for a sleepover still open?"

He shot me a keen glance. "Of course. Are you feeling all right?"

"Yes, but I don't want to be alone tonight."

"Nightmares?"

I finished my wine, unable to make eye contact with him. "They scare the crap out of me. Half the time, I fear going to sleep. I have pills but rarely take them."

"What kind of pills?"

"Just something to help me sleep."

Reed frowned and signaled the waiter for our check.

"I wish you'd dump this guy Schenk and go to a real psychiatrist," he muttered.

"Dr. Schenk is a real psychiatrist, and I don't want to argue about him tonight. We did that at lunch." I didn't enlighten him about my misgivings concerning the psychiatrist I'd had earlier. I needed to think on them more.

Reed raised his hands in surrender. "All right. I won't mention it again. Why don't you move in for a while, until this case is over? I worry about you being alone down in Holly Springs."

Move back? The idea had a lot of appeal. I couldn't help but think back to those nights filled with hot kisses, mind-blowing caresses, and long, slow love-making. I'd missed Reed on every possible level, but would I be able to stay in the guest room as a guest?

"I'll think about it. Let's not jump the gun. I may be able to concentrate better at my place. You're a distraction."

The waiter brought the check and Reed laughed

while placing a credit card on the tray.

"At least I'm good for something."

Oh, he was good for something all right. My heart rate accelerated at the thought.

****

I stepped out of my car in Reed's driveway and stared at the house I'd once hoped to call home. Not much had changed. The crepe myrtle I'd planted along the fence had grown, and Reed still hadn't uprooted the overgrown boxwoods from in front of the living and dining room windows. I sighed and tried to control the tears welling in my eyes. *I should be living here.*

Walking in the front door, I couldn't help but remember my exit. After our discussion, Reed had left for work. I packed, left the house key on the kitchen table along with a note saying where he could find me, and then departed, not looking back. I cried all the way to Linnie's and didn't stop for hours.

Yet now, here I was, happy to be back at the scene of one of my worst emotional upheavals.

"The guest room is all made up," Reed said, leading me down the hallway. "If you need anything, just holler."

"A cup of tea would be nice. I don't suppose you have any of that herbal stuff I bought still around, do you?"

He smiled. "As a matter of fact, I do. I'll make you a cup."

He left and I sat on the bed resisting the urge to peek into the master bedroom across the hall. In a burst of domestic happiness, I'd repainted it a week or so after moving in replacing the boring beige with a soothing light aqua. Had he kept it? And would I find the decorative pillows I'd bought for the sofa in the living room still there? There had been so many little touches I'd wanted to give the house to make it warmer, more feminine.

I entered the hall bathroom and had to chuckle. The bilious wallpaper with the maroon and white hydrangeas hadn't been removed yet. Both of us had hated those nauseating flowers. I washed my hands and face, and then returned to the bedroom. Out of curiosity, I opened the closet. Inside hung one of my old skirts and several tops. The dresser drawer revealed a couple of bras and numerous pairs of panties along with a T-shirt I'd used as a nightgown.

"They were in the laundry when you left," Reed said from the doorway, his voice startling me. "I meant to call you about them, but kept forgetting."

I felt like I'd been caught snooping. "That's all right. At least, I'll have a change of underwear for tomorrow."

"Your tea's ready. I put it on the end table in the living room." He turned and walked away. I sensed he was uneasy, but then so was I. This wasn't the most comfortable of situations.

The tea was in the usual spot. I shifted one of the decorative pillows and smiled inwardly before curling up in the corner of the sofa to sip the smooth chamomile and peppermint brew. I was surprised it hadn't gone stale. Just like old times, Reed sat in the recliner, TV remote in his hand.

"Mind if I catch the news?" he asked.

"Go ahead. Do you know you asked me that every night for six months?"

"Yeah, I guess I did. I wanted to be polite."

"If I'm not mistaken, you requested lessons in being less abrasive. Some must have stuck around."

I sipped my tea, remembering those lessons in civility and politeness.

Reed chuckled, and then sobered. "So you're remembering, too."

He sent me a glance that had my insides quivering. Being here proved just how much I missed him. *Sasha, you're an idiot. You should have gone home. This can only end in disaster.*

No, it could only end in disaster if I let it. I wasn't prepared to do that.

"Of course, I'm remembering. It's hard not to." I tore my gaze from his and sipped more tea. "I thought you wanted to watch the news."

He said nothing, but turned on the TV. For the next half hour we sat in silence. I concentrated hard on the news stories. During a commercial, I slipped into his mind. He was concentrating just as hard. I rose, took my cup into the kitchen, and washed it.

"I think I'll call it a night," I said when I returned. "Where do I find that toothbrush?"

He stood and led me down the hallway. Opening the linen closet door, he rummaged around for a second before finding the item, even coming up with a small tube of toothpaste.

He handed them to me with a smile. "If you need anything else, just ask."

"No problem. I imagine the coffeepot, sugar, and cream are all in the same locations."

"I am a creature of habit. Change something in the kitchen and I'll never find it."

I shifted from foot to foot. In the close confines of

the hallway, his nearness heightened my awareness of him. The remaining hint of the aftershave he'd used this morning still lingered on his skin. It mingled with the citrus smelling shampoo, along with the male scent that was just Reed. A throb deep in my core told me I should turn and leave. But I couldn't. I stood transfixed as though expecting something to happen.

"Sasha," he whispered. His blue eyes turned soft with yearning.

His arms reached for me and I willingly stepped into the protective cocoon. A second later, our lips met.

Heat blossomed from the pit of my stomach to every extremity. I clasped my arms around his neck, kissing him like it was the last time. Oh God, it had been so long and it felt so right, so good. His grip tightened, pulling me closer. Our tongues tangled and his hands roamed up and down my back, stopping occasionally to massage my rear end. The throbbing intensified, leaving me weak. I wanted him so badly I could barely stand it.

Reed pulled away. His hands cupped my face, and his lips brushed mine.

"Go to bed, Sasha. I'm not going to take advantage of the situation. Maybe we can talk later."

I couldn't say a word. He kissed my forehead and walked back to the living room. I looked down at the toothbrush and the toothpaste in my hand. I'd clenched the tube so hard the paste had oozed out the cap.

I turned and closing the bedroom door behind me, stared at my reflection in the mirror. My brown eyes had darkened with desire, but even as I watched, the color returned to normal. I traced the reflection of my lips in the mirror with a fingertip. They still tingled from Reed's touch. I brushed a hand through my black hair lifting the heavy weight from my neck, remembering how the tresses had cascaded through his fingers.

I wrenched myself away from the mirror with a sob. Our engagement had been so right—and so doomed. Could we ever recapture what we'd once had?

****

I sat alone at the kitchen table watching the cold rain slant down, the drops bouncing off the pavers surrounding the pool. The water pounding on the roof at seven o'clock in the morning had a hypnotic effect. I rolled over and went back to sleep. When I'd awakened two hours later, Reed was gone.

Nursing my second cup of coffee, I was grateful that for the first time in many a moon, I had slept dreamlessly. I stared out at the black vinyl pool cover. I'd left on a day not unlike today. The rain, the cold. Only then it had been November. This was February. That cold autumn day had been as depressing as my emotions. Today, I didn't know how to analyze my feelings. Was I exhilarated at being back, even if only for one night? Perhaps I feared that I was building hope of a renewed future with Reed on a hopeless foundation? Or was I just fooling myself?

We shared a kiss, that's all. Nothing to get all hot and bothered about. After all, we were once lovers and are still friends. Why not?

I was lying and knew it. I *was* all hot and bothered and would have ended up in his bed with the slightest encouragement.

Rising abruptly, I poured the remains of my coffee down the sink. *Forget it, Sasha. It was just a kiss. Get dressed, go to the station, and read more files.*

Determined not to brood, I marched toward the back of the house. After showering, I selected the navy blue wrap-around skirt and a white top from the closet, dressed, made the bed, and left.

I had peeked inside the master bedroom as I passed. It was neat and uncluttered, the bed made. The aqua walls made me smile.

****

"Glad you could make it. Shall we make lunch plans?" Mike said as I entered the conference room a little before eleven.

"You know, if we're going to solve this case, we need to get along, and sarcastic remarks about my times of arrival ain't gonna cut it," I replied. "May I remind you, I am not an employee of the police department, but a private individual who lends her expertise? I come and go on my own schedule."

He heaved a sigh and tossed the file he was reading onto the table.

"All right, you win, but for the life of me I don't understand why women can't tell time."

"Will you get off that horse?" Jill snapped. "I know plenty of men who show up late because they can't turn off a football game. So give it a rest."

The conference room door opened, sparing me listening to the partners argue. Bobby Jack walked in looking only slightly like a bum. He'd shaved, but with an obviously shaky hand. Several razor nicks dotted his face. His slacks were wrinkled and his polo shirt had a damp patch down the middle as though the coffee hadn't found its way to his mouth. He squinted through bloodshot eyes.

"Mike, the rest of the St. Louis reports came in overnight. Why don't you and I go through them, while Jill and Sasha work on the last of the files here?"

Mike shrugged. "Sure, although I don't expect to find anything from St. Louis."

Bobby Jack shot me a glance. "Never can tell. Jill, would you mind getting a cup of coffee? I'd like to talk to Sasha privately for a minute."

"No problem." She and Mike left, closing the door behind them.

"Sasha, I want to apologize for last night. I don't remember everything I said, but I know I can sometimes be damn nasty when I drink."

"That's all right. I think I understand."

He ran a trembling hand through his hair. "I wish to God I did. Have you talked to Cindy?"

I nodded. "I'm so sorry. I don't know what to say."

"It's my own fault." He hesitated. "I called a friend this morning—a recovering alcoholic. He's taking me to an AA meeting tonight."

"That's a wonderful idea."

For the first time since meeting Bobby Jack, I was uncomfortable in his presence. His defenses were down and he made no attempt to prevent me from entering his mind. Shame, fear, anger all swirled together, along with a determination to set things right with his family. I breathed a mental sigh of relief for Cindy and prayed they'd make it.

"At any rate, thanks for calling the cab. Did I pay my tab at the bar?" He bit his lip and hung his head as if inspecting his shoes.

"I took care of it. Don't worry."

"I owe you." He turned and left the room.

81

Jill returned and resumed her seat, setting the coffee on the table. I decided to probe for more information on her sister.

"Tell me more about Lisa. You said she's an actress. That must be interesting."

"She came out of the womb acting," she said with a laugh. "Lisa was a drama queen from day one. She used to raid Mother's closet and play dress up. By the time she was five, she had added dialogue. When she was eight, she insisted on going to an audition for *The Wizard of Oz*."

"Did she get the part?"

"They went with a short, experienced adult to play Dorothy, but she did get the role of a munchkin who stole every scene. After that, there was no stopping her."

"So your sister's been at this for quite some time. Does she ever teach acting? You know, like spreading her experience and skills around?"

"She's a regular cast member at the St. Louis Repertory Theater, and often gives talks and recruits from local drama societies and classes."

Oh, God, Reed had nailed it. Good thing I hadn't said anything to Jill about my vision last night.

"St. Louis has several universities and isn't short on talent. Mary Alice Anderson got her start at the St. Louis Theater," Jill continued, mentioning a hot new Hollywood actress.

"Is Lisa good?"

"She's damned good." Sisterly pride oozed from her voice.

"Did she ever want to go the Hollywood route?" I wondered if my nightmare had taken place in Los

Angeles. It was possible if the dream had been precognitive.

"I don't know. By Hollywood standards she's considered an older actress. Hard to break in at that stage of your career."

"Seems to me talent should be the benchmark, not age."

Jill shrugged. "You'd think. Besides, if Lisa ever left St. Louis, it wouldn't be for California, but New York. She goes two or three times a year to take in the Broadway and off-Broadway shows."

Someone tapped discreetly on the door, and then opened it. A uniformed officer poked her head in.

"Excuse me, Detective Conway?"

Jill looked up with a smile. "Yes."

"The desk sergeant just called up to say you have a visitor waiting in the lobby."

"A visitor? Who?"

"I don't know. I didn't get a name. He just said a visitor."

Jill rose. "Better go see who it is. Might be someone from my old precinct, or one of my informants. Mike and I left an open case to come here. Excuse me."

She walked out and I sat back. My finger played with the tab on one of the file folders in front of me. Swell, did this mean I'd have to add New York to my list? And of course, I was assuming Lisa Parker was the victim. If I'd learned anything over the last three years, it was to never assume.

I opened the folder and read the first paragraph before closing it again. It was no use. My mind kept drifting back to Reed and last night.

Did I want to renew the relationship? Did I even want to try? And if I did both, would the results be the same as two and a half years ago? Sadly, my logical mind said yes in spite of my heart saying, "Go for it."

Maybe this case could prove the catalyst to a new understanding between us. And in the back of my mind, I wondered if Reed also wasn't right about Dr. Schenk. Oddly enough, other than yesterday, I'd never tried to enter my shrink's mind, maybe because, deep down, I didn't want to know what he was thinking about my abilities or me.

Perhaps I should call Linnie. What can a trip down to Gladden County hurt? It would ease my...

The conference room door stood open and from the corridor I heard footsteps and two women laughing. Jill entered with another lady behind her. She stepped aside and I sucked in a startled breath, doing a double take.

Charlie's sketch had come to life.

Chapter Six

"Sasha, I'd like you to meet my sister, Lisa Parker. Lisa, Sasha Bellwood," Jill said, her eyes crinkling from her smile.

Internally, I sensed happiness and relief. She could now keep a closer eye on her sister.

Lisa stepped forward, hand outstretched. "I'm pleased to meet you."

I reciprocated and motioned toward a chair. "Have a seat. Jill mentioned you're from St. Louis. What brings you to Memphis?"

Lisa removed her red wool coat, hung it over the back of a chair, and then removed a matching stocking hat. Her long blonde hair fell past her shoulders, the curly ends draping over a black sweater. She flicked a strand out of the way and took a seat. She smiled, her blue eyes radiating mischief.

"Well, I woke up at the absurd hour of five o'clock this morning and decided it was time to see my big sister." She tossed a glance toward Jill. "Must have been your phone call the other day. Suddenly, I needed a change of scenery. Figured Memphis was as good a place as any."

Jill's grin widened. "I'm so glad you're here. Coffee?"

Lisa made a face, wrinkling her nose. "God, no. I'm saturated with the stuff. Got a diet soda handy?"

"I'll go get it." Jill moved toward the door.

"Aw, don't bother. Just tell me where the vending machines are and I can do it. I've been in a car for almost five hours. I need the exercise." She rose and held out her hand, palm up. "I will, however, let you treat."

Jill laughed and forked over a dollar bill along with some change. She was still laughing as Lisa left the room.

"Jill, I'm not sure this is a good idea."

"Why not? It's perfect. She's here where I can keep an eye on her."

Just as I suspected. I shifted in my seat. "But my vision said nothing about where this murder, or attempted murder, occurs."

"Sasha, she'll stay with me. We'll eat together, use the evenings to chat, and generally be joined at the hip. Her routine will be broken for a while. Hopefully, we can nail this guy before she leaves. Besides, we aren't even sure the vision involved Lisa."

I bit my lip and fiddled with a file folder in front of me. Maybe she was right. If my latest vision of a classroom, *and* if Lisa did teach occasionally, was true, then the danger level had subsided somewhat. And Lisa's hair was longer than that of the woman in my vision. I still didn't like her being here and knew the rest of the group wouldn't either. Did Jill realize my vision also said nothing about *when* the murder would happen? I opened my mouth to remind her, and then closed it again.

Jill was smiling and relaxed. I had no problem reading her. The anxiety and fear levels had dropped to reasonable levels. I couldn't escalate them again without more information.

"I guess with you as a chaperone, she's safe enough. And if she does go out, make sure it's with someone you trust."

"She doesn't know anybody here. Where would she go? The only people I'd introduce her to are cops." She chuckled. "Maybe I need more of a social life."

Lisa breezed back in the room, a soda can in her hand.

"A buck and a half for a can of soda? And at the police station no less. I didn't expect to get robbed here."

"You didn't. I did. Wait until you pay two bucks for a cinnamon bun the size of a quarter."

Lisa resumed her seat, chugged a good portion of liquid from the can, and shifted her gaze to me. "Do you work homicide, too? I always thought it was kind of a gruesome job—looking at dead bodies all the time."

"I'm not officially a cop. I just help out from time to time."

I wasn't sure Lisa could handle my specific role with the Memphis Police Department right now.

Her eyebrows rose. "Oh? Doing what?"

"Checking out old files. Giving my insight, so to speak. It's a volunteer position."

"That sounds interesting. I do some volunteer work at home, too."

"Yes, Jill told me you're an actress."

She gulped more from her soda can. "I'm a regular at the St. Louis Repertory Theater. Our last production ended Saturday night, which gives me a few weeks until the next one begins. Having time on my hands drives me nuts."

"When Lisa can't be someone else onstage, she tends to get cranky," Jill said with a smile.

She wrinkled her nose at her sister. "I just hate inactivity."

"What do you do between plays? Volunteer-wise, I mean."

I wasn't being particularly subtle with my questions, but hoped to glean enough information to decide if Lisa was the woman of my nightmare.

"I sometimes give seminars on acting at the local community college or for drama clubs. Occasionally, I go to high schools, too. St. Louis has a lot of talented amateurs. The Theater often uses them in minor roles."

"What do you do for fun?"

"Clubbing until all hours of the night," Jill answered.

Lisa stuck her tongue out and finished her soda. "I like the nightlife. So what? My schedule is after-hours oriented."

I breathed easier. If she was a night owl, then the early morning jogging didn't fit in.

I fiddled with a folder. "I'm a morning person. Up early and in bed by eleven. I'm so boring I could cry."

"Oh, I don't need much sleep. I can keep my focus with only about four or five hours of shuteye. I'm usually up and at 'em by eight."

I had breathed too soon. I was trying to formulate how to ask if she jogged when Jill came to my rescue.

"Still jogging five miles a day?"

"I only do three miles, and it's three days a week. I'm not that much of a health nut. How about you, Sasha? Do you jog?"

"Only to my car when it's raining," I admitted.

Lisa laughed while I sat tapping my fingers on the table. Questions regarding her shopping habits or her favorite St. Louis mall sounded silly.

Before any of us could speak again, Mike, followed by Bobby Jack, entered the room. Both carried folders.

"I told you nothing would show up from St. Louis," Mike said. He stopped speaking when he saw Lisa, his eyes widening. "What the hell?"

"Mike, this is my sister, Lisa Parker. Lisa, my partner, Mike Young."

Mike didn't acknowledge the introduction, but turned to Jill.

"What the hell is she doing here?"

Lisa grimaced and raised an eyebrow. "Well, gee, nice to meet you, too."

He jerked his head in her direction, a flush darkening his face. "I'm sorry, but this is an official police investigation. You really don't belong here."

Bobby Jack stepped forward, his hand outstretched. "I'm Detective Beauregard. Don't pay any attention to Mike. We aren't actively discussing anything at the moment."

Lisa smiled and accepted his hand. "Thank you. I don't mean to interrupt anything official. Jill wasn't expecting me. I had to come by to get the keys to the house."

"As a matter of fact, the three of us were just planning on having lunch," Jill said, sending a warning glare toward her partner. "I'm sure you'll understand if we make it an all girl event."

Bobby Jack answered before Mike. "No problem.

Mike and I can go over things. I have some personal business to get out of the way, too. Have a good meal."

Jill jerked her coat from the hall tree while Lisa and I shrugged into ours. Jill was pissed as hell. Getting out sounded like a good idea.

Out in the hallway, Lisa said, "That was your partner? What an asshole! How do you stand him?"

"I don't. As soon as this case is over, I'm asking for a transfer—again," Jill replied through clenched teeth.

"What was all that business about information from St. Louis?" she probed.

"Oh, nothing important. Just some unfinished reports and such. We were transferred to this precinct a few days ago and still have some loose ends on other cases to tie up. Where should we eat?"

I trailed behind the sisters easily reading both of them. Lisa was confused and insulted by Mike's attitude. Jill was mad enough to hurt someone. Mike's words could have been disastrous if he'd gone on.

The last thing we needed was for Lisa to suspect she might be the subject of a killer's fantasy.

****

We returned to the station an hour and a half later. Lunch had been at a nearby deli with the talk mostly about St. Louis and Lisa's life. I didn't begrudge them the time. It gave me a chance to slip into both their minds for a look-see.

Jill's anger at Mike had diminished. The happiness at seeing her sister replaced it.

Lisa was puzzled by the events at the station, but refrained from asking questions. She was also worried about Jill. The early morning call just to say hi had piqued her interest. Mike Young held a spot in her mind reserved for contempt. She assumed the reason for her sister's call was discontent with her partner.

Reed had joined Mike and Bobby Jack. They sat at the conference table, file folders strewn across its surface. All of them looked up as we entered.

"How was lunch?" Bobby Jack asked with a smile.

"Fine," Jill answered. "Anything new in the files?"

"Nothing."

Mike said nothing, but stared first at Lisa, then at his partner. He frowned and resumed reading.

I tossed my coat over the back of a chair, as did Jill. Lisa stood near the doorway shifting from foot to foot, making no effort to show signs of remaining. I read she had no problem sensing Mike's disapproval of her presence. She also wondered why. To her, it seemed personal.

"Uh, Jill, perhaps I'd better head for your place. You have work to do."

"That's an excellent idea," Mike murmured. "No offense, but you're a distraction at the moment."

"Lisa might not take offense, but I do," Jill snapped as she unhooked a key from her key ring.

Mike, not yet accustomed to people sneaking into his mind, had few defenses. I easily crept in to read his emotions. He was angry with Jill, believing she'd asked Lisa to come. What surprised me, however, was his attraction to his partner's sister. He liked what he saw and believed what he'd said about distractions.

I also clued in on Bobby Jack. Still in the throes of a whopping hangover, he couldn't keep me out. He was counting the minutes until he could get out of here, and wanted the rest of the day to go quietly. I also read despair. His life was falling apart and he had no control. The latter worried me, but it was his problem. My friend would have to climb out of his hole alone. I had personal problems of my own. Namely Reed.

Reed's gaze shifted from person to person in the room until finally settling back on Mike Young.

Lisa pocketed the key. "Detective Young, I can see where my presence might be inappropriate while you were investigating a crime, but you're rude. A simple, more diplomatic, do you mind leaving us alone for a while, would work."

He ran a hand over his face. "I apologize for being abrupt. This is a new situation for me and I'm afraid I let my frustrations gain the upper hand."

He said what needed to be said, but didn't mean a word of it. Lisa sensed the same, and then nodded.

Reed's phone rang. "McIntyre...okay, that's a surprise. I'll be there in a few minutes." He hung up. "Sorry, but I have to go. A new witness on a cold case I'm working just showed up."

"Perhaps I'll see you later," Lisa said with a smile.

"I look forward to it." Reed left the room.

"How long will you be staying?" Mike asked Lisa.

"I haven't made up my mind yet." She turned to Jill. "Can I get anything for dinner on the way home?"

"Sure, whatever you want. I don't care." She was still irritated with Mike.

Mentally exhausted from all the eavesdropping, I pulled out of everyone's minds.

"Great. I'll do something Italian and simple. Nice to have met you all."

Lisa whirled for the door and ran full tilt into a man coming in. She careened backward. His arms reached out, embracing her and preventing a fall. It was Charlie Kendall.

"Whoa, sorry about that," he said, smiling into her face. Then the smile slipped and he stared. "Holy cow, it's my drawing."

Lisa stepped back. "Excuse me. What drawing?"

Charlie gazed around the room, realizing he'd just made a mistake.

"Charlie's a sketch artist," I said, hoping to avoid any more awkward questions.

"And you sketched me?"

He recovered fast. "In a sense. Your sister showed me your picture the other day, and I drew a sketch for her."

"Oh? I'd like to see it."

"Uh, it's still at my place. Jill had to leave suddenly and didn't take it with her." He stared hard at her face, his finger lightly tracing her cheekbones. "You have fabulous bone structure."

Her eyes flared wide. "Well, that certainly is a new pick-up line."

Charlie laughed. "I'm sorry. It's the artist in me. I'm a sculptor. I would love to do your bust."

"This gets better and better. First my face, and now my bust. Should I be concerned here?" Lisa asked her sister with a laugh.

"I have no idea. Sasha? Bobby Jack?"

"Charlie is harmless," I asserted.

"Thanks loads. Just what a man wants to hear from a woman," Charlie replied.

"Charlie is brave, honest, and trustworthy," Bobby Jack added with a grin.

"Terrific. Now I sound like an overgrown boy

93

scout." He smiled at Lisa. "My name is Charlie Kendall. And you, of course, are Jill's sister, Lisa…sorry, I can't remember the last name."

"Guilty, and it's Parker."

"Are you going to be in Memphis long?"

"Haven't decided yet," Lisa answered with a shrug and a sidelong glance at Mike. "I may stay just to irritate some people."

"That sounds intriguing. Why is it I have the feeling I just walked into an argument?"

"Because you did," Jill said. "Mike seems to find Lisa a distraction to the investigation."

Charlie's eyebrows rose. "In that respect, I have to agree with him."

Mike sighed loudly and tossed the folder he was reading farther onto the table.

"I'd like to remind all of you that we are here for a purpose—to catch a killer before he strikes. *Anyone* from the outside would be a distraction. I apologize for not having made myself clear on the subject."

"Mike's right," Bobby Jack replied, closing the folder in front of him. "Why are you here, Charlie?"

Charlie actually stopped staring at Lisa and transferred his gaze to the rest of us.

"I forgot to turn in my bill for last month's services when I was here the other day. Since I was in the neighborhood, I dropped by. Good thing I did. I ran into Captain Stryker. He told me my services may no longer be needed. Seems they're thinking of going strictly with computer programs."

"Oh, Charlie, no," I cried. "But you put so much life into your drawings. The people you sketch are the people I see in my dreams."

He shrugged. "Everyone's scaling back. Face it, I'm an anachronism. A dinosaur. Technology has won."

"In your dreams?" Lisa said, a puzzled look on her face.

I waved my hand. "It's a long story." Turning my attention back to Charlie, I declared, "You are not a dinosaur."

"We're all dinosaurs," Bobby Jack murmured.

I didn't need to slip into his mind to see anger and frustration. It was plainly visible on his face.

"No, we're not. Charlie, you're the best. I can't believe they'd do this. What am I going to do?"

I know I sounded selfish, but I didn't care. I needed Charlie's talent. I needed to see the faces of the victims as though they stood in front of me. Unfortunately, I feared a victim *was* standing in front of me.

"Get along, I imagine," Mike said. "The computer programs are as lifelike as a photo these days what with digital, 3-D imaging."

"Well, that's cold," I snapped.

"But true," Jill said. "I wouldn't be surprised if someday detectives become obsolete. Wasn't there a movie like that? Where policemen were replaced with robots?"

This upset me more than the news of Bobby Jack's leaving. They might dump the always genial and smiling Charlie Kendall for a stinking computer. The rumors Reed had talked about last night must be true. Was I next on the chopping block?

"Damn it, there's not a computer program born that can hold a candle to your work. My visions come to life through your pencil. It's like you have a direct line into my brain."

95

"Visions?" Lisa asked. "What are you? A psychic or something?"

"Yes." I tried, but couldn't keep the anger at the turn of events from my voice.

"You're kidding," she said. "I've never met a psychic before. Are you trying to find someone who's missing?"

"No, she's trying to prevent someone from harm," Jill said. "Look, I'll explain it to you later."

Charlie looked at his watch. "I have to get going. My class is about to begin." He turned to Lisa. "I meant what I said about sculpting you. Would you pose for me?"

Surprise crossed Lisa's face. "Lots of firsts today. I've never been asked to be an artist's model either. Let me think about it."

"Sure, no problem. How about dinner tonight? I'd like to show you Memphis."

She threw a quick glance at Jill before answering. "Um, thanks, but can I take a rain check? I just got in. I'm tired from the drive down. Maybe tomorrow or the next day. Can you give me a call? I'm staying with Jill."

She rattled off her cell phone number while Charlie wrote it on a slip of paper.

"Thanks, I'll be in touch." He waved and left.

"Guess I'd better go, too," Lisa said.

Before she could move, Mike's cell phone rang. "Young…uh-huh…how long ago? Any specifics yet? Witnesses?…Just a shot in the dark. We're on our way."

"What's up?" Jill asked.

He hung up and I sensed the eagerness surging

through him. His eyes snapped with excitement.

"That was Lieutenant Giles. The body of a woman was found in a dumpster behind a business across from Overton Park. She was dressed in jogging clothes."

Chapter Seven

Perhaps a lack of corpses was the source of Mike's frustrations and lousy attitude. He wanted the action of his job. So did Reed. He'd admitted cold cases bored him. I just had a hard time figuring out how anyone could get a charge out of homicide.

"Overton Park? Jogging clothes?" Bobby Jack said. "It's a popular park for jogging. Any ID?"

"Don't know yet."

"Any description?" I asked. If she had long blonde hair tied up in a ponytail, then the killer in my nightmare had struck, although not in the way I'd seen it.

"No. You ready, Jill?" Mike asked, rising from his chair.

Jill grabbed her coat from where she'd dropped it a few minutes ago.

"I'm ready." She kissed her sister on the cheek. "Duty calls. Go straight home, okay? I'll see you tonight."

A lot of emotion swirled around the room. I feared we'd been too late again. Lisa was puzzled as to why Jill told her to go straight home. Jill was ashamed to hope that the body was connected to my vision thereby eliminating her sister from the victim list. Mike was impatient to get started, and Bobby Jack was angry at being left out in the cold. Useless, unnecessary, a dinosaur.

Mike jerked the door open. A man filled the doorway, his face a mask of anger. Jill gasped, retreating a step. Mike glared at the intruder.

"Young, I wanna talk to you," the man growled.

"I have nothing to say."

"Well, I do."

"What's going on?" Bobby Jack demanded.

Mike waved a hand while Jill stared with a wary expression. A lot of unrestrained fear swirled in their minds.

"Nothing of consequence." He pushed the man back with his forearm. "If you'll excuse us, we're on a call."

"You haven't heard the end of this, Young." The guy scowled but allowed Mike and Jill to pass. Mike slammed the door leaving Bobby Jack, Lisa, and I alone.

"And who the hell was that?" Lisa asked.

I drew a deep breath, glad the turbulent emotions had gone. "I have no idea, but he's obviously a charter member of the Mike Young fan club. Boy, was he ever mad—and scared about something."

Lisa stared while Bobby Jack laid a folder in front of him with a precise movement, the edges squared with the edge of the table.

"Ladies, if you'll excuse me, I have a few personal things to see to. I may be gone the rest of the day. Lisa, it was a pleasure meeting you. I hope you enjoy your stay in Memphis. Sasha, if you need me, just call."

He rose and walked from the room, his back straight as an arrow. Tonight was the AA meeting. I crossed my fingers the outcome would be a success.

The man I'd worked with for three years had been cast aside like the proverbial old shoe. I wanted to cry.

Lisa didn't leave. Instead, she slid into a chair.

"Lord, I admire Jill."

"How so?" I asked.

"The thought of seeing the body of someone who's been murdered is disgusting. How does she do it? I'd be puking my guts out." She shook her head, a furrow marring her brow.

"I guess it takes a certain amount of intestinal fortitude to constantly see the scarier side of life—and death. Cops have to view everything with an objective eye. They can get angry at the crime and the person who committed it, but can't let that emotion cloud their judgment. They need to stay cool."

My mind slipped back three years ago to the murder of Janine Henderson, Linnie's receptionist. I'd been horrified. Linnie had been angry enough to kill the murderer with her bare hands. Reed, while angry, had maintained a professional demeanor.

"She does things I wouldn't dream of doing. I once watched her clean her gun. She handled it like I would a potato or something. Guns scare the crap out of me, but she carried on a simultaneous conversation like it was no big deal."

I closed the file folder and glanced at the clock on the wall. They'd only been gone a few minutes. The chances of me getting much accomplished were slim and none.

Lisa leaned back in her chair, clasping her hands behind her head.

"So tell me about this psychic thing. How does it work? Do you, like, interpret dreams?"

"I have the dubious talent to have precognitive dreams—or nightmares rather."

"I'm not sure I understand what that means."

"I have a dream, usually of someone being murdered. Then Bobby Jack and I try to find the killer before my dream comes true."

"Holy cow, that's heavy. How long have you been doing this?"

Without going into elaborate details, I gave her a brief history of my abilities and how I came to work with the police department. I also told her about the personnel shifts of the last few days.

"I knew something was bugging Jill when she called. She didn't come right out and say it, but I had the impression she wasn't happy about the move." Lisa tossed me a glance and rolled her eyes. "Or maybe it has more to do with her snarky partner."

"He's not the nicest or most diplomatic of people," I conceded. "He's not happy with the change either. Thinks working with a psychic is a waste of time and effort."

"Yet the powers that be think new personnel will make things better? Go figure."

"That's why I was so upset with Charlie's news. He adds another dimension to case. His drawings come to life."

"Now there's an interesting guy. Clue me in. If I accept his dinner invitation, I'd like to know a little something about him," she said with a grin.

"I'm not sure what the definition of a Renaissance man is, but whenever I see Charlie, that phrase comes to mind. He sculpts, paints portraits, draws, and does all very well."

Lisa narrowed her eyes and stared toward the corner of the room. "If I remember my history correctly, a Renaissance man was well-educated for his time and did lots of things very well. I believe the general philosophy was that man should seek out all knowledge and develop his skills as much as possible."

By stretching my imagination, I could see Charlie artistically as a latter day Leonardo DaVinci or Michelangelo.

I tapped a pencil on the folder. "A couple of years ago he painted a mural on the wall of a building in an underprivileged part of town. He captured the heart and soul of the neighborhood. Won awards from several civic groups and from the city for his efforts."

"Does he actually make any money from his work or is he more the starving artist type?" she asked.

"I never asked, but he has his own gallery in the South Cooper Square area. I'm ashamed to say, I've never been there. Unfortunately, the only drawings I've ever seen are sketches he does for the police. Every once in a while he also teaches art history at the local community college. Don't know if he's doing it this semester or not."

"I suppose you'd tell me if he was married." She traced the wood grain on the table with the tip of her finger, not looking at me.

"To the best of my knowledge, he's not, but to be honest, I don't know him all that well."

"How old is he?"

"It's never come up, but I'd say in his early fifties, maybe late forties."

She looked up and arched an eyebrow. "Sounds as if he and I have some things in common. I might take him up on dinner. Could be an interesting evening." Lisa glanced at the clock. "Wow, two o'clock already? I'd better get out of here and let you go back to work." She rose and headed for the door. "Nice to have met you, Sasha. I'm sure we'll see each other again."

I listened to her footsteps disappear down the corridor. Mike and Jill would be at the scene by now. I rose and paced, unable to keep my mind from the object of their investigation. Was this the woman of my nightmare? Could the dream sequences have been out of order with the mall the first contact? I had no idea.

I sighed and wandered to the vending machines down the hall, and then returned with a can of caffeine-free soda. I sat, popped the top, and pulled a folder toward me. I needed to focus on what was in front of me. Jill and Mike wouldn't be back for hours.

I tried to concentrate on the papers, but pictures of Lisa, dead bodies, and a nebulous killer kept intruding. Suddenly, I wanted to talk to Reed. He'd soothe my troubled thoughts.

I shook my head. *No, best not go there.*

Instead, I pulled out my cell phone and dialed my former psychiatrist and closest friend, Linnie McIntyre.

****

It was nearly five before Mike and Jill arrived back at the station. Jill walked with a slow step and a weary expression on her face. Mike didn't look any different, but I squeezed into his mind for a quick peek. He was disappointed about something.

"What did she look like?" I asked without preamble.

After inviting myself down to see Linnie tomorrow, I'd finished reading the files. Nothing that held any significance to this case had popped up. I'd even skimmed the St. Louis reports.

"What are you still doing here?" Mike said.

"Waiting. I have to know. Is she the woman of my nightmare? Is she the sketch?"

Jill heaved a sigh. "No. This woman had short dark hair and wasn't a jogger. Turns out the clothes were not of the jogging variety, but of the hooker kind. She's a known prostitute who usually works along South Third."

"That's a long way from Overton Park."

"She obviously met a john and had issues. Her face was pretty banged up. Preliminary COD is blunt force trauma. Lots of forensic evidence. It won't take long to find the guy. Someone had to see something," Mike said. "We were called out in case she was connected to your vision or whatever. She wasn't, so we're back here."

The frustration in his voice was evident. He didn't want to be "back here" at psychic central. No wonder he was disappointed. He was hoping the case would be solved and he could return to real police work.

"Did Lisa go home?" Jill asked, massaging her scalp with her fingers.

"She left around two."

"If you have any sense, you'll send your sister packing back to St. Louis where she belongs," her partner snapped in an irritated tone.

"She's my sister and I feel better with her here."

"You called after I told you not to and begged her to come down."

"I did not. I simply called to ease my mind. She came on her own."

"You're acting like a sister, not a cop. It's going to screw up your instincts."

"It's human nature to protect those we love," Jill argued back.

Their arguing allowed me to read them. Mike had serious doubts about Jill's ability to do her job with Lisa present. In his mind, she'd ignored his advice and taken control. He didn't like it. He didn't view his suggestions as that, but meant them as orders. I wondered if this attitude crept over into his personal life. How many other people had he pissed off over the years? I thought of the man in the doorway as they had left earlier.

Jill was contemplating turning in her request for a transfer today. She'd had it with interfering male partners. The three years she and Mike had been together professionally had reached the end of the line. Resentment and anger at his words had never been higher. She was ready to bust a gut.

"You know, Lisa being here isn't all bad," I said. "We were talking earlier. I think Jill might be better able to concentrate on her job with her sister in Memphis. She'll have a different routine than she would at home. It'll be easier to keep an eye on her."

"What do you know about it? You're not a cop. You don't know the stresses a personal life can have on your job performance," Mike said. He didn't quite sneer, but came close.

Biting back an angry retort, I remembered the hell I had gone through three years ago with a serial killer everyone knew and liked. And I had first hand knowledge about stress in the workforce. My bust up with Reed was proof of that.

"Yes, I do and let's just leave it at that."

Mike took a deep breath and turned for the door. "Excuse me, but I have a report to write. So do you, Jill. I'll be in my cubicle."

"I want to relax for a few minutes—if that's all right with you, *mein Fuhrer*."

Mike glared and left.

"Damn, that man pisses me off," she said in a sharp tone. "One of these days, he'll go too far with giving orders to people he has no business giving orders to—if you get my drift."

Her words were only slightly incoherent given the state of her anger.

"I get it."

She whipped out her cell and dialed. "Hello, Lisa. Did you get into the house all right?...No problem. What's for dinner?...Sounds good. Keep mine warm. I have to write a report. I should be home around nine or so. We can talk then. Make sure the doors are locked. Okay?"

She hung up, a worried look on her face.

"Don't worry, Lisa will be fine," I said.

"Even with her here, I still worry. She can be a terrible ditz at times."

"Can't we all?" I tried to keep my tone light to soothe Jill's troubled mind. "What does she do that's ditzy?"

"She's impulsive. Take coming down here as an example. And like I said, she's not the greatest judge of character when it comes to men. But I refrain from making comments. I won't do that again."

"Why? What happened?"

"She flirts. Talks to strangers at clubs and in bars.

106

Not the brightest thing to do. That's how she met Joshua Brennan."

"Who's Joshua Brennan? A boyfriend?"

Some of the anger at Mike had eased from her mind.

"An ex-husband. She met him at some dive her friends took her to for her twenty-first birthday. I didn't like him from the start. Told her so, too. Had quite a dust up over him. The upshot was she married the jerk three months later. Took her less than a year to realize I'd been right. The miserable scumbag verbally abused her and when she moved back home with me, stalked her. Finally had to get a restraining order."

An uneasy ripple skipped through my psyche. "How did he react to that?"

"Screamed and carried on."

"Jill," I said slowly. "Do you know where he is now? I mean, do they run in the same crowd?"

"No, he eventually moved to Southern California—San Diego, I think." She blinked and stared. "You think *he* might be the man in your nightmare?"

I shrugged. "How long has it been since she's seen him?"

"Years. At least seven or eight. I'm sure she'd mention seeing him—unless she didn't want to upset me. Maybe I'll draw her out about him tonight, just to make sure."

I hesitated before making my next comment. "Jill, don't take this wrong, but in a way, Mike could be right about your focus. It might not be as sharp as you think."

She bridled. "I'm fine."

"I just meant, you're concerned about Lisa and madder than hell at Mike. The combination's

107

distracting."

She bit her lip and looked away. "I'm fine. I'd better get busy on that report. See you tomorrow." Turning, Jill left.

A few seconds later, Reed entered. Lines grooved deep into his face. My heart crimped at his expression. He sat with a sigh and shook his head.

"I wondered if you were still here."

I told him about the body found near Overton Park. "I just wanted to make sure it wasn't the woman of my nightmare. Did you get good information from your new witness?"

"Reasonable. Seems she thinks her boyfriend of the moment four years ago may have been the killer."

"Four years? And she's just now coming forward?"

Reed shrugged. "They recently broke up. Not sure if she's telling the truth or out for revenge. Are you going to Holly Springs tonight? You're welcome to stay with me as long as you like. I don't like the idea of you being alone. That cottage you rent is too isolated."

"It's on an estate with a wall around it. I'm fine. Thanks for the invitation, but I need some time alone. Things are…moving fast. I need to think."

What I really needed was the ability to step back and gather my thoughts. Being with Reed these last few days brought our relationship—past and present—into sharp focus. This case should take precedence over all else. My—our—personal life didn't matter.

"If you change your mind, give me a call. I'll be there." He nodded, turned and left.

I blinked tears from my eyes. He had carefully masked his thoughts, shutting me out.

****

I remembered little of the drive home to Holly Springs. My mind skittered from one subject to the other. The psychic air rippled like the disturbed waters of a quiet lake in the wind before a storm.

While I could enter people's minds, read their emotions, and to a certain extent, their thoughts, I didn't have the ability to carry on telepathic conversations. I didn't count murder victim, Kathy Watson, the woman who started this whole psychic snowball rolling three years ago. Technically, she contacted me—after her death. I had never been able to communicate directly with anyone still alive.

I gathered impressions, feelings, sometimes from long distance—a new wrinkle. Right now, I sensed fear, anger, exhilaration, resentment, and oddly, lust. Unfortunately, I was unable to pair the emotions with specific people.

A microwaved dinner was the only thing available in my limited pantry. I picked at the unappetizing meal, eating little. Most of my sustenance came from the contents of a bottle of wine.

Too early to go to bed, I wandered into the living room, put some soft music on my tablet, laid down on the sofa, and closed my eyes.

Dr. Schenk had been hammering me for months about astral projection and dual consciousness, and I had tried with limited success.

Relaxed and only a little popped from the wine, I let my thoughts drift to Reed. Funny how things happen. Our first contact had been abrasive—he the skeptic and me defensive. In spite of our differences, the attraction had grown, surprising me. I didn't have a lot of luck with men, but with Reed, it had just felt right, as natural as breathing.

And speaking of breathing, mine had slowed, along with my heartbeat. I had the sensation of floating, not unlike my hypnosis sessions with Linnie a few years ago. This was about as far as the astral projection thing had ever gone.

Suddenly, I experienced a swift rush. I couldn't explain a rush of what. Just a rush. Then, my mind no longer saw my living room. Instead, I hovered near the ceiling of Reed's home office.

He sat at the computer working the mouse in quick movements. I peeked over his shoulder. He was playing a game, mindlessly going through the motions to keep busy. I had no entry to his mind. Perhaps the astral projection prevented me from doing two things at once.

He continued clicking until the game ended. Reed leaned back in his chair, and then resumed playing. Not a fan of computer games, I had no idea what he played, but he played it fast and furious. Finally, he quit, shut down the computer, and headed for the bedroom.

He undressed, slid beneath the covers, and turned out the light on the nightstand. It was a routine I remembered well. He'd always come to bed after me. If I'd been awake, we'd cuddle, kiss, and make love.

Reed sighed and flung an arm across his forehead. "Sasha, I miss you," he whispered into the dark.

His words ripped me apart, tearing at my gut until I wanted to cry. I hovered, breathless and yearning to ease his anguish, yet knowing anything I'd do would be temporary. I had to leave, get out before my soul shredded any further. The room blurred and fuzzed out.

I returned to my home with a thud, like a clunky landing in an airplane by an inexperienced pilot. I opened my eyes. The room whirled, disorienting me until the spinning slowed, and then stopped. I sat up and looked at my watch—ten o'clock. I'd been out of it for an hour.

I buried my face in my hands. If this was astral projection or dual consciousness, I wanted nothing to do with it. Seeing Reed's emotional nakedness was worse than an invasion of privacy. It was an attack on what we all hold dear—our private individuality, our desire to remain ourselves.

I'm not sure I understood what I was thinking. I did know, however, that what I'd done was wrong. Invading the minds of criminals was one thing. Invading the minds of friends, even unintentionally, or spying on their movements with a presence they didn't suspect smacked of voyeurism. Thank God, I was seeing Linnie tomorrow.

I wiped the tears from my cheeks, and snatching the tablet from the table, turned off Mozart. Like Reed, I needed mindless drivel to numb my mind.

Reality shows should do the trick. I searched for the TV remote before spotting it on the entertainment center. Without thinking, I willed it to come to me. It rose and wobbled through the air until dropping into my lap.

I sobbed again. My abilities were overpowering me. I couldn't live like this much longer.

Chapter Eight

The black stalks of last year's cotton crop, some still topped with an occasional white puff, flew past as I drove southwest toward Gladden County and Linnie. I used a less congested shortcut along state and county roads. A quick glance at the speedometer told me I was going much too fast. I lifted my foot from the accelerator. It was only forty miles. No need to hurry.

Sleep had been elusive after last night's events. In spite of my fears and tears, I'd played with the telekinesis. It got easier with every attempt. I'd even managed to levitate the footstool in front of a chair—just an inch or so, but it was progress. Still upset with the responsibility of all these abilities, I'd gone to bed, only to toss and turn most of the night. I finally fell asleep around four and didn't wake up until almost ten. It was now a little after eleven. Linnie had invited me for lunch.

Marilyn "Linnie" McIntyre had been my best friend since the fourth grade. She was one of the few people outside of my family whom I trusted with knowing about my psychic abilities. She had also been my psychiatrist.

Now, happily married to Reed's younger brother, Bill, she had moved to Gladden County, Mississippi. She still counseled at the local mental health clinic, but preferred a less hectic life. They were expecting the birth of their first child any week now.

I pulled into the driveway of their rambling Victorian home in the heart of Hollister, the county seat. Bought after their marriage two and a half years ago, Bill referred to the place as "The Rambling Wreck." Renovations never seemed to stop. The front of the house with its twin turrets on the corners had a fresh coat of light yellow paint and the white trim gleamed in the late winter sunlight.

I didn't stand on ceremony, but walked right in the front door. No one locked their doors in Gladden County, not even Sheriff Bill McIntyre.

"Okay, I need a shrink bad," I called out as I entered the spacious foyer.

"It'll cost you," Linnie's voice echoed from the back of the house. She waddled out of the kitchen, her belly sticking out like the prow of a ship.

"Holy crap! You look like you're smuggling a beach ball."

"I feel like I'm smuggling the Rock of Gibraltar." She leaned forward as far as she could and brushed my cheek with her lips. "I hope that crack about needing a shrink was a joke."

Linnie looped her arm through mine and led me into the living room.

"Hmm, all Victorian, all the time? Since when did you go in for antiques?" I asked, eyeing the furnishings.

"Since we bought this monstrosity. A generous supporter of the sheriff who happens to own an antique store in town gave me a deal I couldn't refuse."

"Yes, but is it comfortable?"

"Not overly, which is why Bill and I spend most of our time in the back parlor. This is for show and

113

entertaining company. Come see the dining room. We just finished it a couple of months ago."

We wandered across the hallway and into another homage to Victorian decorating.

"Let me guess, you eat in the kitchen."

Linnie grinned. "You got it. Bill protested loudly at renovating rooms we had no intention of using for ourselves."

"But you convinced him otherwise."

"Of course." Her grin faded. "Now, why do you need a shrink?"

I waved a casual hand in the air. "Just a joke."

"Uh-huh. Come on, let's go sit down. I need to take a load off."

She led me toward the back of the house and the family room. This was where the homey furniture lived—a traditional sofa, love seat, and Bill's "I'll-never-give-it-up-you'll-have-to-bury-me-in-it" recliner.

"How are you feeling?" I asked as Linnie carefully sagged into a corner of the love seat.

"My back hurts, my legs hurt, my ankles are swollen, I haven't seen my feet in months—by the way, do my shoes match? I can't eat any more than six bites of food at a time without getting indigestion, I haven't slept the night through in three months because of bathroom calls, and I can feel the stretch marks popping out every few minutes."

I had to laugh when she finally paused for breath. That was so Linnie.

"Yeah, but it'll all be gone in a few weeks. Where's Bill?"

"Making sure his newest deputy knows what he's doing. He's riding along with him for a little while.

He'll be here for lunch. Damn, I should have asked you if you wanted something to drink before I sat down. It takes a derrick and a crane to get me back up." She scooted toward the edge of the sofa.

"I don't need anything, and if I decide I do, I'll get it myself."

She slumped back against the cushions. "Glad you said that. I'm parched. The iced tea is in the fridge."

I found the glasses and the tea, poured, and returned to the den.

"Does Bill wait on you hand and foot?" I said, handing her the drink.

"Of course. Spoils me rotten. I'm conniving on how to make it last after the baby's born." She took a sip as I resumed my seat. "Okay, spill it, what's bothering you?"

Damn, Linnie knew me too well. I couldn't hide crap from her. Never could. With a sigh, I leaned back and drank a large gulp of tea.

"I'm getting bombarded."

"With what?"

I started with the changes in the department, letting my frustration be heard.

"Tough about Bobby Jack and Cindy, but my advice is to stay out of it. He has to decide if he wants help on his own. My guess is the whole psychic experiment within the department will be eliminated. They may consult with you on a case-by-case basis only if they have no other alternative. What else is giving you fits?"

I told her about the vision and its results, not bothering to hide my worry concerning Lisa.

"And it's the same woman? You're sure?"

"There are differences, but far too many similarities. And I'm not sure I can work with Mike Young. He's a total ass." I took a deep breath. "And then there's Reed."

She stared into her glass. "Reed? How does he figure into this?"

"He's acting as a kind of liaison between Bobby Jack, the new team, and me."

"And how does that make you feel?" Her gaze rose to my face.

I rattled the ice in my glass, refusing to meet her eyes. After the break up, Linnie said I should have fought harder for the relationship.

"Sasha?"

"It brought back a lot of memories. Some good, some bad. I, um, stayed at his place the other night."

Linnie's eyebrows rose. "Oh, really? Care to discuss it?"

"We'd been out to dinner. It was late and rather than drive down to Holly Springs, he suggested I sleep over." I bit my lip, and then blurted, "That's not quite true. He asked me to move in until this case was closed."

"And are you?"

I shook my head. "I can't, Linnie. I just can't."

"Why not?"

I launched into my reasoning, leaving nothing out. That included the kiss and the old feelings being re-born, along with my hurt and distrust of renewing the relationship.

"Have you told this to Dr. Silberstein?" Linnie asked with a frown.

"I don't see him anymore. He retired shortly before

Reed and I split. He suggested another psychiatrist in his practice, Dr. Julian Schenk."

"I didn't know Silberstein had retired. Why didn't you tell me?"

"Because you and Bill were smack dab in the middle of wedding plans. I didn't want to rain on your parade. Later on, it seemed silly to bring it up."

"Did Silberstein help? How about this Schenk? I've never heard of him."

I gave her the lowdown on Schenk and what he had me doing, but refrained from admitting to my little secret of telekinesis or to a successful astral projection or whatever he'd called it.

A horrified look crossed her face. "Sasha! That's crazy. What's he up to? Reminds me of Pennington."

I stiffened in my seat. "He's a *parapsychologist*. You got me involved with Silberstein because you knew little about the subject."

She finished off her iced tea and set the glass on the end table with a hard click.

"A parapsychologist should help you through the visions and the consequences. This guy is asking you to expand on things that may or may not be possible. Something's wrong."

I wanted to argue with her, but couldn't. She echoed what Reed had said on more than one occasion. And damn if I wasn't starting to believe it myself. I was floundering both emotionally and mentally. Would it be like this the rest of my life? Was life even worth living this way?

The direction of my thoughts frightened me, but I wanted to think before mentioning anything to anybody. I came here to talk to Linnie. So why not talk? I had no idea why I was so reticent. *Is this the beginning of suicidal tendencies?* I raised the glass with trembling hands, draining the last watery drops of tea.

Stop thinking like that. You're tired, worried, upset, and God knows what else.

The back door slammed and footsteps resounded across the kitchen floor.

"Hi, Sasha, how's it going?" Bill asked, entering the room.

"Fine. How about you?"

He made his way over to his wife, kissed the top of her head, and placed his hand on her bulging stomach.

"No complaints." He smiled and kissed Linnie again. "How's Bruno? Active today?"

"Bruno?" I pushed my darker thoughts to the back of my mind and fell in with his cheerful banter.

"Bill seems to believe I am carrying the next Ole Miss super quarterback."

"Nonsense. Linebacker. Number one pick for the pros."

"And yes, the little beggar's been active. I almost wet my pants earlier when he—or she—kicked me in the bladder."

"It's a boy," he said with a smirk. "God help a girl who's this big."

"Maybe there'll be girls' football by the time she enrolls at Ole Miss. She can make the team as a kicker," I said, trying to maintain a straight face.

Linnie laughed while Bill rolled his eyes. "God forbid."

I had no problem tapping into their happiness and anticipation. Linnie, anxious and uncomfortable, looked forward to motherhood. Bill was proud and couldn't wait for the birth. He took fatherhood seriously. They both oozed love for each other and their soon-to-arrive child.

God, I envied them. A ripple floated through my mind that Reed and I once had the same ambitions.

"Don't forget, you have to assemble the crib and changing table in the nursery," Linnie said.

"Your wish is my command. Let me change clothes and eat." Bill kissed her again and left the room.

"I'm surprised you don't know whether it's a boy or a girl," I said. "I'd think the suspense would be killing you."

She grinned. "It is, but we both decided we wanted to hear the doctor say 'it's a boy' or 'it's a girl.' I don't care as long as it's healthy."

"Bill seems to have his mind set."

"I have the strangest feeling that if a girl pops out, he'll try to shove her back in."

I was in mid-cackle when a familiar voice called out from the foyer as the front door shut.

"Linnie? Bill?"

Reed was here. I shot a suspicious glance toward my best friend.

"Back here, Reed," she answered, and then looked at me. "Yes, I invited him for lunch, too. Live with it and don't even try to enter my head."

I didn't need to enter her head to know she had matchmaking on her mind.

Reed entered the room and went over to kiss Linnie's cheek. Straightening, he looked at me.

"Hello, Sasha."

He didn't seem in the least surprised to see me here. I didn't enter either of their heads, but sensed collusion all the same. I'd be polite and casual if it killed me.

"Hello, Reed. I didn't know you were coming down. You should have stopped by Holly Springs. We could have ridden together."

He looked taken aback as though anticipating anger. "Didn't think of it."

I said nothing further and rattled the ice in my glass again as a message of my irritation to my best friend.

"Could I get you some iced tea?" Linnie asked. "Or would you prefer beer?"

"Nothing right now, thanks." He settled on the opposite side of the sofa from me, but kept his gaze on his sister-in-law. "How are you feeling? No offense, but you look enormous."

Linnie stuck her tongue out. "I *am* enormous, you jerk, and it's all your brother's fault."

"What's all my fault?" Bill said, reentering the room. Now dressed in jeans and a long-sleeved T-shirt, he made a beeline for the recliner.

"My present physical condition, of course."

"Hmmm, I don't seem to recall any complaints at the time."

"You'll probably hear plenty of them while she's giving birth," I said.

"I'll bet. When's lunch?"

Linnie struggled to her feet. "Give me another fifteen or twenty minutes. Care to help, Sasha?"

"Sure." I rose. Anything to escape Reed's presence. I couldn't deal with him being so near, yet so far away—especially after what I'd witnessed last night.

"And don't forget the crib and changing table.

Reed can help."

"Yes, dear."

In the kitchen, she handed me several items from the fridge.

"Here, make a quick fruit salad, will you, while I check the chili."

"Chili?"

"Yeah, I know, but I'm pregnant and have these cravings. I'll deal with the indigestion later." She stirred the pot on the stove. "What else is bothering you?"

I cut up an apple before answering, and then laid the knife on the table. My hands had begun to shake.

"I feel so overwhelmed, Linnie. There are times when I wonder if life's worth living." I waved a hand at her frightened expression. "No, I don't think I'm ready to end it, but I feel so damned guilty all the time."

"Guilty? About what? The old not being able to solve everyone's problems thing again?"

I nodded. "The last two visions I had were after the fact. Both victims had already died, but we never found the killers. And then there was you."

"Me?"

"If I hadn't come to you with my vision of Kathy Watson's murder, your receptionist, Janine would still be alive and you wouldn't have been attacked. Because of me, your practice fell apart."

I sat back in the kitchen chair, bit my lip, and tried not to let the tears well in my eyes.

"Is that why you haven't been down to see me in forever?"

I nodded. "That and I didn't want to intrude on you and Bill."

Linnie pulled out a chair and plunked her butt into

it. "Silly girl. Sasha, let's get something straight. Your actions had nothing to do with any of what happened. Jeff Hammond was a predator, a serial killer. If you hadn't stopped him, he may never have been caught. Yes, Janine died. I almost did. But my issues with my practice were just that—mine."

"But…"

She held up her hand, cutting me off.

"Even with Bill around, I had trouble staying in my own house. I kept seeing Jeff there. Kept re-living the attack. I compared every temp who came into the office to file and answer the phones to Janine. I spent more time with *my* psychiatrist than I did with my patients. When Bill asked me to marry him, I decided to quit the business for a while. The change of scenery and lifestyle has been ten times better than any session with Dr. Garland."

"I must say, you do look more relaxed than when I last saw you. That was the day you found out you were expecting. We had lunch at that trendy little Germantown restaurant."

She smiled. "Of course. I had the urge to buy upscale baby clothes."

I blinked the tears from my eyes and laughed. Linnie could always make me laugh.

She leaned across the table and clasped my hands. "Now, no more guilt, okay? I'm happy. Bill was just what I needed. And I'm even beginning to counsel again. Next fall I'm opening a small, limited practice here in Hollister."

I don't know how she did it, but a weight lifted from my shoulders. She was happy, fulfilled. Could there be hope for me, too?

"You win," I said, picking up the knife again and cutting another apple. "No more guilt. And you may be right about Dr. Schenk, too. I'll give going to a regular shrink some thought, but only after this current case is closed. I also think you're right about the psychic program with the police department going south. Maybe I need a long vacation."

"What you need is Reed," she said in a firm tone, rising clumsily.

"Linnie, don't start."

"It's true. The two of you belong together."

"I can't get past how he tossed me out of his home and his life."

"It wasn't all his fault, you know."

I looked up, outraged. "How was any of it my fault?"

"You know. You just won't admit it."

Before I could answer, Bill wandered in.

"How much longer, babe?"

"As soon as Sasha finishes cutting up the apples, and adds the grapes, raisins, and walnuts. Another five minutes."

He turned his gaze on me, a hungry look on his face. "Chop faster."

I laughed. "Assembling a crib must work up an appetite."

"A room full of geniuses couldn't figure out how to get that thing together," he muttered. "The instruction booklet is fifteen pages long and written in really bad English. It'll take hours."

Linnie smiled and patted his cheek. "We'll make it a group project after lunch."

Bill grumbled, but left the kitchen with a resigned

look on his face. In the family room, someone turned on the TV.

I finished the apples and tossed the rest of the fruit into the bowl, then set the table.

"Come and get it," I called out to them.

Sitting across from Reed reminded me of those cozy Saturdays we'd spent together. We'd talk, laugh, and watch movies or sports. Gradually, the talking, laughing, and togetherness faded. I blamed Reed for not being there for me, for not understanding, for not…

Okay, some of what happened may have been my fault, but he was the one who ended it. Keep that in mind.

Luncheon comments were few and far between until Linnie suddenly groaned, clutched her side, and screwed up her eyes as if in pain.

"What's the matter?" Reed asked in an anxious voice.

"Linnie?" My heart accelerated. Was this it?

Bill's spoon clattered back into the chili when he leaped to his feet.

"What? What? Oh, crap! Now?" His eyes opened wide and his voice had taken on a panicked tone.

Linnie sighed deeply, and then relaxed, opening her eyes again.

"No, no, I'm fine. False alarm. Just one of those Braxton-Hicks things."

"A who-what thing?" Reed asked.

"Braxton-Hicks contractions. Kind of a dress rehearsal for the real thing. I've been having them for a month. Sometimes they're little twinges. Other times they stab. Only lasts a few seconds." She resumed eating, shoving a large spoonful of chili into her mouth.

Bill collapsed back into his chair. "Don't do that! You scared me to death."

"I can see where he's going to be a lot of help when the time comes," I commented.

"Probably drive you to the wrong hospital or call your hairdresser instead of the doctor," Reed added with a chuckle.

Linnie's laugh boomed. "I have a whole police department at my service. I'll get there."

"That's it. Make fun of the prospective father. I can't wait until it happens to one of you," Bill said. His eyes held a teasing frown.

I made the mistake of glancing at Reed. The humor had fled his face as he stared back. His mind was open and I had no trouble reading his emotions. Naked and raw, his envy for Bill and Linnie was a palpable thing.

It could have been us. Was that my thought or had I read his mind?

Confused, I lowered my eyes and ate, the spicy chili heating up my mouth. I chased it with fruit salad and iced tea. I wanted to cry. *I can't handle this now. Maybe it was my thought. God knows, I believe it.*

While I participated in the conversation during the rest of the meal, I remembered nothing of what was said. I was tired—grotesquely tired—and wanted to go home. I needed to think, but couldn't eat and run.

The men returned to the nursery. I helped Linnie clean up before trooping upstairs to join the fun of crib assembly.

We assigned the job of reading the instructions to Linnie as the rest of us tried to follow what she said.

"That makes no sense," Bill griped with a frown.

"Hey, I'm just the reader here," she said from the

comfort of a rocking chair.

"Look, Reed and I will hold the sides and footboard upright while you tighten the screws," I said to Bill.

"Who wrote these instructions? Some shut-in in China who never saw a crib before?" Reed complained.

It was slow going, but we finally had the crib sixty percent assembled when Bill's phone rang.

"Aw, crap. McIntyre here...Was anybody hurt? Call the paramedics and alert The Med in Memphis we'll have one coming their way, and then call the state boys...I know, it's a lousy stretch of road. I'm on my way."

"Accident?" Linnie asked when he'd hung up.

"Yeah, a bad one out on State Road 101. Some trucker trying to avoid the scales on the interstate came around the curve at Hooper's Bend too fast. Slammed head on into a family in a minivan."

"Oh, no. I take it there are injuries," I said.

"Big time." He rose from where he'd been sitting on the floor. "I've gotta go. This could take a while. Will you be all right? Those whosy-whatsis contractions have me worried."

"I'm fine," Linnie said.

"I'll stay with her until you get back," Reed replied.

"Me, too," I added.

Bill nodded, kissed his wife, and left.

Linnie cleared her throat. "I guess the two of you can handle the rest of this."

"Probably a lot better than my brother could. What's next?"

Reed and I finally finished the crib and set it in the

126

corner of the yellow and white room. Linnie had done an excellent job of decorating. A wallpaper border of alphabet blocks and teddy bears ran just under the ceiling. A chair rail graced the wall. Below, cheerful yellow and white checked wallpaper gave the place a happy, gender-neutral look. Plush yellow throw rugs graced the pine floors. A chest of drawers and a bookcase holding children's books had already been assembled. Once the changing table was finished, all that the room needed was the baby.

I didn't talk much after Bill had left. My mind turned toward the conversation at lunch. Maybe it was putting the crib together that had me so melancholy all of a sudden wondering if motherhood would ever happen to me.

In my mind's eye I saw a laughing Reed holding an infant. He made cooing noises and tickled the baby under the chin setting off a chorus of giggles. I reached out my arms and he placed the child in them, his eyes full of love as I nursed our...

I pulled my thoughts away from what could never be. Or could it? Was I seeing what I wanted to see, or was this a vision of things to come? I no longer knew what was real and what was imagined. Talking to Linnie today had helped, and I made a vow to do so again soon.

"Okay, time to start this changing table. It's got to be easier than the crib," Reed said interrupting my thoughts.

He opened the box and slid the components out onto the floor.

"Doesn't look too complicated," Linnie said, glancing at the instructions.

"Neither did the crib," I reminded her.

"What tools do I need?" Reed asked.

"According to the instructions, a Phillips head screwdriver, an Allen wrench, and there should be a baggie full of little plastic clips and some hardware."

Reed reached into the pile of table pieces. "Got the baggie. Now where's the Allen wrench?"

"Look in the box marked 'Legs,'" I suggested.

He opened it. "Good. Everything's here. Now, what did I do with the screwdriver? I was just using it on the crib."

I knew where he'd left it. I'd seen him put it on top of the chest of drawers on the other side of the room when we moved the crib into place.

I should have warned them, but suddenly I no longer wanted to keep new adventures in psychic phenomena to myself. I wanted to talk about the latest wrinkles—well, at least one of them—in my abilities, but couldn't think of any way to bring up the subject that didn't make me a candidate for the funny farm.

I closed my eyes. So much was happening so fast I couldn't keep up. I needed Linnie sharing and offering her opinion. But Reed? My biggest fear was he would totally withdraw. He hadn't been able to handle the easy stuff two and a half years ago. What the hell would he do with this?

Oh, God, help me. What do I do?

"Sasha? Are you all right?" Linnie asked.

I didn't answer. My mind tumbled down a turbulent stream unable to come to a conclusion.

"Sasha?" Her voice sharpened.

I opened my eyes. She stared at me with a worried look. Reed's piercing gaze held me spellbound. I read

128

concern and fear in his mind.

"What?" I asked.

"Linnie asked if you were all right. You haven't said a word in the last five minutes. Is it a vision?"

Shaking my head, I made a decision and concentrated on the screwdriver atop the chest. Slowly it levitated, and then drifted through the air toward Reed.

Chapter Nine

I was too busy concentrating on the telekinesis to read Linnie and Reed's internal reactions and only vaguely noticed the external. Linnie opened her eyes wide and stifled a gasp with her fingertips against her mouth. Reed sucked in an audible breath, his eyes narrowing into ominous slits.

The screwdriver danced in front of him. He snatched it out of mid-air with a scowl, and then dropped it at his feet as if it scorched his fingers. The effort had drained my psychic energy, but I still caught flashes of their emotions. Pain from their thoughts stabbed deep in my soul.

"Oh, my God," Linnie breathed.

"You've come a long way, baby," Reed said, a hard edge to his voice. "How long has this been going on?"

"A couple of weeks."

Linnie moistened her lips. "I'm stunned. Can you do it with anything?"

"I started with a TV remote and I'm working my way up. So far, the largest thing I've moved is a footstool, and that was only an inch off the floor."

"Is this one of Schenk's little suggestions?" Reed asked. His tone had not softened.

I shook my head. "No. I discovered it on my own." I told them about the first incident. "I just thought, and when the remote responded, tried it on other things."

"What does this new doctor say?" Linnie's amazement was giving way to clinical interest.

Reed breathed hard. "I'm sure he'll have you moving houses in a few weeks."

"Reed, please. Sasha doesn't need sarcasm. What does Schenk have to say?"

"I haven't told him yet."

"Why not?" Reed demanded.

"Because I'm working on a case and don't need any more distractions—psychic or otherwise."

"I'd say this qualifies as a pretty big distraction." His tone still held an edge to it. "So you have another power. What's its use, Sasha? How are you going to help somebody with this?"

"I don't know, but I'm sure there's something I can do with it. That's why I go to a parapsychologist. And I don't think of them as powers. I have abilities, dammit."

"All right, you have abilities. You also have a shrink who's using you, encouraging you to expand on pow—excuse me, abilities—not even you suspected you had. He's planting things in your mind for his own purposes."

The fact he could be right angered me further. "How the hell would you know? You aren't in my shoes. You try going the psychic route and see how you react. It's scary."

"Then quit experimenting. Stop seeing Schenk!"

"Knock it off, you two," Linnie said from the rocker. Her face had lost its stunned expression and had returned to normal. Her forehead wrinkled. "Sasha, I wish you'd reconsider returning to a regular

131

psychiatrist. Dr. Silberstein was a respected parapsychologist. But that doesn't always means everyone in the profession is on the up and up. Let me investigate Schenk."

"No, let me," Reed said. He reached for a piece of the changing table and picked up the screwdriver.

"I'll investigate," Linnie insisted. "I know the right people to contact. If this Schenk finds out, he won't be as concerned if it's a doctor asking questions, but a cop will raise a red flag, especially if the shrink is up to no good. Sasha, is there anything else you need to tell us?"

Her gaze bore into mine. I swallowed a lump in my throat nervously.

"I did have a successful astral projection the other night. Actually, it was more like dual consciousness and didn't last long," I hastened to add. No way would I admit to invading Reed's privacy.

"What the hell are you talking about?" Reed had fished a couple of screws from the package.

I moved to hold the two pieces of changing table together for him. My hands shook.

"I'm not sure I can explain it."

"Astral projection is like being in two places at once. Your physical body is separated from your psychic. Dual consciousness is basically the same, only the subject is aware of what's going on," Linnie said.

"And you, an intelligent woman, believe that crap?" He turned the screwdriver with a vicious twist.

"It's rare, but it happens." Her gaze once again transfixed me. "And where did you go?"

I shifted from foot to foot. "Not far. I was on the sofa in the living room and took a psychic stroll into the bedroom."

I didn't exactly lie. I just didn't mention the bedroom was Reed's.

"I see."

Her fingers drummed on the arm of the rocker and I feared she did see.

"I'm sorry, but I haven't had the best of it the last few days. I'm sure Reed can finish this without me. I'm tired and want to go home."

"Running away, as usual," Reed commented. "Rather than sharing and discussing the matter, you retreat."

I let loose of the two pieces I held and stepped back. He grabbed to steady them.

My eyes stung with unshed tears. "Stuff a sock in it, McIntyre. Linnie, forgive me, but I have to go home. I need to think." I cast a glance at Reed who was putting in the supporting screw. "In peace and quiet. I'll call you soon."

"Sasha, wait!"

I left the room as she struggled to get out of the chair, ran down the stairs, and out to my car. I drove down the driveway letting the tears flow. The pain from earlier jabbed my psyche again. I'd been unable to distinguish the source, but one of the emotions read earlier had been fear. Not fear *for* me, but fear *of* me.

Either my best friend or the man I loved was afraid of what I had become. But not half as afraid as I was.

****

I sat on the sofa in my living room, the strains of Vivaldi's *Four Seasons* drifting from my tablet. I hadn't moved in two hours trying to digest Linnie's and Reed's comments.

If Linnie had spoken Reed's words, I'd be more

receptive, but his tone had angered me. It was like we had regressed to square one and our first meeting three years ago. I was irked because he was right. I didn't share. Who could I tell? Linnie? She and Bill were about to experience a magical moment in their lives. I couldn't whine to her about being able to move automobiles into parallel parking places with my thoughts.

Reed? I'd once confided in him. Why had I stopped? *Because your dreams became god-awful nightmares and you didn't want to burden him with the tragedy they inevitably provoked.* He'd never understood that, and I had never been able to explain it.

My tears had ceased on the drive home. Now, I had to think, to plan. How should I use my abilities? I faced the fact that with the current economic situation, the psychic program was likely to fall victim to the police procedural axe. Cities were cutting budgets to the bare bones. Should I beg to remain with the police department in some capacity? Help on a limited scale only when detectives had reached a dead end? Stay out of any and all situations regarding dreams and visions of murder?

No, I can't do that. I have an obligation to tell what I know, even if it hasn't happened yet.

And what about Schenk? Should I dump him for a regular psychiatrist? Would it make any difference? I could ignore Reed's warning about the man, but Linnie's opinion carried a lot of professional weight.

Vivaldi ended and Copeland's *Appalachian Spring* came on.

If the rumors were true, and the psychic program was about to bite the big one, what would I do with my life? Money wasn't an issue. I could still live off the trust fund inherited from my grandmother. But I needed something to keep busy. That had never been a problem. After the last few years, however, I wondered if working at the discount store would stimulate my mind.

Maybe I'll buy a flowing robe, a turban, a deck of tarot cards, and open a psychic parlor. If that doesn't work I can always join the carnival.

I wanted to laugh, but couldn't. It hit too close to home.

I'd kept my thoughts away from Reed, but now let his image enter my mind. The astral projection had opened my eyes. Our break-up had devastated him as much as me. For the first time, I wondered if my own insecurities had caused me to deliberately sabotage our relationship. I had never quite gelled with the opposite sex. Had I been afraid to lean on a man, including the one who said he loved me? And exactly what were my fears in that department? I'd avoided talking about them, especially to Linnie. Hell, I didn't think about them if I could help it.

My landline rang interrupting my thoughts and I hurried to answer. Even a telemarketer was preferable to the last couple of hours of my thoughts.

"Sasha? Jill Conway here."

"Oh! Hi, what can I do for you?" I sucked in a startled breath. I'd been so self-absorbed, I wondered if I'd blocked any outside influences trying to enter my psyche. "Has something happened?"

"No, everything's fine. Look, I know this is short notice, but I wondered if you'd like to join me for dinner tonight. Nothing fancy. Just girl talk. I'd like to get to know you better, especially since we're working together."

I had no trouble reading the worry in her voice. She probably wanted to talk about Lisa. I glanced around my living room. Dinner out with a quasi-friend sounded a whale of a lot better than my own company. Not even Aaron Copeland and *Appalachian Spring* helped.

"Sounds like a good idea. Where do you live?"

"East Memphis, not far from Audubon Park."

"I'm not in the mood to drive that far tonight. Suppose we meet at Barney's in Olive Branch at, say, seven o'clock? It's right on the main street and easy to find. They also have a big parking lot."

"I'll find it. That's why Google has maps," she said with a light laugh. It sounded forced.

I hung up and stared at the phone. Jill had something on her mind besides Lisa. Whatever it was, it had to be important.

****

Barney's looked like a chain restaurant, but wasn't. Over the years, it had grown from a small diner in a small town to a large establishment in a medium-sized town. The red, white, and blue neon sign out front welcomed without being garish, while the weathered gray exterior gave the customer a sense of comfort.

Inside wasn't much different. The original diner had been replaced by a full bar with the kitchen area behind it. Booths hugged three of the four walls, and tables dotted the floor. Photos on the walls depicted Barney with customers, on fishing trips, and a myriad of other Barney activities. The present Barney was his grandson. On a busy Saturday night, most of the tables were full. I got the last booth and waited for Jill. She arrived a minute later, scanned the room, waved, and then joined me.

"This is nice," she said sliding into the seat opposite me. "Thanks for coming on such short notice."

"Dinner out is always better than a frozen dinner at home. Did you have any trouble finding the place?"

"Nope, drove right up like I'd been here before."

A waitress stopped by, set two placemats and two bundles of silverware wrapped in paper napkins in front of us, then filled our water glasses. Both Jill and I ordered white wine.

When the woman left, Jill unrolled her napkin, placed it on her lap, and fiddled with the silverware, all without looking me in the eye. If she was trying to shield her emotions from me, she failed. Worry clouded her mind. I reached across the table and stilled her restless hands with mine.

"Jill, what's wrong? Is it Lisa? Why aren't you with her tonight?"

She took a deep breath, blinked, and turned her gaze onto me. "Lisa's out to dinner with Charlie Kendall. She went jogging today."

Troubled, I sipped my water. "Where?"

"Audubon Park. It's about five blocks from my house. She drove. I tried to talk her out of it, but Lisa can be stubborn. So I lied and said there had been a couple of assaults in the last few weeks and to be careful. She said she's always got her eyes open. I can't say much more without spilling the beans. She'd probably laugh."

"Did she notice anything unusual?"

"Claims the park was crowded, she felt safe, and called me a worry-wart. I suppose I am. What exactly was it you saw in that dream again?"

The waitress brought our wine and took our dinner order. Still full of Linnie's chili, I opted for the Caesar salad. Besides, my appetite had fled with her question.

"I'll have the Hot and Spicy Chicken Sandwich, fries, and a side of coleslaw," Jill said, a hint of impatience in her voice. She repeated the question when we were once again alone.

"I saw a woman with blonde hair tied up in a ponytail and wearing sunglasses jogging on one of the trails. A man kept pace for a while before falling back. I don't think he's into jogging much. That was it. I viewed it through the man's eyes."

She bit her lip. "I don't know if Lisa wore sunglasses or not. You're into feelings. What were this guy's emotions?"

I took a healthy drink of Pinot Grigio. "Lust. He wanted her...wanted her bad. And then the scene fades away."

"And next you visualized the same woman at the mall—through the killer's eyes again. And what were those emotions?"

"Look, Jill, this isn't..."

"What were they?" She used her cop voice and her cop eyes, hard and demanding.

"Kind of the same. Not necessarily lust, but extreme attraction. He couldn't help staring."

"But she didn't notice him?"

"Not really. The scene didn't last all that long. And I'm not sure it was the same woman."

I took another sip of wine and wished I hadn't come.

"Lisa asked for directions to the Wolf Chase Mall

this afternoon. Said she might go out there tomorrow."

"If it's any comfort to you, I haven't viewed or felt anything wrong in a while. If you're so concerned, go with her. Shop 'til you drop. I still can't guarantee that the woman in my vision was Lisa. Yes, she looked a lot like your sister, but I'm not about to point the finger and say, 'There she is!' "

Jill took a long pull of her wine. "I'm sorry to be such a...a..."

"Pain in the ass," I finished for her.

For the first time tonight, she laughed. "Yes."

"Let's get off this subject." I leaned back in the booth. "Who was that guy who stormed into the conference room yesterday? He looked mad enough to chew nails."

"That was former Officer Steven Winslett."

"Former?"

She nodded. "He worked at our old precinct and is the main reason Mike and I are here."

"What happened?"

"Mike discovered Steven Winslett was accepting money from a couple of marijuana growers as a payoff for his silence about the operation. I guess Winslett's extortion escalated and involved a threat of some kind. One of the growers finally had enough and contacted Mike."

"Why Mike?"

"Mike knew the guy. Arrested him a couple of times several years ago. He knew Mike was honest."

"Mike wired the man, taped the conversation, and headed straight to Internal Affairs. They investigated and Winslett was quietly fired yesterday. That's why he showed up at this precinct."

139

"Must have been messy, especially for you guys," I commented. "Is that why you ended up with us?"

"Yeah. Winslett was well-liked in the Fourteenth. He shared his good fortune with his buddies. Gave them loans, big screen TVs, played the big shot. When word got out, we got a lot of heat."

"What an idiot. Why didn't he just keep quiet?"

"Guess he had this need to feel important, not to mention rich. At any rate, we became pariahs—you know, cops don't rat out other cops kind of thing. The brass thought it would be better all around if we left."

"You said the guy was fired. Why not arrested?"

"I'm not in the loop on that, but Mike suspects the hierarchy wants to keep it in house. The department has had a few unfortunate incidents involving personnel in the last year."

I remembered. A cop had been charged with habitually raping his step-daughter. Another had been arrested for selling old evidence out of the property room, on Internet sale and auction sites no less. And a third had created a major scandal by having an affair with the wife of a suburban mayor. All of those incidents had occurred in several precincts on a citywide basis. Sounded like the Fourteenth had been added to the list. I could see how IA would want to keep it from the public eye until they could finish their investigation.

Our food arrived. I stabbed a piece of lettuce and chewed, not really tasting the dressing or the Parmesan cheese. Jill ate without enthusiasm, too.

"And this Winslett came to call Mike out?"

"I haven't talked to Mike yet about it. He was not in the mood to chat. Mike wasn't cleaning up paperwork the other day; he was testifying at the IA hearing. I might call him later tonight. There are a couple of things I have to discuss with him."

We ate in silence for a few minutes. Then Jill put her sandwich on the plate and gripped the edge of the table with white-knuckled hands.

"Damn Mike Young. He may have done the right thing, but his holier-than-thou attitude pissed people off. If the truth about Winslett ever got out, the hush up could destroy public confidence in the police department."

All of the corruption incidents had come to light through a "tip" from insiders to reporters. "Did he threaten to leak things to the press?"

"I don't know. With Mike there are no gray areas. I doubt he ever gave a warning ticket in his life, and he makes enemies amongst his peers like you wouldn't believe. Several of our colleagues have told him to shut the hell up. It makes the department look bad and brands all cops as on the take."

"And what's your opinion on all of this?"

"I'm with our colleagues. Let internal problems be handled by IA. If we jerk the weeds out now—quietly and without fanfare, it'll look better in the long run. But I'm afraid the animosity he generates will spill over onto me."

"Guilt by association?" I asked.

"Maybe. Not only is the bastard opinionated as hell, but he's going to ruin my career. Sometimes I wonder if that's what he had in mind all along."

She jerked open her purse and fumbled in her wallet, withdrawing a twenty and tossing it on the table.

"Here, this should cover me. I'm sorry, Sasha. I

should never have bothered you tonight. I'm angry and upset on several levels. I'll see you on Monday."

With that Jill slid from the seat and walked quickly toward the door. As I stared after her, a ripple of uneasiness made me shiver. Darkness crept into my consciousness, pressing against the edges of my mind. Something was in the wind. I hoped it wasn't murder.

Chapter Ten

I jerked awake shivering and took a moment to re-orient myself. I'd dozed off on the sofa after coming home from my aborted dinner with Jill. A second glass of wine had helped put me under.

The dream, while not of nightmare proportions, had been strange and troubled me. I struggled upright, a hand pressed against my stomach. No nausea, thank goodness. If it hadn't been for the emotions, I would have dismissed it as an ordinary night vision. At least, ordinary for me.

A quick glance at the clock on my DVR read ten-thirty, so I hadn't been asleep for long. I rose and headed for the kitchen where I yanked a bottle of water out of the fridge, and then gulped half of it down, all the while trying to interpret what I'd seen. Dream analysis had never been my strong point, and I needed guidance.

I reached for the phone, intending to call Dr. Schenk, and then stopped. My doubts about him stilled my fingers even though I needed to talk. If not Schenk, then who? Linnie? No, not after today. My actions had disturbed and frightened her enough already. That left Reed. But would he even want to talk to me?

Dropping the phone, I sat at the table, tears filling and then overflowing from my eyes. Pathetic. I couldn't even call a friend. I had none. I felt isolated and always on the edge of an emotional precipice.

Sniffling, I wiped the tears from my cheeks and picked up the phone again, staring at it for a full minute. *Go to bed. So you had a weird dream. So what? You have them all the time.*

My fingers, however, refused to obey, and punched in Reed's number. He answered on the second ring.

"Sasha?"

How did he know? Oh, of course, caller ID. I opened my mouth. My lips moved, but emitted no words.

"Sasha?" His tone sharpened.

I sucked in a deep breath, and then to my horror let it out again as a sob.

"Sasha? Are you all right?" Fear throbbed in his voice.

"No. No, I'm not," I finally managed to say between hoarse hiccups.

"What's wrong?"

"I…I had a dream."

"A nightmare? Another killing?"

"No, I…I…"

"I'm on my way. Give me half an hour."

I tried to gather my self-control. "That's…that's all right. I'm sorry to bother you. I just wanted to talk. No need for you to make the trip."

"Too late. I'm already out the door. Take a deep breath and try to relax."

He hung up in typical Reed McIntyre fashion with no goodbye. I laid the phone down and gripped the edge of the table. Tea might help. Nice soothing herbal tea, but my hands trembled so much I couldn't hold the kettle still under the faucet. My emotional state was deteriorating fast. I dropped it into the sink and stepped away until backing against the refrigerator. My knees buckled and I slid to the floor. The tears reappeared and I sobbed with no sense of passing time, not so much about the dream, but more about my emotional state.

Reed knocked with his fists, the pounding bringing me out of my daze. I crawled to the cabinets and pulled myself up, then staggered through the house to the door. My fingers fumbled with the latch.

"Sasha! Open the damned door!"

I finally did so. Reed walked in, slammed the door behind him, and snatched me into his arms. I buried my face in his chest and cried some more. Through it all, something brushed the top of my head and I wondered if it was his lips.

Eventually, the tears stopped. Without saying a word, he picked me up and carried me into the living room where he deposited me in the corner of the sofa. Ashamed of my breakdown, I reached for a tissue while Reed smoothed a hand down my hair, tucking a wayward strand behind my ear.

"Stay put. I'm going to make you some tea."

I nodded, unable to speak. His gentle tone nearly renewed my tears, but I hung on to what little dignity I had left.

He returned in less than five minutes with a steaming mug. A cranberry-flavored tea bag floated on top.

"How did you get the kettle boiling so fast?" It was a silly question and had no reference to anything, but it was the first thing that popped into my head.

Reed smiled and perched next to me. "No kettle. Just a mug in the microwave. Now, what's frightened you?"

"I...I'm not sure I was scared, just...just...I don't know. I'm so confused and so tired of it all."

"Tired of it all?"

"I'm so tired of the responsibility. I hold people's lives in my hands or my mind, if you prefer. They die if I fail. I can't live with this much longer."

My hands trembled, sloshing the tea onto my shirt. Reed took the mug from me and held it to my lips.

"Drink."

I obeyed and let the tart liquid slide down my throat. He put the mug on the coffee table.

"Have you called Schenk?"

"No. I didn't want to talk to him and I couldn't talk to Linnie. Not after my performance this afternoon." I turned my gaze to his worried face. "One of you was frightened of me. I actually scared two of the people I love best in the world. Do you know how that makes me feel?"

He ran his hand down my cheek, and then threaded his fingers through my hair.

"Your actions surprised us. Any fear was short lived. Thank you for calling me." He reached for the mug again. "Sasha, you've got to stop thinking you can solve every crime you see. It's not possible. You have to do the best you can and move on. Give up the guilt. It's not your fault."

Reed held the mug to my lips, but this time I wrapped my hands around his as I sipped. Warmth from both his flesh and the liquid surged through me. He had echoed Linnie's words of earlier.

"I know. I keep telling myself that."

"Then it's time you started believing it." He frowned. "Maybe this should be your last case. You take everything on a personal level. That's not how a cop works—nor should it be."

I released my grip on his hand. "I'm not a cop."

"My point exactly," he replied, setting the mug back on the table. "Don't get all defensive, but Linnie was right. You should be seeing a regular psychiatrist. I'm sure she can recommend someone. Someone who can maybe temper these dreams you have so often."

"You think I'm having these awful nightmares because I want them?"

"I think you're so accustomed to having them that you subconsciously call them up." He ran a hand through his hair. "I know that sounds confusing, but I'm no shrink. Call Linnie tomorrow and get a name. You need help, honey."

I leaned forward, picked up the mug and took a long swallow. Some of what he'd said made sense. I no longer trusted Schenk to the extent I had a week ago. And the dreams along with my guilt at not being perfect were eroding my mental state.

"All right, Reed. I'll call her tomorrow. I promise."

He smiled and moved to the other corner of the sofa. "So, what was this nightmare about?"

I sat back cradling the mug in my hands. "It wasn't a nightmare. Just a strange dream. If it hadn't been for the emotions, I'd have dismissed it."

"What emotions?"

"Anger—no, rage—scary rage, contempt, and a dozen others swirled through my mind."

"See any people, any places?"

I shook my head. "No. Just lights and noises."

"What lights?"

"Bright lights flashing like a strobe through utter

darkness. They confused me and blinded my vision." I took another sip of the cooling tea.

Reed wrinkled his forehead. "And the noises? Can you identify them?"

"No. They were odd blaring noises, loud and then fading away. Like a trumpet. The lights and the noises all jumbled together."

"Like in a nightclub?"

"I don't know, maybe."

"More tea?" he asked, and then continued when I shook my head. "Something must have triggered it. Maybe it was the affair this afternoon. What did you do after you left Bill and Linnie's?"

I told him how upset I'd been and about my less than successful dinner with Jill.

"Jill's actions worried me. Could I have tapped into her mind? But I'm not sure her anger was intense enough to morph into rage."

"I don't know. You said she was angry with Mike?"

I gave him the gist of our dinner conversation.

"I'd heard rumors there were problems in the Fourteenth Precinct. Doesn't surprise me Young's at the center of it, although I agree with him."

"I thought cops protected each other in times of trouble."

"Not always. Not when it comes to breaking the law. And Winslett isn't the only one going down. Another cop was fired today and another two days ago. And I'll tell you something you might not have homed in on—Mike Young was attracted to Lisa. The look he gave her was not that of a cop, but of a man. Jill noticed and wasn't too happy about it."

I finished the tea and set the mug on the table. "I tapped into enough to know that in spite of his harsh words, he was attracted to Lisa. I missed Jill's reaction." I bit my lower lip. "I should have picked up on it. Wonder why I didn't."

"Probably because you've been bombarded with a lot of emotions from a lot of people, including me." He finished with a smile and rose. "Do me a favor. Pack a bag and come home. Stay with me until this case is decided—one way or another."

Had he realized he'd used the word home? Whether or not he had, it did the trick. I wanted home, and I wanted Reed. I wanted the comfort of belonging again.

"All right. I was getting tired of the drive anyway."

"Good. Do you need help?"

"Not with packing," I replied in a dry tone. "Thank you for being there, Reed. Lately, I feel as though I've been in a crowded room with everyone chattering a mile a minute, while I talked to myself."

He smiled and kissed my forehead. "From now on you can talk to me. I'll answer."

That was what I needed to hear. I walked into the bedroom and packed a large suitcase.

****

"Can I make you a cup of tea?" Reed asked a few minutes after arriving at his house and dropping my suitcase in the spare room.

I wasn't sure I wanted to be treated as a guest tonight. "No thanks, I've had enough tea to float a boat. I think I'll unpack and just go to bed. It's been a long day."

"I think I'll wind down for a while on the

computer. See you in the morning."

I spent the next twenty minutes unpacking and stowing my clothing in the closet and dresser. As I laid out my toiletries in the bathroom, I heard the beeping sound of a fast motion computer game. Reed never used to do that. Was this now his routine to stave off boredom or loneliness?

I washed my face and brushed my teeth before slipping back into the spare room and changing into my sleeping T-shirt. I was standing in front of the dresser mirror brushing my hair when Reed tapped softly on the door and opened it.

"Find everything? I didn't change the sheets from the last time you were here," he said.

"Doesn't matter. I'm fine."

He nodded and closed the door. I laid the brush on the dresser and sat on the edge of the bed staring at the floor. Tired as I was, my mind refused to shut down. The only emotions I tapped into were mine as I relived my life with Reed three years ago. The horseplay in the pool, the me-Tarzan-you-Jane prelude to making love, the intimate dinners with candlelight in the dining room all crowded together in a kaleidoscope of memories. And then, there were the nights of making love— sometimes slow and sexy, and other times out of control, hot and fast with true animal lust.

The heat built in my core, spiraling outward, clawing and nibbling until my entire body was on fire. I wanted Reed with an intensity I'd not felt in years.

Control yourself.

Easier said than done. Tremors radiated throughout my body. The desire, the need had taken over. I stood. Of their own volition, my legs walked me to the door. I opened it and crossed to Reed's room. I didn't bother knocking, but stood on the threshold. The nightlight in the bathroom spilled a feeble glow over the carpet. In the dim light, Reed propped himself up on an elbow.

"Sasha, are you all right?"

"No, no I'm not."

I peeled off my T-shirt and advanced to the side of the bed. He lay back and stared, then opened his arms. I didn't hesitate, but let their comforting warmth close around me.

"Sasha," he whispered before tangling his hands in my hair and bringing my mouth to his.

We didn't speak, but then we'd never felt the need to do so. Our hands and lips said it all. I slid under the sheet, my restless hands caressing his chest. He slept raw, his erection full and hard. My hand encircled it. A groan gathered deep in his throat.

His lips trailed down my cheek to my neck where he nibbled on the sensitive tendon before moving on to my breast. I almost screamed when they fastened onto the nipple, the wet heat of his mouth sending wave after wave of gushing warmth along my nerves. He sucked and laved first one then the other. I couldn't control the tremors wracking my body.

Neither could he. He also trembled and gasped as my hand stroked his shaft. His mouth left my breasts making its way to my navel while his ever-busy fingers no longer caressed my heated skin, but found the wetness between my thighs.

Then his lips returned to mine as he positioned himself over me. Panting, I raised my knees and opened for him. He slid in to my heat in one swift thrust.

Oh, God, it felt so right, so wonderful. I was home

and never wanted to leave again.

For a moment, Reed lay still, and then began the ancient movement that promised indescribable pleasure. Two and a half years of celibacy had built up a powerful need. I burned like a Roman candle, and it didn't take long for the fuse to ignite the powder. I thrust and lunged with him, my legs wrapped around his waist.

His breath seared the side of my neck and my nails scored his back. The fire built to five-alarm status, and then the Roman candle took off. Fireball after fireball exploded. I screamed and thrust with each spasm hoping to prolong the experience forever.

Then Reed lunged hard, almost driving my head through the headboard. He cried out, ballooned inside me, and erupted, renewing my orgasm. His hands clenched in the pillows until the pulsations ceased.

Exhausted, he rolled over and lay next to me. For the next few minutes, the only sound in the room was our gasping breaths gradually returning to normal. He picked up my limp hand and brought it to his lips.

"God, Sasha, how I've missed you."

"I know." My voice still had a breathless quality.

"I didn't mean for this to happen."

"I started it. Never did have any self-control where you were concerned. It's been a long two and a half years."

He was silent for a moment, and then said, "For me, too."

His admission didn't surprise me. If I'd learned one thing about Reed McIntyre over the years, it was that his passions ran deep and he didn't waste them on something or someone he didn't care about.

"It was just like old times," I whispered.

"But much too fast."

He leaned over to kiss my lips. I knew what was coming and welcomed it. His erection had not decreased, and the fires within my core rekindled. His arms held me tight as he rolled onto his back, pulling me with him.

This time our hands and mouths took a leisurely pace, building the flames like a slow-burning fireplace on a cold winter's night. The night spiraled away into hues of intense color.

****

"Sasha, for the love of God, wake up!"

Slowly, the nightmare faded and I awoke to Reed's frightened voice. He was kneeling next to me on the bed and shaking my shoulders.

I brushed at his hands. "I'm okay."

He released me and swept the hair from my eyes. "You scared me. You were screaming and crying."

"A nightmare, that's all. Just another goddamned nightmare." I sat up and fumbled on the nightstand for my cell. "Where the hell's my phone?"

"What do you need a phone for? Schenk? Talk to me. I'm here." His tone had a hard edge to it.

"Bobby Jack. I need to talk to him."

Fully awake now, I remembered I wasn't in the guest room, but Reed's bedroom. My purse with the phone in it was on the dresser.

Reed said nothing, but rose, pulled on a pair of jeans and stalked out of the door. I stumbled after him, picking up and struggling into my discarded T-shirt of a few hours ago. Thank goodness the nausea hadn't appeared. A quick glance at the clock read six-ten.

I located my cell and dialed. The nightmare had been disjointed, not the usual type of dream. I had no idea if it was relevant to anything involving the current case. Then it dawned on me that Bobby Jack was no longer my boss. I should be calling Young or Jill.

It was all a moot point. He didn't answer. I got his voice mail, but hung up without leaving a message. Only now did I think about Reed. And for the first time, I understood what he'd been saying. I had brushed him off.

I hesitated. I didn't trust Young. His skepticism was like salt in a gaping wound, and recalling one of our conversations, wasn't sure if maybe he didn't have it right about Jill being professionally unstable. But I trusted Reed.

Gripping the phone in my hand, I made my way into the kitchen. Rain drummed on the roof. Reed sat at the table staring out into the saturated darkness through the patio doors. The coffee pot burbled. He made no attempt to block my intrusion into his head. He was intensely sad and hurt.

"Reed, I'm sorry."

"Get a hold of Bobby Jack?"

"No. He didn't answer and I didn't leave a message." I sat across the table from him. "You're right. You're here and can help."

"Are you sure you *want* to talk to me? Or is it because you can't get a hold of anyone else?"

I bit my lip at the bitterness in his voice. "No, I want to tell you. Just give me a moment."

I laid the cell on the table and folded my hands. I needed to organize my thoughts, to put what I'd dreamed into sequence. The coffee pot beeped. Reed rose and poured two mugs of coffee, and then set the cream and sugar on the table. I doctored mine before beginning.

"It's all so strange, so jumbled. I'm not even sure I can call it a nightmare."

He blew on the liquid in his mug and took a sip. "I can. You were yelling, 'no, no,' and gasping as if you were crying in the dream."

I inhaled a shaky breath. "I remember rage and a feeling of impending doom. And then there were those weird lights again like from the first dream tonight." I glanced at the clock. "Or last night rather."

"Go on. Did you see a person or a place?"

"I think I see a restaurant, like the place where Jill and I ate. And I hear that blaring sound again. I think its music."

"You think? Usually, you're very clear."

I sipped from my mug. "Everything is so jumbled and disjointed. I'm not even sure if it refers to this case or not. It might just have simply been a bad dream."

"What else did you see? Something must have frightened you enough to make you cry."

"I saw a door. Black? Maybe dark blue or green. I'm not sure. It wavered in and out of focus. Kind of like viewing something through a waterfall."

"Was it inside or outside?" He raised his mug to his mouth and drank.

"I'm not sure, but I sense cold. I'm guessing outside."

"Was it raining?"

"Could be." I followed his lead and gulped more coffee. Rain pounded on the roof. "The current weather could have had something to do with it."

"What happened next?"

"Bear with me. I have gaps in my memory." I closed my eyes for a second, and then opened them again. "I'm inside the house now. I hear voices. They're arguing, but I can't distinguish the words."

Reed frowned, got up and refilled his mug, gesturing toward me with the pot. I nodded. He topped mine off and resumed his seat.

"Are the voices male or female? Can you tell? Is it just two people or more?"

"I'm not sure. I sense more than two." I shivered while adding the cream and sugar.

"Are you cold? Let me get you a sweatshirt."

He rose, but I stopped him. "I'm not shivering because of the cold, but about what happens next." I took a deep breath. "Suddenly, everything is swimming in a red haze. Fury—gut-wrenching fury, and this horrible sense of death rolls over me. Then I hear gasping breaths or maybe sobbing. I'm helpless. I know something is wrong, but can't do a thing about it. That's all. I woke up to you shaking me."

Reed swiped a hand over his face. "Could be just a strange dream, like you said. The only problem with that is your dreams over the last few years have meaning."

I blinked tears from my eyes. "Why does this happen to me? Is there any way to block the images without having to resort to drugs? Am I doomed to this invasion for the rest of my life?"

His hands covered mine. "I don't know, baby, but a psychiatrist with no ulterior motives should be at the top of your priority list. Hear me out," he said when I opened my mouth. "Linnie's worried, too. Give her a call."

"And what about the case? What about Lisa?"

"You've done your job. Now it's time for Mike and Jill to protect her and find the guy."

"Reed, we both know my job is far from finished. They'll need future things I see to narrow the playing field. But you're right about one thing. I do need to talk to a professional." I squeezed one of his fingers. "You've been a great help. I'm glad I talked to you."

He smiled and raised my hands to his lips. "How about breakfast? Bacon and eggs? Pancakes? Your choice."

"Waffles. Big, thick, fluffy Belgian waffles with gobs of butter and enough syrup to float the QE II."

He laughed, released my hands, and rose. "Whatever you say, ma'am."

I couldn't keep the amusement from my voice. "You sound like Bill with Linnie."

His laughter rumbled again. "Bill is completely henpecked and loving every moment of it. He adores her. Now, do you want bacon or sausage? I have those little links you like so much."

I was touched he kept some of my favorite food in the freezer. Before I could reply, his cell phone rang from the direction of the living room. He left to answer while I rose to scrounge out the sausages and the waffle mix.

"McIntyre here...hi, you're up with the birds this..."

A long silence ensued. I ceased my activities and stood in the doorway making no effort to hide my curiosity. Reed continued in a lowered voice.

"I see. When did it happen?...I have no idea where

he's staying at the moment. Did you get a hold of his partner?...I know, this is going to hit the fan. Can't keep it out of the public eye now. You got an address?" He scribbled on a pad of paper kept on the bar. "Got it. I'll be there shortly."

Reed hung up and shook his head.

"Is something wrong?" I asked, knowing the answer. His mind was shuttered, but I still caught a mental whiff of fear.

"That was Detective Brannon."

I'd first met Brannon when he'd worked on the Jeff Hammond case. Older and nearing retirement, he was the quintessential policeman—all business and to the point.

When Reed didn't elaborate, I demanded, "And? What did he want?"

"He's at a homicide and wants me to come."

The sense of foreboding from earlier during my dream clamped around my chest, squeezing until I wanted to gasp.

"Why? You're cold cases."

"Mike Young's been murdered."

Chapter Eleven

My fingers clenched around the doorjamb while the room spun, and then tilted like a possessed carnival ride. The heaviness in my chest squeezed. I couldn't breathe. My legs shook uncontrollably.

Reed closed the distance between us in a few long strides. His arms encased my trembling body helping to hold me upright. "Don't faint on me now," he said, guiding me toward the sofa.

I sat with a thump. Gradually, the room stopped spinning and my ability to breathe returned. I gulped air and placed my fist against my heart in the hopes of taming its erratic pounding. "I won't faint. What happened?"

"I don't know, a neighbor found him and Brannon wants to see you, me, Bobby Jack, Jill, and Charlie down at the station at ten o'clock."

"Charlie? Why Charlie? Does he have an eye witness and need a sketch?"

"I have no idea. Are you sure you're all right?"

I nodded. "I'm better. It was such a shock. Reed, do you think my dream is related?"

He ran a hand through his hair. "Possibly, but if it is, it's lacking details—other than the front door color."

Oh God, how could this have happened? I buried my face in my hands. Reed sat next to me and pulled me into his arms.

"Relax, Sasha."

"I can't believe it. Mike? I take it he was at home?"

"Brannon didn't say, but that's the impression I had."

"I've got a great candidate—that guy from the Fourteenth who barged in the other day."

"Maybe, or any one of several other cops from there who were fired and/or pissed."

He picked up the TV remote from the coffee table and pushed a button. Within seconds, the screen filled with the early morning news. Mike Young took center stage. The media had been pushed back, but the cameras still caught the outside of the house surrounded by yellow crime scene tape. Plainclothes detectives and people wearing vests identifying them as forensics personnel came and went. I couldn't distinguish the color of the front door. It stood open and the camera angle was from the opposite direction.

The TV reporter was interviewing a couple of bystanders.

"He was a nice man," the woman said, smoothing a strand of hair for the camera and pulling the lapels of her robe closer to her throat. "Always felt safe with a cop living across the street. Can't understand it. This is a good neighborhood. We've never had trouble like this before."

"It's them damned kids," the man with her stated, glaring for the audience. "Drugs and gangs everywhere. Should shoot them all on sight. Maybe then they'd think twice about breaking into law-abiding citizens' homes."

"Uh, yes, thank you," the commentator said hastily before turning his attention back to the camera. "That's all we have at the moment. Police haven't released the name of the victim yet. All we know is the victim is a police officer with the city, and this looks to be some sort of home invasion. Back to you at the studio, Dave."

Reed clicked the TV off, and then leaned over to kiss my temple.

"Can I get you anything? I guess a big breakfast is out of the question. How about more coffee?"

"Tea would be nice, and toast. I need to eat something."

"Sounds good to me, too." He rose. "I'll be back in a few minutes."

Reed left the room. I slumped back against the cushions for a minute, and then followed him. I sat at the table, my feet tucked next to my butt and pulled the T-shirt over my knees down to my ankles. He dropped four slices of bread into his toaster and heated the water for my tea in the microwave.

Glancing my way, he asked, "Are you sure you're all right?"

"Reed? Let's assume that my nightmare did relate to Mike. If that's the case, it was after the fact. I woke up a little after six. Brannon called forty-five minutes later. The scene looked busy on TV, which means he'd been there a while."

"I'd say at least an hour. So this dream was post-cognitive? Isn't that unusual for you?"

"Somewhat. And why would I suddenly dream emotions from an incident that already occurred? That's never happened before." I tucked my feet closer to my behind and wrapped my arms around my knees. "Why wouldn't I dream it, at the very least, in real time?"

The microwave dinged and he removed the

steaming cup of water, placing it in front of me along with an herbal tea bag.

"We were occupied during a large portion of the night. Don't know about you, but I only caught catnaps between kisses. Maybe you needed more time to assimilate what was happening. By the time you did, the murder had occurred."

His theory made sense. I dunked the tea bag into the water. The smell of peppermint and chamomile tickled my nose.

"Is this a new wrinkle?" I asked. "If I'm involved with strong emotions of my own, could they block the intrusion of the outside feelings of others?"

The toaster popped. Reed placed the slices on a couple of plates. I smiled inwardly as he buttered mine, and then added cinnamon with sugar on one and cherry preserves on the other. They were my favorites. He hadn't forgotten.

"If so, then that's a good thing." He set the plate in front of me. "It means you can control what tries to sneak into your mind."

I bit into the cinnamon slice first, the sugary spice nipping at my taste buds.

"For a while, maybe." I swallowed and chased the toast with a sip of tea. "I wonder if it was an extension of the dream I had earlier before I called you. The ones with the lights and noises. Or was I integrating the two?"

He sat next to me and chewed on his blueberry jam covered bread. "You mean, the first one was just a weird dream and you transferred the images to the second?"

"Something like that. I wonder when Mike was

killed."

"I don't know. Brannon will fill us in on more details at the station."

"When are we due?"

"Ten. I'd like to get there a little early to see what I can dig up, though."

I sighed and finished my breakfast, downing the last of the tea in several long swallows. Today would not be pleasant.

****

Detective Brannon met us as we walked in the station's front doors thirty minutes ahead of schedule. Brannon hadn't changed much in the last three years. His hair and mustache had more salt than pepper now, and he'd put on a few pounds, but still looked like a bulldog ready to fight.

"Good morning, thanks for coming in. Please follow me."

He led us down a hallway and stopped in front of a door marked Interrogation Room 1. He opened it and waved me inside.

"I'll be right back, Sasha." He closed the door.

I took a seat at the Formica-topped table. A few minutes later, the door reopened and Brannon walked in.

He advanced to the table, slapped a large file folder in front of him, and then sat.

I remained silent. I sensed Brannon was angry and not happy with having drawn this assignment, especially considering the shenanigans at the Fourteenth. Cops hated investigating other cops.

He nodded in my direction. "Good to see you again, Sasha. It's been a long time. How're you doing?"

"Pretty good, considering."

"I've got to ask. Did you have any visions about this?"

I was stuck between the old proverbial rock and a hard place. Both yes and no were lies.

"I'm not sure. A couple of disjointed dreams that didn't make sense. I had impressions and sensed things, but didn't actually see anything that led me to believe Detective *Young* was in danger."

"I know you're working a case at the moment. Want to tell me about it?"

"There's not much to tell." I gave him the story of the nightmare and its usual aftermath.

"Tell me about your relationship with Mike."

"I'm not sure we had one. He was a very vocal skeptic regarding my abilities. He was also controlling, overbearing, and a major league ass. If you're asking if I liked him, then the answer is no."

Brannon nodded and wrote on a legal pad in front of him. "Where were you between ten and one last night?"

"With Reed at his place in Germantown."

"Thought you two had broken up."

"We did, but are still friends."

"Friendly enough to stay overnight with him?"

"Upon occasion." I kept my answer brief. My sex life was none of Brannon's business.

"What do you know about the stink being raised at the Fourteenth?"

"Enough to know it stinks. Some guy named Winslett barged in here the other day demanding to talk to Mike. Neither had particularly pleasant expressions on their faces. I heard through the grapevine more than one cop over there was pissed at Mike for outing the dirt to Internal Affairs. My guess is that's where you'll find your killer."

He wrote fast. "Maybe. Do you know if Young and this other guy, Winslett, talked?"

"Haven't a clue. Young and Jill were leaving to investigate a body found near Overton Park. He shoved Winslett out of the way. Winslett was damned angry. Looked like bacon could fry on his forehead. That's all I can tell you about it."

"What did you observe about Detective Young's relationship with his partner, Reed, and Charlie?"

"He irritated Reed, and Jill had her issues with him. I know he didn't like women on the police force."

"Young didn't exactly keep his opinions to himself so she must have known how he felt, yet she stayed partnered with him for several years. It doesn't take that long to figure out you aren't a match."

I shrugged. "All I know is she told me she requested a transfer. As for Charlie, I don't think he met Young but once. For details, you'll have to ask them."

Brannon finished writing, set the pen down on the pad, and leaned back with a smile. "Thanks, Sasha. You don't have anything to worry about. I had to do this."

"I know. How did Mike die? Was he shot?"

He hesitated. "You're not a cop and I shouldn't tell you this, but you'd find out soon enough anyway. He was bludgeoned. His head was bashed in pretty bad. No weapon as of yet. Killer must have taken it with him."

I sucked in a startled breath. The image of a golf club flashed in front of my eyes. I opened my mouth to speak, and then closed it again. Had I seen it in my dream or was it just an image? I couldn't remember, but told Brannon anyway.

"A golf club? You're sure?"

I nodded. "But whether or not it's connected to the murder is anyone's guess. Can I go now?"

The detective rose, a deep frown on his face. "Sure. Stick around in the conference room. You may be needed."

I didn't question why, but made my escape stopping by the vending machine for a soft drink along the way.

In the conference room, I took a seat and popped the top. Tilting the can back, I let the fizzy liquid slide down my throat. Separating us was standard operating procedure, but still I wondered how Reed would explain our evening. Would he mention the dream and why I was at his place? If he did, then Brannon would talk to me again.

Restless, I wandered to the window. The relentless drizzle had stopped, but the heavy cloud cover coated the day with gloom. I closed my eyes and concentrated on filling the gaps in my memory. The dream had been disjointed making me wonder if I'd viewed things from several points of view. Strange how I'd forget the golf club, but remember unrelated lights and noises along with a lot of rage. And there was something I was missing about the door. A window, maybe, reflecting back the face of the killer?

I opened my eyes and finished the soda in three long gulps. It was no use. My memory would either place the missing pieces like a jigsaw puzzle or remain locked away. Experience had taught me not to push it.

The door opened and Reed stepped through.

"So, did you get the rubber hose treatment?" I

asked.

He smiled. "Not quite. They were just routine questions."

"What did you say about us?"

"Only that you stayed the night. I told him to go to hell when he asked why. He also asked about my relationship with Young. I told the truth. He was rude and I wanted to deck him on more than one occasion, but never had the opportunity. I don't know Jill and Charlie well enough to comment. Is that about what he asked you, too?"

"More or less. Does he really suspect one of us?"

He shrugged. "I doubt it, but he has to cover his ass all the same, especially with the brouhaha going on over at the Fourteenth."

I told him about the golf club image. "Only problem is I don't know if it's relevant to this dream."

"Brannon asked if you'd had any visions last night. I told him you mentioned a dream, but it didn't seem like anything alarming."

"I told him anyway. I'm not even sure what I'm seeing." I explained why.

"Wouldn't be the first time you picked up vibes from several people at once."

Reed had not closed the door and now, Bobby Jack strode into the room. For once he didn't look like an unmade bed. His clothes were pressed, he was clean-shaven, and his eyes, while still tinged with red, were clear.

He rubbed his hands together. "Looks like I'm back in charge, at least for this case. Shame about Young, but I understand he ruffled more than a couple of feathers over at the Fourteenth. The man pissed off a lot of people everywhere he went."

"I'm surprised Brannon didn't want to talk to you."

"He did when the Lieutenant told me I was back in."

"You seem rather cheerful about it all," Reed commented in a dry tone.

"I'll admit I was mad as hell when I was first told about being yanked off the case. I resented Mike and Jill coming in. Guess it's all water under the bridge now. I'll finish this case, go into rehab, take that desk job, and try to make things right with Cindy."

"Oh, Bobby Jack, I'm so glad. You look ten times better this morning than you did the last couple of days," I said, blinking tears from my eyes.

"Not hung over you mean. The AA meeting helped."

Charlie entered the room. "Whew! Glad that's over. Never been interrogated before. Not a nice experience. Hi, Bobby Jack."

"Hi. This is just routine," he replied with a smile. "And I'm going to talk to the powers that be about reinstating you, too."

Charlie looked perplexed. I didn't blame him. The jovial attitude was out of place. "Uh, thanks, but I haven't actually been laid off yet. Maybe it's for the best. Gives me more time to concentrate on my work."

"Your sketches are better than any computer, so I'll give it a shot. In fact, why don't I do that right now? Sasha, is there anything I need to know about this case?"

While he and Charlie talked, I'd tapped into Bobby Jack's emotions and the result troubled me. He was positively overjoyed at being back in charge. Mike was gone and he hoped Jill would soon follow. His happiness bordered on frenetic, and nowhere did I sense he thought about his wife and family. I wondered if he'd lied about attending the AA meeting. For the first time, I was reluctant to tell him anything.

"Nothing to report," I said, keeping it simple. A quick glance at Reed confirmed he also found Bobby Jack's demeanor odd.

"Odd, you'd think the violent death of someone you worked with would have come through. Well, I'll go have that talk. I'll be back in a little while." He left with a bounce in his step.

Reed turned to me. "Did you find that conversation bizarre?"

I shook my head. "Not only bizarre, but downright scary. I got news for you, he's glad Mike is dead and can't wait to unload Jill."

"I don't know Bobby Jack all that well, but it seemed strange to me," Charlie added with a frown. "I know he's had some drinking problems the last few weeks, but I wonder if he traded one vice for another."

"Drugs?" Reed said with a raised eyebrow.

"I circulate in the art world. I've seen a lot of weird behavior due to drugs—extreme highs and lows. This was definitely a high."

"Oh, God, I hope this case is over soon. He needs help," I said.

"He can only get it if he wants it," Reed reminded us. "Right now, he's on top of the world. What happens when he crashes?"

Charlie shook his head. "A cop on drugs? Doesn't he see enough abuse to know what it does to people?"

"Cops are people, too," Reed said. "And I never

met an addict yet who didn't think he could handle the problem. They have to hit rock bottom before admitting they need help."

I moved from the window and tossed my empty can into the trash. My earlier joy at seeing Bobby Jack appearing much better had now evaporated. Had he gone from bourbon to something worse? Anger stabbed my psyche. Damn it, why couldn't he admit he'd screwed up and do something about it? Then I was immediately contrite. *He is trying. He's acknowledged he has a problem. I just hope he can kick both habits assuming there are two to kick.*

Reed came up behind me, placing his hands on my shoulders. "Are you all right?"

"Yes. Just sad. My connection to Mike was brief, but Bobby Jack?" I shook my head, unable to continue.

Charlie looked around the room. "I could use another cup of coffee. How about you?"

"No, thanks. I'm full of liquids."

He left and I resumed staring out into the dreary day. The fine drizzle had resumed promising to keep things miserable.

Why would Brannon want to talk to Charlie? He'd barely said hello to Young. My initial shock had worn off and I speculated on the grilling ex-officer Winslett would receive. His confrontation with Young here had been seen by several people. And Lord only knows what was going on over at the Fourteenth Precinct. They were all probably getting the third degree.

My thoughts were interrupted by Jill's arrival. I turned from contemplating the weather and the fates of others to stare at the late Mike Young's partner.

Her face was pale and dark circles under her eyes

indicated a bad night's sleep. She ran a shaking hand through her slightly messy hair, as if she'd forgotten to brush it this morning. Her eyes, however, were dry and showed no signs of redness due to tears. Without thinking, I tapped into her emotions.

I read relief mixed with extreme fear and only a tinge of sadness. She was also irritated as hell about something. Surprised, I pulled out. If my partner of the last few years had just been murdered, I would have had a few other emotions swirling through me—like anger and grief even if we hadn't always gotten along.

"Hello, Sasha. I figured you'd be here. Did you have a vision of Mike's death?"

Nothing like getting to the point. For some reason, I didn't want to discuss last night with her. I was still unsettled by her behavior at Barney's and would tell her about the dream later, if the need arose.

"No, but then I'd had a full day and took a sleeping pill. I'm sorry for your loss." I hated telling lies, even little white ones. They always come back to trip you up.

She shrugged. "Mike could be a real bastard, but he didn't deserve this. I've been here since seven this morning. I just got off the phone with a friend at the Fourteenth. The shit is really hitting the fan. She said reporters are jammed in the lobby demanding to know if it's true a couple of cops have been fired recently for illegal activities."

"I guess a leak was bound to happen sooner or later. Shame it had to take a death to do it."

Before she could answer Charlie walked in with a steaming cup of coffee.

"Good morning, Jill. Sorry to hear about Mike. Can I get you some coffee?"

Her eyes narrowed and a frown creased her forehead. "No, and the next time you take my sister out to dinner try to have her home before one in the morning."

His eyebrows rose. He walked over to a chair and sat down, then took a sip.

"I didn't realize a thirty-year-old woman had a curfew. If she did, she didn't say anything to me."

So this was the source of Jill's irritation. Lisa had been out late. I understood the aggravation, but not the fear. It was out of proportion to the situation. By now, I assumed Lisa was sound asleep.

She licked her lips and took a seat next to him. "I'm sorry, Charlie, but you drew the picture. When I woke up at one and she wasn't in bed, I had a moment of panic. Thank God, you brought her home a few minutes later. What dinner takes eight hours?"

"We ate at Giovanni's, and then took a road trip to Tunica. Lisa had a yen to gamble. Won a hundred bucks on a quarter slot machine, too." He sipped again. "You know, you really have to chill out. She was with me—unless you don't trust me to keep her safe."

Jill had the grace to blush. "I do. I apologize. I over-reacted, but I'm so worried about her."

"Not all of my dreams come true," I interjected. "Sometimes, we manage to find the killer before he strikes."

I'd lied again, but Jill needed some comfort. And if *this* little white lie eased her mind, then so be it.

"Thanks, Sasha. I guess everything is getting to me. And now my partner is dead. I was thinking of asking for a few weeks leave of absence. Lisa and I could go someplace like the Bahamas or Cancun and just vegetate until this all blows over."

I didn't have the heart to tell her that my dreams often had no timeline.

"That's a good idea," Charlie replied. "Take some time off. A change of scenery often helps. It beats winter in Memphis."

I turned my attention to Charlie. "Why are you here? Did you have a problem with Young?"

"No, not really. I bumped into him in the lobby a day or so ago. He got snotty and asked what I was doing here. I didn't like his tone and told him it was none of his business. We got kinda loud. Several people heard us. That's all."

He sipped his coffee and didn't make eye contact with the rest of us. Curious, I tapped into his energy, and then backed out again. He hadn't quite told the truth. He and Mike had argued over Lisa.

I rubbed a hand across my forehead and dared a glance at Reed, who threw me a questioning look. I shook my head. I'd tell him later.

"I'm sorry, Charlie, but that was Mike," Jill said with a frown. "Confrontational. He hated civilians in police stations unless they were reporting a crime, witnesses, or being booked. Said they cluttered the place up. He had little use for husbands, wives, or significant others just visiting."

"No wonder he rubbed people the wrong way," Charlie replied.

"Mike had a habit of making enemies," she concluded.

"Do you think Brannon will be back soon?" Charlie asked from across the room. "I should be at my studio preparing for a class tonight."

A moment later, Brannon entered.

"Anything new?" Reed asked.

"Some."

"What happened?" I added.

"A man walking his dog about five-thirty this morning passed Young's house and noticed the front door wide open and the foyer light on. He thought maybe Mike had just been out getting the paper and walked on. When it was still open as he passed again on his way home, he investigated and found Mike on the floor of the living room. He called nine-one-one."

I wanted to ask the color of the front door, but held my tongue. No need to tip my hand yet.

"What was the cause of death?" Reed asked.

"Blunt force trauma to the head. Someone nailed him from behind. Wound was just above the right temple. He bled a lot before he died."

"From behind, yet the wound is near the right temple?" Reed asked. "Sounds like he turned at the last moment."

Brannon nodded. "Possibly. And once he was down, the killer kept right on banging away."

"Do you have the murder weapon?" Jill wanted to know.

"Not yet, but we're looking for an eight iron."

"An eight iron? As in a golf club?" I said.

Brannon nodded again and looked at me. "His golf bag was in the foyer. When you told me you had an image of a golf club, I had someone check the bag. Everything's there except the eight iron. Whoever used it also did a number on the living room. Smashed the TV, lamps, DVR, Internet router. Anything breakable was a pile of rubble."

"Which makes this up close and personal," Reed said. "An ordinary thief would have whacked him once and been done with it."

Charlie shuddered, while Jill bit her lip and frowned. I sensed a huge jolt of fear surge through her.

"Sounds messy," Reed commented, sipping his coffee again. "And angry."

"It was," Brannon confirmed.

I said nothing. Instead, my mind filled with an image of a golf club descending again and again in uncontrollable rage. A background of red seeped everywhere. Blood? Anger? It was one of those gaps in my memory clicking into place. Then the vision faded. I didn't dare look at Reed.

"Any idea when this occurred?" Reed asked.

"Coroner has a preliminary as sometime between ten and two, possibly later. By the way, Detective Conway, a representative of Internal Affairs would like to see you in interrogation room three."

Jill nodded and left.

Between ten and two, maybe later. After my first dream, yet prior to the second. Maybe I'd nailed it. My own emotions while making love with Reed had stifled the vision of a murder.

"Why are we all here, Detective?" I asked.

Brannon heaved a sigh. "Because all of you had a confrontation with Detective Young in the last few days."

"So did half the Fourteenth Precinct if what I heard is true," Reed commented.

"We're questioning everybody over there, too."

"Do you need me for anything else?" Charlie inquired. "I have other things to...well, hello gorgeous."

I turned and stared at Lisa standing in the doorway.

Chapter Twelve

Oh, swell. With all the turmoil of the morning, Lisa Parker was the one person I didn't need to see. She wore jogging shorts, a bright red sweatshirt, and had her hair pulled up into a ponytail. Sunglasses dangled from her fingers, and an iPod hung around her neck along with a visitor's badge. I sensed not only surprise at finding all of us here, but a definite sense of uneasiness along with a dash of fear. She paused in the doorway and surveyed us.

"Well, hello yourself. Didn't expect to find you all here." Her voice held a hint of suspicion.

"Why are *you* here?" Reed asked.

"I'm going jogging and can't find the house key. I used it last night, but must have misplaced it. Rather than search forever, I thought I'd borrow Jill's. Where is she? I stopped by her cubicle. It was empty so I figured she was in here."

"She's still being interrogated," Charlie informed her.

"Interrogated? What the hell for?"

"Haven't you heard?" I replied.

"Heard what?"

"Mike Young was murdered last night," Reed said. If nothing else, he was blunt.

Her eyes went wide and she stifled a gasp. "Murdered? Oh no, poor Jill. How? Do you know who

177

did it?"

"Not yet."

"Is that why Jill's being questioned? They don't think she had anything to do with it, do they? I mean, I know the guy was a pain in the ass, but Jill'd never off anybody."

Lisa's sense of fear deepened, but I couldn't quite figure out why. Maybe too many emotions floating around.

"No, no," Charlie said in a soothing tone. "It's just routine. I guess they're talking to anyone who knew him or talked with him in the last couple of days."

She bit her lip and shifted from foot to foot. "Will they want to talk to me, too?"

"I doubt it," I said.

"He asked me out, you know. Called yesterday morning. I turned him down. I don't think he was happy about it. Jill sure as hell wasn't when I told her. Said I should steer clear of him."

That didn't surprise me. With his involvement in the mess at the Fourteenth, Jill wouldn't want her sister anywhere near possible repercussions—especially in view of my dreams.

"I wouldn't worry about it," Charlie said with a smile.

"What are you doing here?" Jill appeared behind Lisa, who moved farther into the room.

"Hi, I'm going jogging and can't find the house key. Thought I'd snatch yours. Sorry to hear about your partner. Why are they questioning you? That's ridiculous."

Jill frowned. "Jogging? Where?"

"Audubon Park."

"I wish you wouldn't. I told you before, there have been problems in the park. Muggings, attempted rapes."

"Jill, no one mugs a jogger. We don't carry anything of value. Slows us down. Plus, I have pepper spray and a big mouth." She indicated a small pen-shaped object also hung around her neck. It was hidden behind the visitor's badge.

"Please, just go home."

"What the hell is the matter with you anyway? Ever since I came you've been hovering like a guardian angel. Don't go here, don't go there, stay in at night. Are vampires and zombies roaming the streets? I'm surprised you don't lock me in my room once darkness falls." Her voice took on a theatrical tone, but she got her point across. "Maybe I should go back to St. Louis."

"No!" Jill and Charlie said at the same time.

Jill bit her lip. "Sorry. I've been under a lot of stress lately. I don't mean to nag."

"I don't want to see you go for selfish reasons. Have you given any thought to my suggestion?" Charlie asked.

"What suggestion?" I interjected.

"Charlie asked me to pose for him," Lisa said with an impatient gesture.

I glanced at Charlie. He had an eager look on his face, like a kid about to clean out the candy store.

"Are you teaching at the university this semester?"

He swung his gaze onto me. "Just a couple of classes a week in Art Appreciation. It's a freshman elective. Most students see it as an easy two credits. No, I want Lisa to model for me at the studio. I wasn't kidding about the bust. I'd love to catch those

179

cheekbones. I'd also like her to model for my class."

"Since when does Art Appreciation include models?" Jill asked.

Charlie sent her an amused look. "It doesn't. I hold classes for serious artists a couple of nights a week in my studio."

"I don't think that's a good idea," she said.

Lisa drew a deep breath and glanced at her sister with irritation. "Charlie, I'd love to pose for you, but not nude. We'll get together later on, okay?"

His eyes lit up with what I could only describe as artistic anticipation.

"That's great. This project will be a masterpiece. You're the most beautiful model I've ever had."

Lisa laughed. "I'll bet you say that to all the girls."

Charlie grinned. "But of course. I love all my models. I worship them. Just ask ex-wife number three—she still poses for me on occasion."

Jill's eyebrows rose. "You have three ex-wives?"

"Guess I'm just unlucky in love. Call it the artistic temperament."

"I can relate to that," Lisa told him. "I have an ex-husband in St. Louis."

"St. Louis? I thought he was living in San Diego," Jill answered sharply.

"He's back. I ran into him at a club a few weeks ago. Josh seems to have gotten over his problems. He had a good-looking brunette on his arm and said he was happy. Now, about that key."

"Huh? Oh yeah, the key." Jill fumbled with her key ring, detached the key and handed it over. "I take it you locked the door when you left."

"Of course, I did. I'm not stupid. The deadbolt on

the front door is the only one unlocked."

"Sorry, Lisa, I've got a lot on my mind. What other plans do you have today?"

"I'm not sure. I may go to that big mall either today or tomorrow. Haven't decided yet."

"How about having dinner with me tonight?" Charlie asked her.

Lisa didn't make eye contact as she tucked the key into a zippered compartment in her jogging shoe.

"Uh, thanks, but I already have plans."

Charlie looked taken aback, but shrugged. "That's okay. I'll talk to you later about the modeling schedule." He glanced at his watch. "Guess I'd better head for the studio. I have a few things to do. See you all later."

He gathered his coat and left.

I picked up enough on Charlie's emotions to know that while he looked nonchalant, he wasn't happy about the refusal. He wanted to begin sculpting her as soon as possible.

Jill was worried on several levels. I sensed the interview hadn't gone well, but her main concern was still for her sister. She wanted to warn Lisa not to go, but kept quiet. She also worried about this modeling gig for Charlie. For the life of me, I couldn't place the fear in her psyche either.

As for Lisa, she'd lied. She didn't have plans, but most of her mind was taken up with irritation at her sister. Jill was crowding her space. And the fear factor had not lessened much. I suddenly wondered if Lisa knew something the rest of us didn't.

Brannon strode into the room interrupting any further conversation and my emotions analysis.

"Jill, report to the Fourteenth as soon as possible. They also have a few questions for you concerning Mike. The rest of you are free to go." He eyed Lisa. "And who are you?"

His tone wasn't unfriendly, merely brusque. Jill introduced them, and then struggled into her coat.

"I guess I'd better get going, too," Lisa said.

"Be careful," Jill said a trifle absently as her sister slipped out the door.

Her furrowed forehead concerned me. "Jill, why don't you and Lisa join us for dinner tonight? How about The Welcome Mat in Germantown at, say, seven?"

Reed sent me a look from across the room. I don't know why I extended the invitation without consulting him, but something told me Jill's interview with Internal Affairs hadn't gone well, and that the one at the Fourteenth would not be pleasant.

"Oh, you don't need a third wheel."

"We like having dinner with friends," Reed replied.

"All right. I doubt Lisa will come if she has plans, but I will." Jill took a deep breath. "Guess I'd better go face the tigers in the den."

She turned and walked away, her face set in grim lines.

****

I sat at a table in The Welcome Mat lightly twirling the stem of my wine glass between my fingers. The last time I'd been here, it had been with Linnie and Jeff Hammond—the night he'd killed Janine, Linnie's receptionist.

I took a sip from the glass. Reed had gone outside to take a phone call. Through the front windows I watched him pace and talk.

Earlier, after Jill's departure, Reed had gone to work while I grabbed a cab back to Germantown. In lieu of anything better to do, I cleaned. Not that there was much to clean. Reed was a neat man—only the occasional sock on the floor—and kept up on housekeeping with the exception of dusting.

Now, I cleaned to keep my mind off the events of the last few days. I didn't want to think about Mike's murder, Lisa, Jill's problems, or the dreams. It didn't help. I still pondered everything and tried to connect them in one large bundle for easy delivery. That didn't work either.

Something Reed said as we left the station nagged in the back of my mind.

"Did you see how relieved Jill was when Lisa turned Charlie down for dinner?"

No, I hadn't. I'd homed in on Charlie's displeasure and sensed Jill's unhappiness with Lisa's continuing activities, but I totally missed the relief. I chalked it up to him keeping her out until the wee hours. The motive wasn't the point. The point was I'd missed it.

I've missed a lot lately. And my visions have been almost incoherent. Am I losing it? Are the abilities receding?

I was confused. For someone who didn't really like her abilities, why was I so concerned about losing them? Then it dawned on me that my physical powers were growing, perhaps at the expense of my mental abilities. I turned off the vacuum cleaner and called Linnie.

"Sasha, are you all right? I'm so sorry for the other day. I wanted to call, but Reed suggested I wait a day or

183

two."

"I'm as good as can be expected. I was upset and called Reed—just to talk. I took your advice and moved back in with him until this is over. I also decided you were right about consulting a regular psychiatrist."

"Good for you. I know just the person, Dr. Sandra Solomon. She's located in East Memphis not far from my old office. Do you want me to call her and set up the appointment?"

"Yes, if you don't mind."

We hung up and I waited chewing my fingernails until she called back.

"I've got you in for a week from Tuesday at eleven o'clock. Is that all right? Can you hold on that long?" she asked ten minutes later.

"That's fine. Thank you. I forgot to ask, how are you feeling?"

"I was at the hospital last night," she grumbled.

"Why? Is something wrong?" I'd sensed nothing. She's my best friend and I'd never even gotten a glimmer. My spirits plummeted to my toes.

"False labor. Just those damned Braxton-Hicks contractions again. They were so strong I thought it was time. Felt like an idiot when the doctor told me to go home and relax."

I tried to laugh. "I suggest you do as he says. Put your feet up, read a good book, and let Bill do the work."

"I intend to."

We'd hung up, and while I was still unsettled, just talking to Linnie helped.

Reed returned from his phone call, resumed his seat, and took a long swallow of his vodka and tonic.

In spite of concerns regarding my abilities, I tapped into his mind. He wasn't exactly upset, more apprehensive than anything.

"Trouble?"

"Not really. I have a couple of new cases on my desk and a new lead on an old one. I want to get in early tomorrow."

Delving further was out of the question. I learned long ago that if Reed wanted to clue me in, he would and no amount of probing could change things. He'd learned how to shut the door.

"I drove by Mike's on my way home tonight," he said abruptly. "The crime scene tape's still up, but I got a good look at the place. Traditional red brick with white trim. The shutters are forest green."

"And the front door? I assume you saw that, too."

"Forest green."

I finished my wine in a single gulp. "So my dream could have been connected to Mike and his killer."

"Well, it was connected to Mike and somebody. Remember, you didn't actually see the murder, only the image of a golf club."

"There's still something about the front door in my dream that I can't remember. And a lot of people have front doors to match their shutters. Plus, I wasn't sure of the color—only that it was dark. I'd like to see the door up close and personal."

"Won't be a problem once the scene is released. What do you expect to see?"

"Wish I knew."

The waiter stopped by, asking if I wanted another glass of wine. I nodded and glanced at my watch. It was almost seven-thirty.

"I wonder what's keeping Jill."

"Traffic maybe? She might be having a donnybrook with Lisa about the mall and modeling."

"Lord, I hope not. Lisa just might head back home after all."

"I'm not sure that wouldn't be the best solution," Reed said.

"But here, Jill can keep an eye on her."

"Do you know for sure where this abduction takes place? Or when?"

"You know I don't." I tapped my fingers on the table in irritation.

Reed sat back with a thoughtful expression. "I wonder how Jill would react to a little subterfuge regarding her sister's safety."

"Such as?"

"I'm thinking of Keith Simmons."

I quit drumming my fingers and stared. "The man who was my bodyguard during the Hammond case?"

"The same. He quit the force a year or so ago and opened his own security firm. I understand his company provided the bodyguards for Sweet Revenge when he was here for that concert."

"Sweet Revenge? The gangsta rapper who declares through his so-called music that it should be open season on all cops? Oh, I'll bet Keith just loved that."

Reed shrugged. "He doesn't have to like his clients, just protect them."

"But I can't see Jill agreeing to a bodyguard. She'd have to tell Lisa why, and I had the impression this morning that was not an option."

"Who says Lisa has to know?"

"You mean surveillance? Keith follows her

wherever she goes? Maybe even makes her acquaintance at the jog park or something?" I paused for a moment to think. "You know, that might work. If he's a fellow jogger, she might never notice, although how anyone could miss Keith Simmons is beyond me. He's tall, built like a stone wall, and hard not to notice."

"Keith understands that. He'd send one of his less massive operatives."

The waiter brought my wine. Reed ordered another drink.

"Where is Jill?" I couldn't keep the irritation from my voice.

"Give her a call."

I fished the phone from my purse and dialed off the recent calls list. I got voice mail and left a message.

"Jill, Reed and I are at The Welcome Mat. We'll give you another ten minutes, and then order. Hope everything went well. Have an idea about Lisa you might like." I hung up. "Why wouldn't she be answering her phone at this hour? Surely, she's not still being interrogated."

"The Fourteenth's problems are increasing. The rumor mill is grinding them out faster than a wood chipper. Heard today another cop was part of a gambling ring up in Bartlett. He looked the other way for a fee."

"Why would someone have a gambling ring when legalized gaming is less than a lousy hour away down in Mississippi?"

"Some people don't want to take the time to drive. They have a little coin in their jeans and stop by the back of Smitty's Bar for a few rolls of the dice."

I sipped my wine. "Jill's attitude about what Mike

had done with his fellow officers surprised me."

"You mean about how IA should handle it as a private affair?"

I nodded. "That just doesn't sound right. And why would the guys at the Fourteenth want to question her? What could she possibly know? Mike Young kept this close to his chest." I sipped again. "Reed, do you suppose Jill could have had a piece of the action, too?"

"Like having a little scam on the side? Maybe. Once the rot begins, it spreads fast unless something is done."

"She popped off about him last night at dinner, that's for sure."

"Enough to do something about it?" he asked with a frown.

I sipped my wine again. "I can't see that. I can't even see her as a crooked cop. And at no point when I've been in her head, did I get a sense of wrongdoing. It's mostly fear—a lot of fear today—and worry about her sister."

"You're assuming Jill would think of it as wrongdoing. Cops are people. The greed factor hits them just like everyone else. A shot at supplementing your income might be hard to pass up. And they could easily justify it to make it sound legit."

"Oh, boy, what a mess." I glanced at my watch again. "Let's order. I'm hungry and tired of waiting."

Reed sat facing the doors. "She just walked in and she doesn't look happy."

I turned to look over my shoulder. Jill scanned the room. I raised my hand and waved. She acknowledged with a nod and made her way toward us.

I connected and easily read the fear, frustration,

and anger swirling inside her. She arrived at our table, took off her coat, and sat without a word. Her clothes were the same as this morning.

"Hi, you look beat. Was it bad?" I asked signaling the waiter.

"I am, it was, and I'll have a Bloody Mary," she told the server.

"How did it go at the Fourteenth?" Reed inquired.

"I felt like pig on the barbeque." Her eyes filled with tears.

I laid my hand on her arm. "Jill, what is it?"

She looked from me to Reed and back again. "I talked to Internal Affairs, the Feds, my captain at the Fourteenth, my new captain at the new precinct, and several state prosecutors. The upshot is I have been placed on administrative leave—with pay, as of now."

"Administrative leave? What's that?"

"It means they have further questions regarding her activities and relationships within the precinct," Reed answered with a frown.

"Bingo! And I am now an official 'person of interest' in the murder of my partner."

Chapter Thirteen

Jill was a suspect in Mike's death? It was ludicrous. *Or was it?*

"Why do they think you may have killed him? And why bring in the federal authorities?" I asked.

Reed took a long swallow of vodka and tonic. "I can answer that. Some of the criminal activities took place in Mississippi and/or Arkansas, which means they crossed state lines. And since marijuana is a drug the federal agency brought in is the DEA. Is the FBI involved, too?"

Jill nodded. "One of the owner's of the grow house also owns a grow house in Horn Lake. He frequently transported harvested weed to Memphis, sometimes with an escort like Winslett. As of now it's the DEA's case, but the FBI is waiting to assist."

He stared at Jill with a grim expression. "But you also withheld information from the investigators and it came back to bite you in the ass. Right?"

She nodded again, her lips set in a stern line. "I saw and heard things at the Fourteenth, but didn't report any of it. I also knew Mike saw and heard the same things and had taken matters into his own hands. I warned him to stay out of it—that the guilty would be caught sooner or later."

"Only Mike decided to make it sooner," I said.

"I can't tell you the times I told him to back off,

but not Mike Young. He had to speed up the process by starting his own sting operation."

"Did you help him?" Reed wanted to know.

"On a couple of occasions, but I finally told him to find another crusader. I felt uncomfortable sneaking around trying to get the goods on my colleagues. And what was worse, half the time Mike wasn't sure who was doing what either."

"So he launched fishing expeditions," Reed said. "Must have pissed off a lot of cops who were clean."

"Why would a clean cop get involved on the wrong side of a sting?" I asked.

Reed frowned running a finger up and down his glass. "Curiosity, or a suspicion that perhaps Young was on the take."

I sighed and rubbed my forehead. "Terrific. Mike's running a sting on cop A, while cop B is running a sting on him." I gazed at Jill. "What was Mike's reaction to your decision not to help?"

The waiter arrived with Jill's drink. She picked it up with a trembling hand and downed half of it.

"Told me it was my duty as a public servant 'to serve and to protect.' His exact words. I got angry at being lectured and told him he was on the fast track to ruining his career and mine along with it. Then he got personal and made a tacky comment about women not having the guts to do the job when dealing with personalities. Said we were natural compromisers."

"And then you argued," Reed said.

"I'd call it more of a heated discussion," she replied in a cautious tone.

"You argued," he restated.

"When was this?" I asked.

"A month or so ago. I put in for a transfer. The next thing I knew, we'd both been reassigned to the psych ward. I was pissed at Mike. If he'd left well enough alone, the problem would have been taken care of internally. He was pissed at me, because he thought I'd ratted him out to the higher-ups. I didn't."

I ignored the last part of her comments, preferring to focus on three words. "The psych ward?"

She blushed. "I'm sorry, Sasha, but to be brutally honest, that's what a lot of officers and detectives call this divisional experiment. Not many take it seriously."

"That's their mistake."

Reed waved his hand. "Honey, that has nothing to do with this. Keep it for a later discussion. I suggest we order. Our waiter is hovering just out of earshot. Probably wants to turn this table over."

"Like I can eat anything," Jill muttered, finishing her Bloody Mary.

Reed signaled the waiter who trotted over eagerly. I ordered a seafood salad, while Reed opted for a steak. Jill finally settled on an appetizer after requesting another drink.

When the server left, Reed said, "So far, nothing you've told us would give anybody a reason for suspending you. What else happened? Did you lie during the interrogations?"

"Not so much lie as I didn't tell the whole truth."

"Same difference," he said in an impatient tone.

Her brows drew together in a scowl. Before she could answer, I jumped in.

"What happened that made you withhold information?"

"Self-preservation."

"I don't understand."

Jill shook her head and bit her lip. "I was pretty upset about a lot of things the past couple of days. Last night after I left you, Sasha, I went home to think. Lisa had told me Mike asked her out and I wasn't happy about that. I finally called him and said we needed to talk. He agreed and told me to come on over."

"Did you go?" Reed asked. "What time did all this happen?"

"I called about nine-thirty and got to his place around nine forty-five."

I closed my eyes, and then opened them again. That put her at Mike's about the time of the murder if the coroner was right.

"What happened?" I inquired.

"I told him to back off with my sister. His crusading activities had burned a lot of people, and I didn't want her involved with him if someone was out for a pound of flesh."

"What did he say?" Reed asked.

The waiter brought her second Bloody Mary. She took a long swallow before answering. "Said Lisa was an adult and I should butt out. Then he accused me of disloyalty. Said my request for transfer put him in a bad light and could hinder his credibility with the internal affairs investigation. Then he had the gall to ask if I was involved in something, too. Sent me right over the top."

Oh God, my question to Reed not a half an hour ago.

"I yelled at him that I was clean and always would be. He yelled back. I was so angry, I had to get out of there or I'd bust a gut. I ran out, stumbling over his golf bag in the foyer. I grabbed and righted it before it hit the floor. Then I drove home."

"And of course, that's what tripped you up," Reed stated. "The police found your call on Mike's cell phone memory, and your fingerprints on the golf bag."

She nodded. "Mine and Mike's were the only ones on it they could ID. All others were partials or smudged. I guess from caddies or someone like that."

Reed shook his head. "As a cop you should have known your prints would be there."

Jill scowled. "I was scared and panicked when I got the news he'd been murdered. I didn't think. So when they interrogated me, I just didn't tell them I was at his place."

The extreme fear from earlier in the day was now explained. "But surely, they're fingerprinting the rest of the house."

"Naturally," Reed said. "And I wouldn't be surprised if they issue a search warrant for your house looking for an eight iron. And I'm sure you're under surveillance right now."

"The warrant was issued, the search is being conducted now, and I've been ordered to appear for more questioning at the station tomorrow morning at nine o'clock sharp."

I leaned over and laid my hand on her arm. "Jill, I don't believe you killed Mike Young, and I'm sure nobody at the Fourteenth does either."

I spoke with a grain of salt. At this point, I wasn't sure if she had or hadn't brained her partner. I liked Jill, but then I'd liked Jeff Hammond, too, and he turned out to be a cold-blooded killer.

Reed shot me a sardonic glance and raised his eyebrow. Good heavens, did *he* think she'd done it?

She set her glass on the table and fiddled with the silverware. "Did you ever wonder if the last thing you said to someone might be the last thing you say to them? I wish I hadn't said what I did to Mike. Wish I hadn't left on an angry note."

"Water under the bridge," Reed said.

She picked up her glass again and sipped. "Oh well, if nothing else I'll be able to keep a closer eye on Lisa with this leave. She's out tonight at a club with some friends she made while jogging. I hope she's all right."

"Jill, have you considered telling Lisa the truth about why you hover?" I asked.

"Good God, no! I don't want to scare her."

Even though Lisa was an adult, Jill still wanted to protect her.

"It might make her more attuned to her surroundings," I said, remembering the dream scene at the mall.

"It might also send her scurrying back to St. Louis where I'll have no way of keeping in touch. I can't leave Memphis now—not with this person-of-interest thing hanging over my head."

"Reed came up with a possible solution to your constantly being with her."

Jill turned her head toward Reed with a hopeful gaze. He told her about Keith Simmons.

A spark of interest lit her eyes. "A bodyguard? You're right, Lisa would never agree to it, but I like the idea of subterfuge disguised as a distraction. Worked when we were kids. Wave the bright, shiny object under her nose and she forgot about swiping my lipstick. Only this time the shiny object is a good-looking guy. Might work." Our food arrived. "Let me think on this," she said as we were served.

Reed ate, but kept shooting sidelong glances toward Jill, who picked at her appetizer. I didn't have much of an appetite either, but forced myself to eat. I tapped into Jill's emotions. Fear, anger, and a profound sense of having done irreparable damage to her career surged.

I wanted to reassure her, but before I could find the words, she laid her fork down.

"I'm sorry, but I can't continue. I'm going home, assuming my colleagues are finished tearing my house apart. Please forgive me."

In a scene identical to last night's, she pushed her chair back, grabbed her coat and headed for the front doors. I started to rise, but Reed clasped my arm.

"Leave her. She has to deal with it on her own. You were in her head. Did she kill Young?"

"I just don't now. She's harboring a lot of anger, fear, worry, and frustration. It's all mixing together. I'm having a hard time reading anything about murder."

I sat back and pushed my salad bowl away. As far as dinners went, this one sucked.

****

"Reed, what's going to happen to Jill?" I asked the question as soon as we were in the car.

"I'd say her career in Memphis is shot to hell. If she wants to continue being a police officer, she'll have to move."

"But why? What if she didn't kill Young?"

"We don't know that for a fact."

I hesitated. He was right. We didn't. "Like I said, I sensed nothing along the lines of murder."

196

"Unless, she blacked out. You said you saw things through a red haze."

"You mean she was so enraged she doesn't remember?" I paused and bit my lip. "*That* is a distinct possibility. Do you think Mike could have made some kind of sexual advance toward Jill?"

"You mean actually had her pinned down or something and she got away, then used the eight iron to defend herself?" He frowned as he paused. "If that was the case, she'd have said so. It would clearly be self-defense. She'd be home free with Young not there to tell another story. *Or* maybe she's learning to block your intrusions."

I dismissed his suggestion with a wave of my hand. "She hasn't had time yet to learn how. And I suppose you're right about the self-defense angle. But if she's innocent, why can't she stay here? Why would this destroy her career?"

"Just because a person is deemed not guilty of a crime or is released from jail doesn't mean the public will embrace them. Would you feel comfortable working with someone accused, however falsely, of a crime?"

"I don't know."

"The suspicion, that nagging doubt, would always be in the back of your mind."

"But Bobby Jack arrested me for murdering Clarke Pennington. I've never sensed any hesitation on his part about having me around working with him."

Reed sighed as we pulled into his driveway. He killed the ignition and turned to face me.

"That's because the real murderer was found, tried, convicted, and put away. Suppose the crime goes unsolved and ends up on the desk of someone like me a year or so down the line. What then?"

I saw his point, but refused to accept it. Brannon would get to the bottom of the case.

"Do you think Jill will take your advice about hiring Keith Simmons?" I asked, changing the subject.

"Your guess is as good as mine. She seemed receptive, but with time on her hands, she might cling like ivy to Lisa."

Reed entered the house. I followed more slowly. The whole day had been a shambles—news of Mike's murder, the interrogations, the scene in the conference room with Charlie and Lisa, Jill's admissions, and finally a dud of a dinner.

I dumped my purse on the foyer table and wandered into the kitchen where I jerked open the refrigerator door and reached for the half-empty bottle of Pinot Grigio.

Pouring a glass, I looked out the window into the garage. Reed was on the phone.

Older Germantown houses often had kitchen windows with views of a carport or a garage. It was silly. Did the architects think people enjoyed looking at their cars and other junk?

I shook my head and returned to the living room, plopping myself on the sofa. I needed to talk. My concern about my abilities had taken hold in my mind. Reed would listen, put things into perspective, and give good feedback. This entire Lisa Parker thing was muddled. Too many emotions and confusing half-dreams had blurred the original nightmare. I no longer felt confident. I was beginning to doubt my abilities. For the first time I admitted I was scared.

Reed reentered the kitchen. I heard the refrigerator door open, and then the sound of a liquid being poured into a glass. A moment later, he joined me and sat in his recliner giving my wine glass the eye, but saying nothing. I'd had three at the restaurant. He took a swig of his iced tea.

"I just talked to Brannon," he told me.

"What did he say?"

"He confirmed Jill is a suspect, but refused to say if he thinks she's guilty. The search of her place didn't turn up a possible weapon or anything else of an incriminating nature. The warrant, however, was flawed. It only mentioned the house, not her car."

"Her car?"

"Could hide a golf club in the trunk."

"No one's that stupid, especially a cop," I retorted.

"She drove home from Mike's last night and to and from the restaurant tonight. Both excellent opportunities to stop and sling it into the woods, or better yet, onto a golf course. What a lucky find for a duffer."

"You're being cynical."

He shrugged. "Perhaps."

"What else did Brannon have to say?"

"They found a wealth of fingerprints in the house—Winslett's and a couple of other cops from the Fourteenth."

"Of course, they did. Wonder how Winslett will explain it."

"Probably the same way Bobby Jack did."

I looked up in surprise. "Bobby Jack? His prints were in the house?"

"Front door, the inside door knob, a couple on the

199

doorjamb to the living room. According to Brannon, Bobby Jack said he dropped off some files for Mike day before yesterday."

"It makes perfect sense," I said in irritation. "Bobby Jack may have resented Mike and Jill coming in to take over, but he understood why."

"Brannon also confirmed that Young had a golf date with a friend the next morning. Tee off time was scheduled for eight o'clock."

"So that explains the golf bag in the foyer."

Reed didn't answer, but took another drink of his tea, and then turned that penetrating blue gaze on me.

"Want to talk about it?"

"Talk about what?"

"Whatever's bothering you."

A soft glow spread from the pit of my stomach to my fingers and toes. He always knew when I had a problem.

"Guess I don't have much of a poker face."

"You never did."

I heaved a sigh, and sipped some of my wine. "I'm worried, Reed. My abilities are scrambled, like eggs. I see some things, but not everything. I feel some emotions, but totally miss others. I have no idea why."

"You have too many irons in the fire. Schenk is filling your head with nonsense that can't possibly help you. You have a dream about a murder, talk to Schenk, and then come home making screwdrivers move across the room. Everything is running together like a finger painting left out in the rain."

I took a deep breath and told him about my call to Linnie and the appointment with a new shrink. "I don't know. Maybe I let things get out of hand, because I wanted so badly to explore these experiences. I'm at the point where I don't know if what I'm feeling is real or the power of suggestion."

He set his glass on the end table and leaned forward. "Sasha, you have a gift to see into others' emotions. Maybe you have more than that. You must or you couldn't move screwdrivers. If you lived four hundred years ago in Salem, you'd have been burned at the stake or hanged."

His words brought my conversation with Schenk's secretary back to mind with a jolt. Salem—witchcraft. Hadn't she said his book was about witchcraft and reincarnation or something along those lines? Was I nothing more than an experiment to him? A source of information? *Like Clarke Pennington?*

He picked up his glass again and sat back. "I'm sorry, I shouldn't have said that. Your mind is on overload. You can't process everything. That's why you're confused and no longer see clearly. You're reaching terminal velocity."

"Terminal velocity?"

"That's the point at which air resistance and gravity are equal on a falling object. The object falls no faster. You'll always have visions and nightmares. All you can do is report to the police and back away. Let them do their job. You have no business running around trying to prevent a crime or solve one. Jeff Hammond's case should have told you that."

"I 'ran around' as you call it because I was tuned into you, or would you have rather I'd have not bothered to charge into that clearing?" I asked, irked at his words.

"Sasha, I don't want to argue." He sighed, picked

up the remote, and pushed a button. The TV popped on.

I finished my wine and glared at the screen while Reed channel surfed for sports. Of course, I should try to prevent a crime from occurring. And my visions had helped nail Jeff Hammond, along with other cases in the past.

A voice in the back of my mind asked, *but what about Margie Hollis and Rafe Quillen?*

I ignored the mental question, not wanting to think about the failures.

A picture flashed in front of my eyes. Then the edges of my vision darkened. While Reed watched a basketball game, I slowly went under.

As usual, I was aware of being in a trance-like state, but saw or heard nothing of what was happening in reality.

My vision brought me into a park with a bunch of joggers. I viewed the group through the eyes of Lisa Parker. Don't ask me how I knew. I just did. She joked and talked with them as she ran, her pace that of a seasoned runner. The iPod played a tune matching her footsteps. Lisa was still irritated with Jill, but concentrated on her breathing as she jogged.

Then I detached from her body and floated above. Near a large grouping of trees, a shadow lurked, hiding until she passed. Joy, lust, an insatiable need stirred the watcher's soul. I shivered and tried to warn her, but had no luck. Lisa paid no attention. The stranger moved onto the path and commenced running. Lisa's companion joggers had thinned, moving ahead of her by several dozen yards. She jogged alone.

Slowly the man closed the gap. Still Lisa paid no attention to him. Music filled her head.

"Lisa, be careful! Turn your head! Run faster!" I shouted silently but she took no mind. She didn't hear me.

The stranger was out of shape, huffing and puffing at the fast pace. Gradually, he slowed and came to a halt. Anger at his inability to catch her mingled with the lust.

The vision faded and I dropped back into Reed's living room with a mental thump.

Oh God, was this precognition or an event that had occurred earlier? Shaken, I racked my brain for details.

Had to be from this morning, I decided. Lisa wore the red sweatshirt.

Reed glanced over at me, his gaze sharpening. "What is it? You look pale."

I told him what I'd seen.

"It was retro? You're sure?" he asked.

"Pretty sure. Unless she wears the same clothes tomorrow or the next time she jogs."

"I worry about all these visions and dreams happening in the past. Your mind may conjure them up using information already stored. Your vision either happened this morning or will happen at a later date if at all."

"So it means nothing? How can I take that chance?"

He sighed and ran a hand over his face. "Sasha, I'm to the point I don't know what to tell you anymore."

"That's all right. I don't know what to believe myself." I reached for my cell. "There's only one thing to do."

"What's that?"

"Call Jill. Tell her what I saw. If nothing else, she can take up jogging."

"No, not until you know for sure. Jill has enough on her plate at the moment. If this was a retro vision, then there's nothing she can do about it."

I put the phone back on the table. My wires may have crossed, but a woman's life hung in the balance.

How on earth can I prevent a tragedy?

Chapter Fourteen

I was at the point where I dreaded sleeping. Disjointed dreams plagued me. Scenes of joggers and shoppers in a mall woke me at regular intervals. I finally gave up and eased out of bed at five o'clock. I tiptoed into the kitchen so as not to disturb Reed.

While the coffee brewed, I sat at the table and tried to marshal my thoughts. I was picking up a lot of emotions and mental clutter from way too many people. Sifting through what was important had become a full time job. I couldn't keep up the pace much longer. Even I knew I was headed for a breakdown.

"Sasha, are you all right?" Reed asked from the doorway.

He looked wonderful standing there in his boxers and a T-shirt, his hair tousled from sleep. I swallowed the lump forming in my throat and shook my head.

"No, I'm not. Reed, I don't think I can hang on much longer. I don't know what's relevant and what's not. I have no clue what to tell the police or Jill."

He walked over to the coffee maker, poured two mugs full, and returned, setting one in front of me along with sugar and creamer before sitting across from me.

"I don't pretend to have the answers, honey. You need to take control. I can block you from reading me at times. Why not do the same to yourself? Concentrate on that original dream. Forget about Mike Young. Let the police handle it."

"Easier said than done," I muttered while doctoring my coffee. "You're right, of course. You always are."

"Not always."

His guard was down and I slipped into his mind. He was worried about me, but keeping something to himself.

I pulled out and asked, "You're upset about something, aren't you? What?"

"Been snooping again?"

"A little. What's wrong? What aren't you telling me?"

He sighed and sipped from his mug. "Last night I took a phone call from the detective in charge of a couple of unsolved cases. He was turning them over to me."

"What's so unusual about that?"

"The cases deal with Margie Hollis and Rafe Quillen."

Margie and Rafe—two murders I hadn't been able to solve. No killer had ever been apprehended. Bobby Jack had never even come up with a viable suspect in either. He'd handed them back to Homicide after four months.

"My failures." I stared into the mocha depths of my mug.

"Don't dwell on them, Sasha. Not everything gets solved. Let's get back to that first dream. Did you ever see the woman's face or that of the stalker?"

"No. In the park, all I really focused on was the blonde ponytail and the emotions of the stalker. I saw things through his eyes. But if that was the case, how did I describe the woman to Charlie? Unless, this wasn't the first time the guy's seen her. Maybe I was also picking up on his thoughts along with the emotions. And if that's true, then why didn't I know it? Oh, God, this is confusing."

"What about the mall?"

"Possibly. He was walking toward her at one point in time."

"Was either woman Lisa Parker?"

I hesitated and sipped. "I don't know. She certainly resembles my victim."

"Okay, they may or may not be the same person. Are you sure the woman in your mall vision is the same as the woman jogging?"

I sat back and concentrated. "I think so. You think they may be separate incidents with different women?"

He shrugged. "It's possible. What about the actual abduction? What did you dream?"

I set my mug down and propped my elbows up on the table, resting my forehead against my fingertips. I concentrated on that final vignette.

"I saw a building—two stories, maybe three—and the woman walking down the sidewalk. I think it's a side street because the lighting isn't strong. She's carrying a tote bag and has her keys in her hand. I have the impression her car's parked not far away. I got the feeling her mind was on something else—like perhaps where she'd just been—so she's not as aware of her surroundings. Or perhaps she's on her cell. I can't be sure in the half-light." I shivered recalling what happened next.

"Suddenly, an arm snakes around her neck. A knife is held to her throat. A voice says something like, 'Keep going. We'll take a little ride and discuss things.' He forces her into the car and makes her drive away. She's terrified and begging for him not to hurt her. Now, here's where things get fuzzy on me. I don't see clearly."

"Do you see her face?"

"No."

"So you don't actually know if the woman is murdered?"

I sat back and stared at him. "No. I don't."

"And his comment about discussing things indicates they'd had a confrontation of some sort."

"Which means, they know each other," I said slowly. "So why doesn't she notice him in the park or the mall?"

"Because it's not the same person?" Reed frowned. "You may have had two, possibly three contacts, at once."

"And the picture Charlie drew was close to looking like Lisa, but not exact. Yet I recognized her the instant she stepped into the conference room. Why?"

"You may have been feeding off of Jill's thoughts and emotions. She thought the drawing was of Lisa, so you convinced yourself the real thing had shown up. Does that make sense?"

"I guess." I rubbed my forehead, picked up my coffee, and sipped. It was cold. I set it down, not really wanting more anyway.

His hand touched my arm. "Let's quit analyzing this. I'll take a personal day off. We can go do something together. It doesn't matter what or where. We relax and not think about murders or possible murders for a while. The weather's supposed to be gorgeous—sunny and in the mid-sixties—an early pop of spring. What do you want to do?"

Spending the day with Reed lifted my spirits. He'd keep me on an even keel.

"That sounds wonderful. How about the zoo? I haven't been there in ages."

"The Memphis Zoo it is." He laughed and rose. "Now, what do you want for breakfast?"

"You."

He looked at me with a crooked grin. "I think that can be arranged."

We hustled back to the bedroom.

****

Memphis has one of the best zoos in the country. Located in Overton Park, it spans a lot of territory. After over six hours of walking, my legs were telling me to call it a day.

"I don't think I can walk another step," I said with a groan as Reed eased the car into afternoon traffic.

"But it was well worth it. I love the meerkats. They make me laugh, especially the one reclining against a rock and scratching his tummy. Reminds me of Bill watching a football game on TV."

I burst out laughing. "I wonder if Linnie can confirm that."

"I'll ask next time I see her," he replied with a grin. "Want to go out for an early dinner or order in a pizza?"

"Pizza!"

While our day out had helped relieve the stress, my mind couldn't help returning to the visions I'd been having. The exercise had helped clear my head as I recalled my original dream.

"Reed, I think I may have a handle on this dream thing. Suppose I didn't actually see the victim's face like we discussed. I was seeing things through the stalker's eyes, so maybe I was getting the facial image through him, and it's just fuzzy enough for me not to be sure whether or not the woman is Lisa."

"Kind of a second hand vision? Like you mentioned earlier, maybe he'd seen her before and had a picture in his mind?"

"Something like that."

"And the description you gave Charlie was close enough to Lisa to send Jill into panic mode."

"Oh brother, I may be way off base this time."

"Or not," Reed said slowly. "Don't dwell on it. Let your mind rest. Maybe things will be clearer tomorrow or the next day."

"Assuming we have until tomorrow or the next day."

Reed opened his mouth but my phone rang, interrupting whatever he planned to say. I pulled the cell out of my purse and groaned.

"Damn, it's Schenk."

"Ignore it."

"Crap, it's Monday. I totally forgot and missed my appointment."

"So what? Ignore it," he repeated.

I answered anyway. "Hello, Dr. Schenk. I'm so sorry. I totally forgot what day it was."

"Sasha, if I'm here, then I expect you to be here. What's going on that you forgot an important appointment?"

"I've been very busy."

"Have you even worked on the astral projection or dual consciousness?"

"No. I told you the last time we met that I was

working on another case for the police department."

"Have you thought about possible past life experiences like we discussed a few weeks ago? From our sessions, I'm sure you lived many times over. Reincarnation is not unheard of and with your abilities, I'm convinced you were a victim more than once. We must explore this further."

I remembered the conversation with his receptionist about his work in progress on witchcraft. Then I remembered Clarke Pennington and how he tried to use me for his book, too.

"You mean, like was I burned at the stake or hanged for my abilities?" I glanced at Reed. His fingers tightened on the steering wheel and his jaw clenched.

Schenk drew in an audible breath. "So you do know something. Were you in Salem? Or perhaps somewhere in Europe during Medieval times?"

"I know nothing of the sort."

"Come in immediately so we can explore this."

"No. I'm working with the police on something very important. I'll make an appointment when I can."

"Sasha, I demand you come in for a consult. Forget the police. This is too important to put off."

I hesitated and took a deep breath, about to make a major decision.

"Dr. Schenk, my work with the police involves human lives, not your latest book deadline." A strange sense of déjà-vu washed over me. I'd said practically the same thing to Pennington when I had quit my job three years ago.

Even though on the phone, I could feel Schenk's rage.

"I have no idea what you're talking about."

"Sure you do. I'm the psychic. Remember? In fact, I think this is a good time to terminate our relationship. I'm already set up to see another psychiatrist next week. Thank you for your help, but this is what's best for me."

"You can't do this to me. I have too much at stake. Get in here now! I won't take no…"

I hung up. "Shades of Clarke Pennington. Why didn't I see it before?"

"You've seen it now, and that's what counts." Reed said, his hands relaxing on the wheel. "Congratulations. You've just taken a big step toward reclaiming your life."

"And yours?"

He stopped at a red light, turned and stared at me with a somber look. "God, I hope so. Now, how big a pizza do we want, what toppings, and how many bottles of Chianti?"

I laughed, happy for the first time in over two years.

****

I awoke the next morning refreshed and with a renewed purpose to my life. Reed and I made slow, sweet love, slept, and then made love again. It was like coming home.

Schenk called and left messages in my voice mail every few minutes after I'd hung up on him. I finally reported him as a harassing phone caller and turned the device off. I'd never felt so free. Perhaps now I could concentrate on the case at hand and try to decide if the woman in the park, at the mall, and on the street were one and the same.

"What's on your agenda for today?" Reed asked,

buttering his toast.

I sipped from my mug letting the aroma of fresh-brewed coffee further awaken me. "I'm not sure, but I may swing by the mall and see if I can identify the area in the parking lot where I saw the woman in my dream. It's time to ignore all those new abilities I've picked up and buckle down on the case in hand. Plus, there's Mike Young's murder. I saw something in that dream, too. I'm just not sure what."

"I'll check and see if the house has been released. Maybe Detective Brannon won't mind if you do a walk through. The vibes might be stronger."

I nodded. "Good idea. I also want to go home, get some more clothes, pick up my mail, that sort of thing."

"I'm not sure you should go alone," he said with a frown.

"I'll be fine. I haven't felt in danger."

"I just keep remembering Jeff Hammond. He knew he couldn't get to you directly, so he used Linnie and me as distractions to lure you into a deathtrap."

"But he's dead and the only people who know about my dream are cops. I know, I know," I said as he opened his mouth. "So was Jeff, but I didn't know him prior to meeting him that day in Linnie's office. I know the people involved this time around."

"You don't really know Jill."

"Are you suggesting Jill wants to kill her own sister?" I let the exasperation show in my tone.

"No, but she's on the suspect list for Young's death."

"So's half the Fourteenth Precinct."

Reed sighed and finished his breakfast. "Just be careful. Please."

I reached out and squeezed his hand. "I will. I'll go to the mall this morning, and then head to Holly Springs. I'll be home before dark. Promise."

He smiled and squeezed my hand back. "I worry."

"I appreciate it, but I'm a big girl. I can handle myself if necessary. Besides, it's a quick trip. Less than two hours round trip. What could happen?"

Reed left for the station a few minutes later. Too early to go to the mall, I settled for making a list of things to bring from home. It was a long list. For all intents and purposes, I was moving in on a permanent basis. I just hoped this time we could make it last.

I tried to organize my thoughts as I drove to the mall. The best way to tackle this was to drive around the parking lot until I saw something familiar. The problem was I often shopped at this mall, so *everything* was familiar. After an hour of cruising the lanes and spaces, I admitted defeat. The parking lot was a parking lot and nothing leaped into my mind. Frustrated, I finally slid into a slot and headed inside. If nothing else, I could always shop.

Three hours, six stores, a pair of designer jeans, three tops, and two pairs of shoes later, I took a load off my feet at the food court where I munched on Kung Pao chicken.

My mind had remained remarkably clear of visions. I had no idea why. All I knew was it felt good to be normal for a change. *Thank God for small favors.*

I spoke too soon. As I ate, I watched children riding the carousel near one of the mall entrances their laughter and the Wurlitzer blending together. Then the happy scene faded, replaced with that of a blonde woman walking down a parking lane, her hands full of packages. I viewed it through other eyes.

I rose, gathered my bags, and slowly walked to the doors. Once outside, the woman also faded into nothingness, but I was certain I'd found the place in my original dream. The foot traffic was normal. No blonde woman stood out. Neither did a man who watched others.

Shaken, I retraced my steps through the mall and out to my car. I stopped, popped the trunk lid and stashed my purchases inside. Cold descended. A chill of fear raced down my spine. I turned. Twenty feet away a man passed by. He glanced in my direction. My breath stopped in my chest.

In a panic, I unlocked the car door, slid inside, and relocked it. Trembling and gasping, I clutched the steering wheel. I hadn't bothered to even try entering his mind.

On my God, what the hell is going on? The woman in my original dream and the scene I just saw is blonde. Did I project myself into this grim vision?

I had no clue and suddenly wished Reed was here. I also wished I was seeing the doctor Linnie had set me up with sooner than a week away.

Okay, Bellwood, get a grip. What just happened is one of those things. The man was totally disinterested in you—an innocent shopper going to the mall. You're so jazzed up you're seeing things that aren't there.

I heaved several deep breaths. More under control, I inserted the key into the ignition and a minute later left the mall for Holly Springs. This day was rapidly going downhill.

****

The drive home helped calm my shattered nerves.

By the time I pulled into my driveway, I'd convinced myself I was letting paranoia rule. If I was going to be any use to anybody, I had to keep my head on my shoulders.

I got out of the car by the mailbox and retrieved a huge stack of magazines, flyers, and assorted junk. I paid most of my bills online, but did have a few honest pieces—one from my dentist reminding me my check-up was due, another from my auto dealership suggesting my five-year-old car might need replacing, and one from my broker. Hopefully, the latter was good news.

Inside the house, I headed for the bedroom. A few more jeans, tops, sweaters, skirts, and jewelry found their way into my two remaining suitcases. My closet and dresser drawers were just about empty. I next raided my DVD collection. I preferred the old-fashioned way of popping a disc into a player. Streaming movies just didn't feel right. I also wanted popcorn and dim lights for watching *Casablanca*.

Finished, I carted my bags to the foyer, and then slipped into the kitchen to clean out the fridge, dumping the worst offenders into the trash can outside the back door. I also took a moment to text my landlord saying I was out of town indefinitely and asking him to keep an eye on things.

A quick glance at the clock showed it to be nearly four. I figured I'd be at home with Reed in an hour if traffic between Holly Springs and Germantown was with me.

Back in the foyer I stared at my suitcases, sucked in a deep breath, and said a little prayer that everything would be all right this time around. It had to work. I couldn't go through the heartbreak again.

Determined, I yanked open the front door, then screamed and stepped back. My heart lurched and my knees went weak. Dr. Schenk stood on my porch, glaring at me.

Chapter Fifteen

"I want to talk to you!" Schenk said, his lip curling.

"Well, I don't want to talk to you." I tried to slam the door, but he shoved it open. I fell back farther as he entered. I swallowed the lump of fear in my throat. "What the hell do the think you're doing? Get out of here!"

"I have invested a lot of time and effort with you and I'll be damned if I let you just walk away at this stage of the game."

"Game? This is a game to you?"

His breathing increased as he took a step forward. "I have a lot at stake, and by God, you're not going to screw me over."

I retreated a step. "Yeah, you have a lot at stake all right—your next book deal. I understand it's all about witchcraft and Salem. You're using me to further your own agenda. I've been there, done that, and swore it would never happen again. Now, get the hell out of my house before I call the cops."

"Who have you been talking to? Someone's trying to influence you. Has to be a cop. You need to get out of police investigations. I told you that ages ago."

"And I told you, no. You don't own or control me, Schenk."

"Dammit, Sasha, you owe me. I brought out psychic powers you didn't even know you had. Given time, we can develop those powers into a mighty force. With me guiding you, we'll be unstoppable."

We? What the hell did that mean? Was he nuts? "Unstoppable how?"

His eyes blazed with what could only be described as a zealous light. "Just think. With your ability to read minds and predict the future, we can name our own price. And if we develop the astral projection, you can be in two places at once. Governments would pay a fortune to know what their enemies are planning. Politicians would kill to obtain information on their opponents."

I took another step back. He *was* nuts.

"You're crazy. I would never agree to something like that."

His eyes now narrowed into slits. He balled his fists and shook.

"You little bitch. If you think you can walk out on me now, you're dead wrong."

He stepped forward. I had no problem entering his mind. Rage was the dominant emotion. Rage and hate. I was thwarting carefully laid plans for his future. And if I didn't comply, he'd rather see me dead. Terrified, I didn't stop to think, but reacted by mentally pushing him away.

His body flew across the foyer and slammed into the wall. He gasped and sank to his knees. The rage and hate was replaced with fear. He stared with astonishment.

"What…what the hell was that?"

"Get out or I'll do it again. You'll end up in the next county."

He staggered to his feet, a look of uncertainty on

his face, and then came at me again. I repeated my actions—only harder. He sailed into the doorjamb this time.

"Wanna try for demonstration number three, asshole? I might find the door and propel you right into your car."

Schenk didn't answer. The terrified expression didn't need verbalization. His mind slipped into panic mode. He rushed from the house on unsteady legs, and ran. A few seconds later, the car roared down the driveway, the tires spitting gravel all the way to the road.

I drew in a ragged breath, clutched my hair, and stumbled into the living room.

"Oh my God, oh my God," I mumbled, shaking uncontrollably. "The son of a bitch really wanted to kill me."

Should I call the cops? "And tell them what? That my former shrink had murder on his mind, but I thwarted his plans with my telekinetic powers?" I answered out loud. "Yeah, like they'd believe that one."

Reed. I needed Reed. He'd know what to do, how to handle this. Just thinking his name calmed my shattered nerves.

What had upset me the most was the fact that for the first time I'd used one of my abilities in anger. Oh, I'd been afraid, but the anger worried me even if it was in self-defense. And I was more than a little frightened at how strong some of my powers had become.

I rose, gathered my two suitcases, tossed them into the trunk, and headed for Germantown. An hour later, I pulled into Reed's drive.

That hour had given me time to think. If I told

Reed about Schenk, he'd immediately confront him. The results might not be pretty. On the other hand, if I didn't talk to someone about what happened, I'd have the nightmare of a lifetime. Perhaps I could downplay Schenk's thoughts. That way Reed might not get so angry.

I toted my suitcases and shopping bags into the house. The wonderful aroma of garlic made my mouth water.

Reed entered the living room from the kitchen. "Hi, how did your day go?"

"Fine, more or less. Let me get this stuff put away. Something smells divine."

"Chicken breasts smothered in my world-famous tomato sauce," he said with a grin. "Can I pour you a glass of Chianti?"

I remembered that particular dish from a long time ago. It didn't matter that we'd eaten pizza the night before. I love Italian food. "That would be wonderful. I need it."

His grin faded. "Why? Did something happen?"

"Let me get the suitcases unpacked and I'll bring you up to date."

I turned and headed for the bedroom. Twenty minutes later, I sat on the sofa, my feet tucked up under me, sipping from a glass of wine.

"What happened?" Reed asked as he sank into his recliner.

I gave him the skinny on my trip to the mall and the mini-vision I'd had.

"And you think the guy was following you?"

"It was so weird after the vision, that I wondered if I had projected something from it onto myself. In the end, I decided I was being paranoid. The guy was harmless."

He stared at me with slightly narrowed eyes. "So if the guy was harmless, why do you feel the need for Chianti?"

I sipped from the glass as I formulated my response. "Schenk showed up in Holly Springs just as I was leaving the house."

Reed's spine stiffened as his eyes narrowed more. "He showed up at your house? Why? What did he want?"

"An explanation on why I told him to take a hike."

"And what did you tell him?"

I tried to keep my voice cool and detached. "That I didn't think the relationship was working any longer and I needed a change."

Reed, however, wouldn't let go. "And his response to that?"

"He accused me of allowing outside agitators to influence my decision."

" 'Outside agitators?' Like who?"

This was getting sticky. "The police mainly."

"Uh-huh. What else?"

I didn't like lying to him, but knew if I told the whole truth, he'd be furious.

"Not much really. He demanded I return and when I said no, he got a little testy. He finally left."

"A little testy. Sasha, if he contacts you again in any way, I want to know about it. That's harassment, possibly even stalking. We can get a restraining order against him."

"I'm sure that won't be necessary. He knows I won't be coming back," I replied remembering his frantic exit. "When's dinner? I'm starving and that sauce smells great."

He rose and entered the kitchen. I followed. As I set the table, I slipped into his head. He suspected I wasn't telling him everything. And his anger at Schenk convinced me I'd done the right thing by downplaying the incident. I convinced myself that Schenk's I'm-mad-enough-to-kill-her thoughts were momentary and had no real basis in truth. I removed myself from his mind before he had a chance to know I'd invaded.

I set the last fork in place when my phone rang. I recognized the number as Jill's.

"Hey, girl."

"Hi, Sasha." Her voice sounded forlorn and tired.

"How are you holding up?"

"Pretty good, I guess. Spent most of the day over at the Fourteenth asking and answering questions. They hauled in Winslett and a bunch of other guys to grill. A couple of them will probably be arrested for their activities. Now that the media's gotten a hold of this, the department has no other choice, but that's not why I'm calling." She hesitated. "Sasha, Lisa is going to pose for Charlie's class tonight at his studio. I was wondering if you'd like to go with me to observe."

"Observe?"

"I'm sure Charlie's all right, but I don't trust anyone a whole lot lately. I thought that if you went with me, it wouldn't look like I was spying on my sister—which I'm not. I'm just concerned and…" Her voice trailed off.

"But you are spying, Jill."

"Well, I wouldn't be so worried if you hadn't had those dreams. Oh, please help me on this. Maybe I can

223

shake this feeling I have that Charlie isn't trustworthy."

The old guilt I'd worked on eliminating for years resurfaced. Between my dream and Charlie's drawing, Jill was suffering.

"All right, I guess I can come. What time?"

"Class starts at seven. It should be over by ten. Do you know where the studio is located?"

"More or less. Give me an address." I scribbled down the address and hung up, then explained to Reed.

He shrugged. "I haven't got anything better to do. I'll go with you. Always wanted to see Charlie's professional work outside the station. We'd better eat. It's almost six now."

He served up the plates. We said little during the meal, giving me time to think. I wondered if this investigation was going anywhere, or if there was even anything to investigate. Had my abilities finally reached a dead end as far as police work was concerned?

****

Charlie's studio was located just off South Cooper Street in an up and coming art district. Reed found a nearby parking spot and we walked the remaining half block. I paused, gazing at the front window display of unique sculptures, some metal, some wood, and others that appeared to be in a ceramic material. *Kendall Art Gallery* was stenciled along the top of the glass, the tasteful design blending with the items.

Reed pushed the door open. A bell above the doorjamb rang out through the room. The gallery was dimly lit, but we heard voices and followed the chatter before stepping into a large room. A circular dais stood in the middle of the area. It was surrounded by perhaps a dozen or so easels, some with pads of paper on them.

Over in a corner, several people grouped around a table set with a coffee urn and Styrofoam cups. Charlie was among them. He looked up as we approached.

"Good Heavens, what are you doing here?" he asked with raised eyebrows.

Since I saw neither Jill nor Lisa, I wasn't sure how to answer. Reed had no such reservations.

"Jill called and said she was coming tonight since Lisa would be modeling. She asked if we'd like to join her. Never seen your place before."

"The work displayed in the window is gorgeous," I hastened to add. "Is it all yours?"

"Yes," Charlie replied absently. "Jill's coming, too?"

His question was answered when Jill walked into the room, a smile plastered on her face.

"Charlie, hope you don't mind, but I just had to see this firsthand."

Charlie returned the smile. "Not at all. Let me set you guys up with easels and drawing pads."

Jill laughed. "I am not in the least bit artistically inclined."

"I'm afraid I never got beyond the stick figure level," Reed said.

"Well, I'll have a crack at it," I added. "Sounds like fun."

"Atta girl, Sasha. Come on, it'll expand your horizons," Charlie said. "Reed, Jill, give it a shot."

Reed laughed. "Okay, what can it hurt?"

"My efforts will undoubtedly hurt your eyes, but I may as well try," Jill said with a smile.

Charlie disappeared into a storeroom off to the side and reappeared a minute later with three large pads of paper. Within seconds he set everything on easels and on the workstations next to them placed small boxes of what looked like crayons.

The room started filling up. The other students had drifted toward their easels with only a few curious glances at us. A door opened in the back of the studio and Lisa entered wearing nothing more than a sheet draped around her body like a toga. Next to me, Jill drew in a sharp breath.

Lisa stepped onto the dais, and then saw us. She heaved a sigh and rolled her eyes.

"Good grief, Jill, what are you doing here?"

"I was curious and Charlie talked us into joining the fun."

Her tone was light, but I sensed disapproval at her sister's attire.

As if on the same wavelength, Lisa said, "Well, just for your information, I'm not completely naked."

"What a shame," one of the male students chimed in with a laugh.

Everyone joined in, including Jill and Charlie, although Jill's reaction sounded forced.

Charlie clapped his hands. "All right, if we're all ready, let's get started. Tonight, the medium will be charcoal. I want you to concentrate on the draping of the fabric. Show the depth and grace of the folds with good use of shadows and light. Lisa, if you will."

He set a bar stool with a back and arms in the center of the stage. Lisa perched on the seat while Charlie arranged her limbs for maximum effect.

"Comfy?" he asked.

Lisa smiled. "I'm fine."

Lisa was not fine. She was ticked off at us,

especially Jill, for having shown up. I also sensed she was uncomfortable with the pose which allowed the sheet to drop quite low on her chest and back.

"All right, ladies and gentlemen, start impressing me."

Jill made a few lines on the paper with a charcoal pencil. I inserted myself into her mind. Her heart wasn't in this, but she was determined to not appear like James Bond on a mission.

To my surprise, Reed made several quick swipes with the charcoal and managed to capture what looked like a fold near Lisa's shoulder.

I gave it the old college try, but my efforts were not successful. My draping resembled vertical blinds.

Then from the doorway, a newcomer sauntered in, a large sketchpad under her arm.

"Hey-ho, everyone. Sorry I'm late, but you know me, I can't tell time."

As she set up at an easel, I was bombarded with a lot of internal thoughts from others in the room.

"Bitch."

"Show-off. Always has to make an entrance."

"Damn, I was hoping she wouldn't be here tonight."

"Wonder how she feels at not being the model for a change."

The young woman removed her coat and slung it over the back of a chair, then removed her stocking cap. Long, red tresses fell to just past her shoulders.

"Fucking drama queen."

"Why do I let her get to me like this?"

"Wish she'd fall down an open manhole."

My psyche ached from all the negativity.

Charlie stared at her with raised eyebrows. "Celine, I think my Christmas gift to you this year will be a watch with very large numerals on it."

The newcomer laughed until she caught sight of Lisa on the stage. "I see we have a new model. Are you a student?"

"Nope," Lisa replied. "Just passing through."

More thoughts sailed around my psyche.

"Serves her right."

"Not top dog anymore, huh, Celine?"

"Now, the bitch is a redhead. What's next—a Mohawk?"

"Red? What the hell is she thinking? I liked her better as a blonde."

"Why do some people always have to be the center of attention?"

"He can't get away with this. Is she his new conquest?"

Clearly, that last thought came from the newcomer, and while Celine's face registered no emotion, her mind thought otherwise. She was pissed.

I was also getting blasted with emotions ranging from exasperation to loathing to lust, and just plain disgust. I had no idea who thought or felt what, but this Celine person was not popular among the rest of the group. I tried to ignore all the negativity.

"Celine, take your place. We're working with charcoal tonight. I want you to focus on the draping of the fabric," Charlie told her in a cool tone.

I sensed he was not pleased. He took his classes seriously and Celine's flippant attitude irked him.

Or maybe he knows what she's thinking, too.

The room quieted along with the random thoughts.

Most of the students concentrated on their assignment, although the redhead had a few dirty mental remarks for Charlie—and Lisa.

Charlie walked around the room, stopping every once in a while to comment on a work.

"That's really quite good, Reed. Didn't know you had a hidden talent."

Reed chuckled. "Neither did I. Maybe I've found a new career."

"Uh, don't quit your day job just yet," he replied with a laugh before turning his attention to me. He contemplated my efforts. "Not bad."

"You don't need to be nice, Charlie. I know it sucks."

"But you're trying. That's what counts."

I glanced at Reed's pad. A head and shoulders had emerged on the paper, and the folds of the fabric had depth. I was impressed. Mine still looked like a bunch of lines.

"Loosen up a little, Jill," Charlie commented from next to me. "Don't be so heavy handed with the charcoal."

Curious about his choice of words, I slipped into his mind. He wasn't referring to Jill's drawing when he'd said to "loosen up," but to Lisa.

I was glad when class ended. My brain was fogged with all the thoughts and emotions of earlier. I wanted to get home, make love, and get a good night's sleep.

Jill had spoken little over the last couple of hours. As soon as Lisa headed for the changing room, she followed. I imagined Lisa would have plenty to say to her sister.

Most of the students had packed up and left, with

the exception of Celine, who'd cornered Charlie near the refreshment table. I didn't even attempt any mind entering. It was none of my business. Besides, I was tired.

"Well, that was interesting," Reed said as we walked down the sidewalk.

"If nothing else, I discovered I have absolutely no artistic talent."

"Who suspected I did? How was Jill?"

"You mean mentally? Concerned and a little ashamed for following Lisa to the studio. Lisa was ticked off, but found modeling a bore. I doubt she'll do much more of it." I paused. "That Celine girl really set the psychicsphere to humming."

"Psychicsphere?"

"I made it up."

"And how did this Celine set things to humming?"

"Most of the students dislike her intensely. The thoughts and emotions ranged from disgust to out and out hatred. Couldn't tell who thought what, but there were a lot of not so nice comments floating around."

"She's a looker, that's for sure—big blue eyes and long red hair. Funny, she reminds me of someone."

"The red is fake, if I trust what my mind heard."

We had come to the corner. Reed's car was parked just across the street. I casually glanced up the side street and froze with a gasp.

"What's wrong?"

"This is it. This is the sidewalk in my vision. The one where the woman is attacked." I looked at the building next to me. It was the same, or at least close.

Reed gripped my arm. "Are you sure?"

I nodded and closed my eyes as the mental photos

flipped passed. "Yes. Only I'm seeing things through the eyes of the victim. Her car is nearby. She's on her cell phone and as she reaches for the keys in her pocket, an arm comes around her throat. I'm getting all kinds of emotions. Disgust and contempt right before to rage and intense jealousy after. Does that make sense?"

"You're tapping into two sets of emotions. Any timeline? Is the woman Lisa?"

"I'm not sure and there's no timeline. For all I know, this has already happened. Have there been any reports of rapes or missing persons from this neighborhood?"

"I don't know, but I'll check with Brannon."

He guided me to the car and opened the passenger side door to help me in. He stood outside and made a call before joining me.

"Brannon's checking on it. Let's get you home."

As we drove through the light traffic, my mind replayed what I'd seen so briefly.

This had not been the best of days.

Chapter Sixteen

I awoke at two in the morning. By three, sleep was still elusive. My mind tumbled with information—so much so it was hard to separate what was what.

I had definitely identified the place where the abduction might occur, but still had no inkling of who or when. Frustrated with my inability to sort through the garbage, I quietly slid from the bed. Reed continued to sleep.

In the kitchen, I started to make tea, and then changed my mind, pouring a short glass of wine instead. If nothing else it might help me sleep again. With the light from the stove as the only illumination, I flipped on the chandelier and sat at the table. With a pad of paper in front of me, I proceeded to jot down what I considered pertinent events, beginning with my original nightmare, concentrating on each scene in as much detail as possible.

Looking back on it, I now realized the jogging trail could have been anywhere and the blonde woman anyone. The turbulent emotions of the stalker were still disturbing, but I had no evidence he—or she—intended to kill.

The mall parking lot offered much the same. A blonde woman being observed by a man as he walked past was no indication of a crime about to occur. The lust was strong, but once again there was no evidence the people were the same as in the first scene.

The abduction view, however, was another story. I had recognized the setting as near Charlie's studio and I had visualized the threat through the perpetrator's eyes in my original dream. But it was dark and I couldn't tell if the woman involved had blonde hair or not. All I saw was the brown leather-clad arm snaking around her neck and the possibility of a knife being involved. Reed was right—even the words, "We have to talk" didn't sound right for a kidnapping and murder.

So why use a knife at all? To scare the woman? I sat up straight as another thought flashed through my mind. Was there even a knife present or had I imagined it? Did his arm go around her neck or her shoulders?

I dropped my pen and held my head in my hands. *I don't know anymore. The vision is becoming jumbled, like it's changing as I think about it.*

I rose and refilled my wine glass before resuming my seat. For the first time, I doubted what I'd dreamed. My mind had been on overload for years, and thanks to Dr. Schenk, I no longer had confidence in the ability to interpret my visions.

"What are you doing out here?" Reed asked from the doorway.

I jerked my gaze to him. He was bare-chested, but had taken the time to pull on a pair of jeans.

"Couldn't sleep," I explained and told him about my concerns regarding the first nightmare.

While I talked, he rescued my glass from in front of me, dumped the wine in the sink, and made a pot of coffee. I wrote until the pot was full. He poured us each a mug, and joined me at the table.

"Is it possible that nightmare was nothing more

than a nightmare?" he asked.

I doctored my coffee with cream and sugar. "You mean it had no connection whatsoever to a future crime?"

"Exactly. Think about it. The past eight months have been frustrating for you and Bobby Jack. Margie Hollis's killer is still at large. Rafe Quillen was murdered less than a month later. His throat was slit so deeply, he was almost decapitated. No one's ever been arrested for that either." He sipped from his mug. "And Margie Hollis had long blonde hair."

"So you think I projected Margie into the dream?"

He shrugged. "I have no idea, but it's possible. Dreams—especially nightmares—are our brains releasing pent up stress. Face it, this one may have been just that."

"So how did I conjure up the image of Lisa Parker?"

"That morning in the police station was disconcerting to say the least. Mike and Jill are brought in to replace Bobby Jack. You're tapping into everybody's emotions in one way or another."

I sipped my coffee and thought for a moment before answering.

"In other words, I may have tapped into Jill's mind and come away with an image of her sister, which in turn translated into Charlie's sketch?"

"Is that possible?"

"Anything's possible. I knew Bobby Jack was keeping something important from me, but he slammed the psychic door before I could get a handle on what. Jill seemed receptive to the idea of a psychic and was irritated with Mike. I concentrated much of my energy toward him. He was rude, skeptical, resentful—you name it. I wanted to shoot the so-and-so. Then you showed up further muddling the situation."

"And for all we know, Jill had been thinking of Lisa, perhaps worrying about her prior to that morning."

I drew a deep breath. "In other words, I was distracted with everybody else and unconsciously saw Lisa in Jill's mind. I then described her to Charlie. No wonder Jill went ape-shit when she saw the sketch. The park and the mall from my dream world are irrelevant. The abduction may or may not be real."

"The fact that you identified the location is disturbing," Reed acknowledged.

"You know, for the first time I can see how Mike Young felt. I'm a psychic who may have screwed up big time."

Reed smiled and patted my hand. "Not necessarily screwed up, but misinterpreted what you saw. I'm sure you're not the first psychic to do that. You were tuned in to someone, that's for sure. But now I'm thinking maybe you *should* be focusing on Mike's murder."

"Yesterday you told me not to." I ran a hand through my hair and sighed. "You're right as always. Maybe I do need to concentrate on Young."

"Don't push it. Young was an ass, but someone was enraged enough to bash his head in with an eight iron."

"I need to get into his house. That might help. That much rage leaves residual emotion all over the place. I could tap into it."

"I'll call Brannon in a while to see if the scene's been released. In the meantime, it's after five. Suppose we find something to do, and then go out for breakfast. I know a place called the Daily Bread and Bagel not far from here. They open at six and serve a mean Southern-style breakfast."

My mind honed in on another phrase. "Something to do? What have you got in mind?"

He laughed. "Probably the same thing you do. See? Your psychic abilities may be rubbing off on me."

I laughed along with him as he grabbed my hand and we headed back to the bedroom.

****

I took a bite of my blueberry bagel smothered in garden vegetable cream cheese. It was an odd combination, but I loved it. I sighed as I chewed, and then tackled my sausage, scrambled eggs, hash browns, and cheese skillet breakfast. All in all, there were enough carbs and calories here to keep me alive for days.

Reed sat across from me in the booth, sipping coffee, and doing justice to bacon, three eggs over easy, hash browns, and a cinnamon raisin bagel.

"The one thing that always amazed me about you was your ability to pack away food," he said with a grin.

I swallowed and took a large gulp of highly Tabascoed tomato juice.

"I find food more interesting than exercise first thing in the morning. It's a great catalyst to stimulate the mind."

He grinned wider. "For me, an hour's worth of exercise followed by a long hot shower is the perfect start to the day."

"Since when do you exercise?"

"Wasn't talking about jogging."

He said it with a slow smile that made me go all warm inside.

"But I did run once on a regular basis. Still do when I have time," he continued.

The Daily Bread and Bagel was one of those hole-in-the-wall places off the beaten path. Situated in a small strip mall just off Kirby and Poplar, the exterior was unassuming. The interior was even less so. Twenty tables and a no frills décor said it all. The place was packed and from the conversations between waitresses and patrons, I deduced most of the customers were regulars.

"How come I've never heard of this place?"

"They don't advertise, they don't have a website, they don't have much in the line of signage, but somehow people find it. Word of mouth, I guess. I stumbled upon it five or six years ago by sheer accident. I was down at the swimming pool service store one day and decided to grab a quick bite to eat. Needless to say I waddled out of here. I try to get back every couple of weeks. Any more than that and I'd weigh five hundred pounds."

"Well, we can roll out of here together. This is the best food I've ever eaten breakfast-wise." I took another bite of bagel.

Reed's cell rang. "Ah, Brannon calling me back."

We'd arrived at the restaurant around seven-thirty. Reed had called and left a message with Detective Brannon about Mike's house.

"This is Reed...sorry to have disturbed you so early, but I was up and wondered if Mike Young's house had been released yet...would it be possible for

Sasha and I to get in?…I understand, but if the relatives aren't here yet then this would be a good time for Sasha to see if there's more to what she saw in her dream. Even though I'm on cold cases, I'm still a cop. Do they even need to know about it?…Sure, ten o'clock is fine. See you there."

He hung up and gazed at me. "Brannon says he'll meet us at Mike's. Technically, no one's supposed to be let in, but since it's an open case, he'll make an exception. Brannon has the utmost respect for your abilities. Jeff Hammond's death still gives him nightmares."

I shivered. "Me too, on occasion. How did he ever explain what happened to the department?"

"I have no idea, but if he told Internal Affairs that two ghosts exacted revenge on their killer by strangling him, he'd have been shipped off for some major league therapy."

"I'm sure his story must have been confirmed by the others in the clearing. Keith Simmons was there along with four cops."

"I'll say this, the department did a bang up job of keeping the reality quiet. I'm sure the families of Jeff's victims were awarded compensation of some sort in return for their silence that the killings were done by a cop."

"Which brings me back to the Fourteenth Precinct and their problems," I said finishing the skillet goodies.

"They certainly go to the top of the list," Reed agreed as the waitress refreshed his coffee and dropped the check on the table. "We'll see what Brannon has to say."

****

Reed pulled up to Mike Young's house in East Memphis. Even from the curb, I sensed the turbulent emotions still lingering in the air. Lord only knew what lay inside.

"You sure you're all right with this?" he asked.

I heaved a deep breath and nodded. "Yeah, but it won't be pleasant."

Detective Brannon's car slid in behind us. He exited and came around to the driver's side. Placing both hands on the door, he gazed at us.

"You guys ready?"

"As ready as we'll ever be," Reed said.

He led us up the driveway to the front walk finally stopping on the small porch. The forest green door stared at me as if daring me to conjure up something. A solid glass storm door covered it. I took another deep breath as a chill raced along my arms causing the hairs to stand up.

"Is this the door in your dream?" Reed asked.

"I'm pretty sure. Remember, I saw it as though looking through a waterfall, but yes, this is it."

"Any vibes?" Brannon said.

A vague outline of a man—or a woman—reflecting in the glass slipped into my mind. I told them what I saw.

"Well, we know his partner, Jill Conway was here. Could be others besides the killer showed up, too," Brannon speculated.

He took a key from his pocket and opened the door. We stepped into the narrow foyer. A living room was to the left and a dining room to the right. For a moment I couldn't breathe. In my mind, the walls dripped with red, but whether it represented blood or rage I wasn't sure. My guess was rage.

"Sasha?" Reed questioned.

I shook my head. "Where was the body found?"

"This way." Brannon led us toward the back of the home. "Here, in the family room."

Even though I knew what to expect, the destruction was stunning. The TV—a huge, wall-mounted flat screen—was dangling by one support, its screen shattered. Other electronic gizmos on the entertainment pedestal beneath it were also in pieces. Every lamp had been smashed and crushed into tiny ceramic slivers. Mike's decorating tastes had run to the modern side with glass-topped coffee and end tables. These, too, were destroyed. The glass crunched under our feet as we walked. Even the walls had huge holes gouged in them. And of course, blood spatter was everywhere from the wall to the blinds, even on the ceiling. The biggest stain was near the entry to the kitchen. This was where Mike had fallen.

I was bombarded with so many emotions I could barely take it all in.

"Holy shit," Reed said.

"Yeah, ten times over," Brannon concurred. "Getting anything, Sasha?"

"Rage. Incredible rage. I mean the kind of rage that leaves you wondering later if it was all a dream."

"A dream?" Reed asked.

"Like a black out. People wake up and have no idea what they did or even how they got where they are. Remember? That happened to me when I visualized Linnie's attack." My mind slipped back to our conversation about Jill. Could that be the answer?

"Anything else?" Brannon said.

"I sense fear, resentment, contempt, desperation, and a feeling of intense loss. Of what I don't know."

"That's what you sense. Do you see anything?" Reed continued.

"Everything is coated in a red haze. The rage, I guess. And I see the golf club smashing into things, and before you ask, no, I don't see who's wielding it. Any suspects?"

Brannon rubbed a hand over his chin. "Jill Conway admits to being here that night. Said she came to discuss a personal matter with Young."

"A personal matter?" Reed questioned.

"She told us it was to inform him that she was requesting a transfer or a new partner."

I knew differently. Jill had come to warn him off pursuing Lisa. While I didn't want to throw Jill under the bus, the police needed to know the truth.

"That's not quite accurate." I related what Jill had told me during our aborted dinner Saturday night.

"Mike Young was bothering her sister?" Brannon said with raised eyebrows. "Funny, but there was a rumor going around the Fourteenth that Young was gay. Not that it matters one way or the other, but he was in his early forties, never married, and to the best of our knowledge, was never seen in the company of a woman."

"Take my word for it, he found Lisa Parker attractive. Maybe he was bi-sexual, which opens up a whole new line of possible suspects," I replied.

Reed shook his head. "I don't buy that. I think you're going to find the killer sitting over in the Fourteenth Precinct."

"Maybe. As of now, his partner is suspect numero

uno," Brannon said.

"I don't know. This is a lot of destruction for a woman, even one under emotional distress, to achieve," I added.

We walked through the remainder of the house, but nothing had been disturbed. The killer had done the deed, smashed the place to smithereens, and then left.

Back outside, we stopped next to the cars.

"How's the investigation going?" I asked.

"Slow. One neighbor was setting out his trash at the curb and said he noticed a dark-colored car in the driveway. He thinks the time was somewhere around ten. Jill Conway's car is a dark gray Toyota. Another neighbor says he heard tires squealing somewhere along the street around one-thirty or so. By the time he got to the window, the street was empty."

"Any fingerprints?" Reed asked.

"Plenty. Jill Conway's, Steve Winslett's, Bobby Jack Beauregard's, several cops from the Fourteenth, and a bunch of unidentifiable ones."

"And the murder weapon?" he pressed.

"Still missing, but the coroner is pretty certain the blunt force trauma was the result of an eight iron. We screwed up the first search warrant for Jill Conway's home. Didn't include her car. Got one yesterday. No telltale golf club appeared. Nor was there any blood found anywhere in the car. If she'd chucked the eight iron in the trunk, it would have left some trace," Brannon said.

"Unless she used the time between warrants to toss the club in the Mississippi and have a thorough cleaning done," Reed ventured.

"I'm not sure it's Jill," I said in a somewhat

exasperated tone. "After seeing the mess inside, this doesn't feel like a woman's crime. She might have clocked him once or twice, but not to the extent of the damage we found. I agree with Reed. The killer has to be from the Fourteenth. How deep is the rot in that precinct?"

Brannon heaved a sigh. "Pretty deep. Internal Affairs is investigating everyone from the captain on down to the newest beat officer."

"I wonder if the killer is someone Young trusted—didn't suspect was on the take," Reed mused.

"And Jill told me his actions at the Fourteenth had built a lot of resentment—those sting operations and such. It's like he was going rogue to get rid of the bad guys. Suppose one of those stings almost netted a big fish? Only Young didn't realize it yet. Maybe the killer decided that sooner or later he would fit the pieces of the puzzle together, and so struck before the dots were connected."

"Like I said, we're checking on everyone. Oh, and by the way, there are no reports of abductions or rapes in the Art District," Brannon told us easing toward his car. "Thanks, Sasha."

I nodded. "I didn't tell you anything you didn't already know. Sorry."

He shrugged and moved away.

"So my vision about the woman being abducted is likely precognitive."

"Very possible. We can talk about it tonight. I have to get back to the station," Reed said as he drove me back to his house. "What do you plan on doing the rest of the day?"

"I'm not sure. I may have a long talk with Linnie

or just curl up with a book. Haven't done that in a while." My cell rang. It was Schenk. I rejected the call immediately. "Or spend my time dodging my former shrink."

"Is he still bothering you?" Reed asked with a scowl.

"Off and on. I reported him as a harassing caller the other day."

"Let me take care of it."

I didn't like the sound of his voice. "Reed, don't do anything silly."

"Who, me? Silly? Not on your life. I can, however, let him know you do not appreciate his constant calls."

I didn't reply. In a way, having Reed run interference was not an unpleasant idea. I didn't want Schenk causing any future trouble.

I waved goodbye as he dropped me off, then poured a glass of iced tea and sat at the kitchen table. I called Linnie and told her about Schenk.

"Good for you. If he keeps it up, threaten to report him to the American Psychiatrists Association. They have strict standards of behavior and trust me, this asshole ain't following them."

I also told her of his ambitions regarding my abilities.

"Are you kidding me? Not only is he an asshole, but he's twisted as well. The APA needs to know about this guy. Pronto. Call and lodge a complaint."

"I will. How are you feeling?"

"Antsy as hell. I can't sleep, I can only eat a few bites at a time, I have to go to the bathroom every ten minutes, and Bill is hovering."

I chuckled. "He loves you. And in spite of all the

stories about fathers fainting and not handling the delivery well, I think Bill will be a champ in there."

She laughed with me. "I think you're right. I just hope he can take the verbal abuse coming his way during those last few contractions."

I hung up with a promise to come down this weekend—with Reed.

It was nearly noon and I didn't want to eat alone. I had this urge to be needed. On impulse, I called Jill. Even though she was a suspect in a murder investigation, I sensed she wanted a shoulder to cry on.

"Of course, I'd like to have lunch," she said. "This has been the worst forty-eight hours of my life. I need to talk. I'm not sure, but I think I totally ruined my relationship with my sister."

As if to punctuate her feelings, she sobbed into the phone.

Chapter Seventeen

I waited impatiently in a corner booth at a local chain restaurant not far from Reed's. Jill was late. I had been shocked at her loss of emotional control, but then this was about her sister, not a police matter. However, after her initial outburst of tears, she'd calmed down enough to agree to meet me here for a late lunch at one o'clock. It was now almost one-thirty. I pulled my phone out of my purse to call when she came in the door. I waved her over.

"I'm sorry I'm late," she said slipping into the booth opposite me. "I had to pull myself together."

Her eyes held a hint of redness and the puffiness told me she'd had a good cry after our conversation. Mike may have been right about letting her feelings clutter up her job.

"No problem."

A waiter zoomed up to the table. "Good afternoon. Can I get you something from the bar?"

Jill eyed my wine glass. "I'll have whatever she's having."

He nodded and left.

I sipped the rapidly warming Chardonnay. Jill fiddled with her napkin and silverware, refusing to meet my gaze.

"So, why do you think you've ruined your relationship with Lisa?"

She rested her elbows on the table and massaged her forehead with her fingers.

"The last couple of days have been so, I don't know, surreal, I guess. The problems at the Fourteenth are growing by leaps and bounds. I have the feeling most of the cops—many my friends—are caught up in the accusations. Even my name was brought up. Mike's actions pissed off so many people I can't begin to describe it. I heard some of the guys actually applauded when they heard Mike was dead." Her eyes welled with tears and she used her napkin to stem the flow.

"Do they still think you killed him?"

"They got another warrant to cover my car. Thank God nothing suspicious showed up."

I wondered why she was thanking a higher authority. Had there been something to hide? Her wine arrived and we ordered—chicken Caesar salads for both of us.

"What did you talk about with Mike that night?" I asked when the waiter left.

She sighed. "I wasn't happy about him calling Lisa. With the turmoil about to overflow in the Fourteenth, I didn't want her anywhere near the guy. I told him to lay off. He told me to shut up, and that he had every intention of seeing more of my sister. Then I told him she was out with Charlie that night. You should have seen the expression on his face. He was not a happy camper."

"So he was jealous Lisa turned him down but accepted Charlie's invitation. Yeah, I can see how that might upset someone like Mike. He needed control."

"Then our talk turned to the Fourteenth and his silly sting operations. I said that if he'd left everything

247

to Internal Affairs, we wouldn't have been sent to help out in your department. That's when he suggested maybe I had something to hide, and that he'd told Internal Affairs just that. I was furious and left."

"Did you tell IA this?"

She shook her head. "No, I just said I'd been to talk to him on a personal matter, and that I'd run into his golf bag in the foyer on my way out. That's how my fingerprints got on it."

"And Lisa?" I probed gently. I could have slipped into her mind, but at the moment, she had so much going on I doubted I'd glean much from the experience. Plus, I still doubted my own abilities.

"Oh God, I botched things so bad this morning. She came down around seven dressed in jogging gear. I told her I didn't think it was a good idea. She told me to get off her back. I said fine, I'd go with her. She wasn't happy, but we ended up in Audubon Park. I kept my eyes open, scrutinizing every man we passed or who passed us like he was Jack the Ripper. I admit I was being overly cautious, but I couldn't help it."

"Oh dear, I feel responsible for this," I lamented finishing my wine.

Jill waved a hand in dismissal and sipped from her glass. "Don't. It's not your fault you see things. You're psychic."

Our food arrived. I requested iced tea and for the next couple of minutes, we busied ourselves with salad.

"What was Lisa's reaction to your eyeballing every man in the park?" I asked.

"She finally stopped and asked if I was going to act like a nutcase the entire morning. I apologized and said I was just concerned about safety. We finished our jog and went home. That's when things got dicey. Lisa wanted to go to the mall. I said I'd go, too. She got snippy and wanted to know why I'd become the world's most conscientious baby-sitter. I didn't have an answer for that. And then there's Charlie Kendall."

"What about Charlie?"

"I told her I wasn't happy with her posing for him. Even though she was covered up the other night, I don't entirely trust him. He's had three wives and is years older than Lisa."

"Sounds to me like you don't trust your sister."

She sighed. "Sometimes, she's so impulsive, and often does things she knows I'll disapprove of just to tick me off."

"Look Jill, Reed and I have talked about that vision and the drawing Charlie made. The park and mall scenes may or may not have been true. I never got a good look at the woman in either place."

"Yet you described Lisa almost to a 't' for Charlie."

I told her about the theory that I'd accidentally tapped into her mind. "Let me ask, did you talk to Lisa in the few days prior to our first meeting?"

She sipped her wine and paused to think. "Yes. She called me three or four days earlier."

"Was there any confrontation?"

"No, not really. She'd admitted committing to a singles cruise around Christmas. As usual, I tried to talk her out of it, but we didn't argue if that's what you mean."

It sounded as if Jill had control issues, too. "But yet, you could have been worried and thinking about her that morning, right?"

"I may have."

"And even if you weren't thinking about the cruise at the moment, you could have the night before. I may have glommed onto residual thoughts."

A frown marred Jill's brow. "So Lisa was never in danger?"

"I'm sorry, but that's possible." Guilt hammered at me. I may have put both Jill and Lisa through a lot of anxiety. "Why not come clean and tell her the truth?"

She shook her head. "Not yet. There's still that last scene of a kidnapping."

I didn't think now was a good time to tell her I'd identified Charlie's studio as the place of my dream, especially since I couldn't ID the people involved.

"Did Lisa go to the mall?" I asked as I finished my salad.

"Yes. Can't say I was happy about it, but she was pissed. I have the feeling she's about to head back to St. Louis. Then, instead of worrying about her when she's not in my sight here, I'd worry about her constantly."

"Jill, would it help if I talked to her?"

"And say what?"

"I don't know. I'll just chat."

She didn't answer immediately, but finished her salad and her wine before making a decision.

"That might help, but please don't tell her about the sketch, okay?"

"I promise."

After getting Lisa's phone number from Jill, I paid the bill and headed for home. I hoped Reed didn't mind eating alone tonight.

****

Lisa was only too eager to meet me at The

Welcome Mat for dinner in Germantown. I suspected she was still put out with her sister and this was the perfect chance to extend the cooling off period. I arrived early and nabbed a table along the back wall. A few minutes later, Lisa walked in the door, waved and slid into a chair opposite me.

"This is nice," she said shedding her coat. "I'm so glad you called. Things are a little intense with Jill at the moment."

"I know. I talked to her today."

A waiter appeared and took our drink order—white wine for both of us. I used the opportunity to slip into her mind. She was still irritated with Jill, but right now her emotions were centered on having a good meal.

"I love my sister to death, but my God, can she hover. It drove me nuts as a teenager. It *still* drives me nuts."

"She has a lot on her mind."

"I know. There are issues at work and now her partner is murdered. I couldn't believe they searched her house and car. I mean, Jill wouldn't kill anybody unless it was in the line of duty. And take it from me, she's as honest as the day is long. To think she'd accept bribes or anything of the sort is ludicrous."

"They had no choice but to suspend her when her fingerprints showed up on Mike's golf bag. I'm sure she'll be reinstated soon. Was she always a worrier?"

"Pretty much. She felt a strong sense of responsibility for me after our parents died. Those apron strings stretched but never broke. I suppose that's why I up and married my ex-husband, Josh, in the first place. She didn't like him and said I wasn't using good judgment. We eloped just to show her there was nothing wrong with my judgment." Lisa made a face. "Dumbest decision I ever made. He was even more controlling than Jill. All of it also busted up her marriage."

"I never knew she had been married."

"Yeah, a guy named Jim Conway. He was all right, but I think he resented all the time she took looking after me, especially after Josh and I separated."

"Jill said something about your ex being in San Diego, but didn't you mention he was back in St. Louis?"

"Yes. He's with someone else now and that's fine with me. I see him and his fiancée at the occasional club."

Our drinks arrived and we placed our food order. When he left I tried to steer the conversation to her activities.

"Jill mentioned that you might go to the mall today. Did you?"

She nodded. "Lovely mall. I got a few things and even rode that darling carousel. Made me feel like a kid again."

I laughed. "I know. I've ridden it, too."

"And that's another annoying thing about Jill—suddenly she wants me to stay housebound—no jogging, no shopping alone. She doesn't want me to see Charlie, pose for Charlie, and she warned me off Mike Young in no uncertain terms."

I fiddled with the stem of my wine glass. "Cut her some slack, Lisa. She's got other things on her mind besides her job."

"You mean that silly drawing Charlie made?"

I had just taken a sip of wine, and now choked as I

swallowed.

"You know about that? How?"

"Oh, Charlie let it slip the other night when we were out. Besides, he'd mentioned something that first day when I arrived in Memphis. At any rate, he swore me to secrecy that I wouldn't tell Jill. Sasha, I know you have certain abilities, but there are a lot of blonde women who jog and go to the mall out there."

I breathed a sigh of relief. Now I didn't need to tiptoe around the situation any longer.

"That's the conclusion I've come to also. I never got a look at the woman's face and can't swear the man is the same either. Unfortunately, your sister was unnerved by it."

"That's putting it mildly."

"I can see why she wouldn't want you to see Mike on a social basis, but what's her objection to Charlie?"

"She thinks he's too old for me, he has three ex-wives, he's an artist and she has it stuck in her head that all artists fool around with their models—hence she doesn't want me to pose either."

"And how do you feel?"

Lisa sighed and sipped some wine. "Honestly? I accepted his dinner invite because he sounded interesting. Imagine taking clay or some other medium and turning it into a work of art."

"And was he interesting?"

She leaned forward. "Not really. All he could talk about was sculpting me. In a way, it was kind of creepy. Kept telling me how gorgeous I was, how my cheekbones were perfect, my chin, my mouth, and on and on. All that praise and the compliments made me uncomfortable. I finally suggested going down to the casinos. At least there'd be other people around. And as much as I hate to admit it, he *is* way too old for me. I agreed to pose this week for his classes and to let him take photos of my head so he can create his masterpiece. Now, if only he'd stop calling me."

Our food arrived. As it was served, her last sentence showed definite signs of irritation with Charlie. I didn't know him well on a personal level, and wondered if his interest was strictly professional.

"Charlie is calling you? A lot?"

She rolled her eyes. "Just about every day. He wants me to go out to dinner, to lunch, to a club. I don't want to sound mean, but can you imagine me at a club with a bunch of young people and *him* in tow? And to be honest, I was also a little uncomfortable posing for him. I had panties on under that sheet, but no bra. His hand kept touching my breasts while he was adjusting the draping. I don't think it was intentional. I mean, he didn't get this gleam in his eyes. He just seemed to concentrate on how the folds looked. Still, I'm getting to the point where I don't even answer the phone anymore when his number shows up. But he's not as persistent as Mike Young was."

I stopped chewing my chicken Parmesan and stared, then swallowed and chased it with a large gulp of wine.

"Mike Young called you?" I asked even though I already knew the answer.

"I'll say. At least twice a day for two days. Wanted me to go out with him. He didn't make a good first impression, so I kept turning him down. Wouldn't take no for an answer. Finally I asked how he'd gotten my number in the first place."

"And how did he?"

"He got into Jill's personnel file. My name and number were listed as emergency contacts. Can you believe that? Jill was pissed when she heard. He called me on Saturday afternoon. When I told him I would never go out with him, I didn't like him, and to lose my number, he got mad. Called me a stuck-up bitch and that the loss was mine. And then, of course, later that night someone killed him. I felt kinda bad, but only for a moment."

"Did Jill know he called?"

She nodded. "Yeah, and because I was mad, I told her what he called me. She was livid. I also mentioned it to Charlie. He wasn't happy either."

I continued eating. Mike Young was a real piece of work. No wonder Jill had shown up at his place that night. I only had her word for what she and Mike had said. Maybe he'd refused to stop calling Lisa or made some inappropriate anti-woman remark. If so, could that have sent his partner over the edge? I remembered the red haze of my dream and the destruction of the family room at Mike's. Rage was rage, and if pushed far enough, a woman *could* have done that much damage. Especially, a female police officer who probably worked out.

I finished my meal and leaned back. Gazing around the crowded restaurant, I saw a familiar face seated at a table near the front doors. It was Keith Simmons, my former bodyguard while I was dealing with the Jeff Hammond case. I remembered telling Jill about him in the hopes she wouldn't have to worry about Lisa so much. Had she contacted him? Or had Reed? Or was this just a coincidence?

He looked up, caught me staring and smiled before resuming his dinner.

A sense of calm settled within me. If Jill had hired him, then Lisa would be safe.

"So, do you think I'm doing the right thing?" Lisa asked.

I realized I hadn't heard a word of whatever she was saying for the past minute. "Uh, I'm sorry, I was thinking. What right thing?"

"Should I bail on posing for Charlie and just go home? I hate leaving when Jill has so much on her plate. It's like I'm abandoning her."

"If you don't want to pose for Charlie, then don't. I'm sure Jill finds your company a help in these troubling times." I cast a covert look toward Keith as I sipped my wine. Yes, he'd keep her safe. "Why not stay? Spend some one-on-one time with her. I'm sure she'll be reinstated soon. As far as I know, she's not under any kind of travel ban from the department. Why not go someplace like Hot Springs or Nashville for a weekend?"

"Hmmm. That sounds like a good idea. I'll run it by her tonight. Thanks, Sasha. I'm glad we had this time to talk."

"So am I."

The waiter stopped by to clear the table and ask if we wanted dessert or coffee. We both declined. He brought the check. I paid and as we left, I cast a glance at Keith's table. He was also signing a credit card receipt. A moment later he rose.

So he is on the job.

I waved goodbye to Lisa in the parking lot and slid behind the wheel of my car. She drove off. A black

SUV, Keith Simmons driving, followed her tan Prius at a discreet distance.

****

Reed was watching TV when I returned to the house. I gave him the gist of the conversations I'd had with Jill at lunch and with Lisa at dinner. I also told him about Keith.

"Jill called me late this morning after we got back from Young's place asking for his number. It's a smart move on her part. I'm not sure Lisa is in danger, but it helps put Jill's mind to rest."

"Jill wasn't entirely truthful with what she told us about her confrontation with Mike. She didn't mention the harassing phone calls he made to Lisa."

Reed changed channels to a Grizzlies basketball game. "The police have nothing on Jill for Young's murder. If she'd done it, taken the golf club with her, and then chucked it into the woods, there still would have been blood somewhere in her car. Not even detailing could get rid of it."

"Unless she had the brains to wrap the head of the club in a towel or something. Car trunks always have junk like that in them. Don't golfers often have towels attached to their bags?"

He leaned back and looked at me with a thoughtful expression. "Yes, many do. I wonder if Brannon found one on Young's bag. I'll call in the morning and ask."

I fiddled with the fringe on one of the sofa throw pillows—one of my contributions from almost three years ago.

"I was kind of surprised Mike kept calling Lisa. I mean, he didn't like women."

Reed shook his head. "Oh, I think he liked them

just fine. He just didn't like them in jobs that had always been considered male domains."

"Such as cops, firefighters, the military, the board room? He saw them as 'the little woman' at home making dinner, cleaning, raising the kids, and deferring to whatever decision the man made."

"It's hopelessly old-fashioned and chauvinistic, but yes, I can see him thinking that way."

"I was also kind of surprised at what Lisa had to say about Charlie," I said.

"Older men are often attracted to younger women."

"It's strange, but I always considered Charlie in a non-sexual way."

"That's good to hear, although I'm not sure Charlie would be happy to know it," Reed replied with a grin.

"Smartass. No, he was just the nice guy that did these fabulous sketches from my dream images. Now I learn he has three ex-wives and is badgering Lisa to pose for a sculpture, not to mention the drawing classes."

"He's a guy, and an artist to boot. I've been told artists can become damned obsessive about their work. Carving, painting, whatever with no thoughts of eating or the time of day."

"You think he's obsessing with Lisa?"

"I don't know if I'd call it obsessing, but he certainly is engrossed with the idea of her posing for him. Could be he's thinking of a more personal relationship."

I chewed on my thumbnail. "Which Lisa isn't at all interested in. Maybe I should accompany Lisa to her sessions with him."

"You could, but I'm sure Keith will have someone

there, too."

I'd forgotten about Keith. Still, I didn't think two sets of eyes and ears were a bad thing.

"For the class, maybe, but the sculpting poses would be private."

"Then how would you fit in?"

"I don't know. I'm still working on it." I quit nibbling on my fingernail and tossed the pillow aside. "How did the rest of your day go?"

He sighed. "I started re-interviewing witnesses in the Margie Hollis case."

"Bobby Jack and I wanted that one in the win column so badly. I wish we could have solved it."

"You tried."

"Reed, do you think Bobby Jack is using drugs in place of booze?"

He hesitated for a moment before answering. "I don't know, but he was high on the fact that Young was dead, Jill was compromised, and he was back in charge."

"How sad. To be glad a colleague, even someone like Mike Young, is dead so you can get your job back is not a pleasant thought. He was almost giddy. If he had taken something, what would have caused such euphoria?"

"A lot of drugs give you that fantastic high at first—coke, heroin, methamphetamine. If he'd taken meth and had a couple of drinks, that may have upped the high."

"You mean mixing the two can be a wild ride?" I asked. I knew next to nothing about drugs.

"From what I've heard it can produce intense highs and emotions—happy as a lark one minute, and ready for suicide the next."

"Damn."

I felt for Bobby Jack. He'd been my friend and partner for close to three years. His drinking and now possible drug use, personal life, and encroaching reassignment had left him depressed and desolate. Now he was back in charge of a department that was likely to close soon. Then what would he do? If he didn't get his problem under control, I saw a lot of nights in bars like the one when I'd poured him into a taxi. His anger and resentment would only build. I hoped the rehab would set him straight and that Cindy would take him back. He needed a supportive wife.

"Sasha, you can't take on the woes of the world," Reed said in a gentle tone.

"I'm not taking on the world."

"No, but Bobby Jack, Jill, Lisa, and Charlie have to work things out for themselves."

He was right, of course, but I wanted to help my friends. Especially Bobby Jack. He was coming apart at the seams, and I feared I wasn't a good enough seamstress to put him back together.

Chapter Eighteen

Reed left early for the office the next morning. I sat at the kitchen table sipping my third cup of coffee when my phone rang. It was Bobby Jack.

"Sasha, are you coming in today?"

"I don't know. With Mike dead and Jill on suspension, I wasn't sure anything was happening."

"Of course, it's happening. I'm back and we can concentrate on your dream again. We might not have much time left."

I realized that in all that had occurred over the past week, he wasn't up to date on my theories about that nightmare or my possible misinterpretations. I agreed to come in. I didn't want to deliver that kind of news over the phone.

I hung up and poured the rest of my coffee down the kitchen sink. My colleague had sounded like his usual self today. Maybe that was a good sign.

I walked into Bobby Jack's office an hour later. He may have sounded like his old self on the phone, but his eyes were bloodshot and his face bore the ravages of sleeplessness—or perhaps a hangover.

"Sasha! It's good to see you. Great to be back in the saddle again. If we can put this dream of yours into perspective, then we might be able to mark it closed." He picked up a couple of file folders and handed them to me. "Here are some complaints from female joggers in Audubon Park who say they were approached by—"

"Bobby Jack, there's something you need to know."

"—strange men. Some made suggestive comments—"

His vaguely manic babbling concerned me. "Bobby Jack, there's something you need to know," I repeated in a louder voice.

"What?"

I proceeded to tell him about how off I may have been with this particular dream, and how I could have come up with Lisa's face in the sketch.

He stared at me for a few seconds before frowning. "You're not sure? You've always been sure."

"Look, I can't be one hundred percent right all the time. The only thing I could identify for certain was the building in the last scene as being Charlie's studio, and I'm not certain now that the man had a knife *or* spoke in a threatening tone to the woman."

He sat back in his chair with a look of disbelief in his eyes. "Then this may be nothing at all?"

"It's possible. Reed thinks I should concentrate on my dream about Mike Young's murder."

"You had a dream about Young? When? What was it?" His eyebrows shot up along with his voice.

I told him the details of that night.

"So you didn't actually see the killer, but honed in on the rage?"

"I'm hoping to return to the house in a few days. Maybe by then, some of the anger will have dissipated and I can get a clearer view of the killer and his or her thoughts."

He raised his coffee mug to his mouth with shaking

hands and drank. "As of now, all you can see is a red haze?"

I nodded. "I'm sure that represents the rage. I'm not sure about the lights and the sounds, but sooner or later, I'll figure it out."

"Let's hope so. If we can solve this one, the psychic program may get a new lease on life."

I thought he was being delusional, but played along. "We can only try."

"In the meantime, why don't you take a look at the files I gave you and concentrate on that dream again. Maybe there is something to it."

I left for the conference room, the folders in my hand. It seemed like a waste of time, but I'd do it to make Bobby Jack happy.

The psychic program consisted of Bobby Jack, me, and a couple of detectives, usually new to the department, who were called in to investigate whenever necessary. They'd done so with the complaints I now read two days ago, after Bobby Jack had been reinstated.

One of the complainants was a brunette. I closed the file immediately. The other woman was blonde. The detective had noted her hair was long. The problem was the guy had spoken to her inappropriately and she'd told him to shove it. When he followed her to the parking lot—still making comments—she'd called 9-1-1. A complaint was filed, and the guy had been given a warning. That was two weeks ago, about the time of my dream. However, there were no further complaints, so I assumed the man had not reappeared.

Mall security had filed a report from three women about men following them in the parking lot. One of the women was blonde. But according to her, the man had skulked behind her as she entered the store. Not after as in my dream.

I returned the files to Bobby Jack.

"I don't see anything here to pursue," I told him.

"Are you sure? The blondes could have been the visions you had at the park and the mall."

"There is nothing to connect the two. I never actually saw the woman's face in either incident. I may have just had a weird dream."

"And what about the abduction scene? You said it was near Kendall's studio."

"I'm not convinced it was an abduction. The image changed when I saw it the other night." Poor Bobby Jack. He grasped at any straw, no matter how weak, to keep this psychic thing alive.

"The other night?"

I told him about Reed, Jill, and I attending Charlie's drawing class.

"Well, I think it's important. Bear down on that image. If you recognized the place, then it's got to be true."

"If you don't mind, I'll think I'll go back to Reed's. I may be able to concentrate better there where it's quiet."

"Reed's?"

"Yes, I'm staying with him until this is all over. I was having a tough time of it a few days ago. He offered to let me move in for a while."

"I see. Okay. Good luck and keep me informed if you come up with anything new."

"I will."

I left the police station more irritated with Bobby

Jack than I'd ever been—even when he'd arrested me for Clarke Pennington's murder. For the first time in almost three years, I wanted out of this business. The experiment with a psychic as a consultant was about to end. Between it and Schenk, I'd nearly become unglued. I could offer my services if and when the Memphis Police Department—or any police department in the area—wanted it.

I just hoped Bobby Jack could come to terms with everything.

****

In the car, I put in a call to Detective Brannon requesting the full police report on Young's death. He said he'd e-mail it to me.

On impulse, I decided against going back to Reed's. If I needed to concentrate on that final scene in my dream, then maybe returning to Charlie's studio would help. I found a parking spot nearby and walked to his place. I gazed into the window of Kendall Art Gallery. Sculptures sat on velvet runners while discreet lighting shone down on them. I pushed open the door and entered. The same small bell as the other night tinkled from overhead.

I stopped to admire a horse's head done in wood. The proud lift of the head and the mane standing out as if in a strong wind made me think of a wild mustang on the open range. Next to it was another figure done in clay of a mother and child embracing. The look of love on each of their faces was exquisite.

"May I help you?" a voice said from behind me.

I turned to find myself staring at the redheaded woman who'd arrived late to the class the other night.

"Oh, hello. Actually, I'm just looking. I was here

for a class and thought I'd take a look around."

"I think I remember you. I'm Celine Davis, Charlie's assistant. Did you enjoy the class?"

"Yes, very much, although I wasn't very good. I didn't do the model justice."

Celine's nostrils flared for a moment. Resentment and anger clouded her mind. "She was much too stiff for a model. Being an artist's muse isn't easy. I'm sure you'd have done much better with me posing."

"Do you model for Charlie, too?"

The smile slipped from her face as she stared. "Yes. I'm his main inspiration at the moment."

She's lying. Charlie isn't focused on her at all now that Lisa is in the picture. At the moment, she's angrier with Lisa than Charlie. If she can get Lisa out of the picture, she's sure Charlie will come back to her.

Celine plastered the smile back on. "How well do you know Charlie?"

"I met him about three years ago. His drawings are so wonderful. They almost have a life of their own."

I remembered some of the thoughts of the others in the room that night. Not many had been kind to Celine. Then I remembered one comment in particular.

"I love your hair. It's such a vibrant shade of red," I said.

She twisted a lock of the long tresses around her finger. "Thank you, but I'm thinking of going back to blonde. Charlie liked it better."

"Is Charlie here?"

"No, I'm afraid not. Would you like to leave a message?"

"Class is tomorrow night, isn't it? I'll wait until then. In the meantime, is it all right if I just look around?"

"Certainly, if you need anything, just holler. I'll be in back."

Celine left the room. As I wandered from sculpture to sculpture, I couldn't help but to speculate on a *blonde* Celine. Could she have been the woman in my vision here at the gallery? I had no idea and mentally cursed. Doubts about everything were strangling me.

I left the studio and walked around the corner to the side street in my dream. It was a street, nothing special about it. I passed several parked cars as I strolled down the sidewalk. Then, without warning, my vision dimmed and I heard voices. I stood still waiting for the images to form. They didn't. I listened to a conversation instead.

"You bastard, you can't do this to me!"

"You've left me no choice. You're obsessive and interfering with my work."

"I'm obsessive? How about you? How do you think I feel about what's happened? You never once took my feelings into consideration. It's all about you, asshole."

"And that's the way it should be."

"You arrogant jerk. You haven't heard the last of this. Not by a long shot."

The voices faded. One second they were there, the next they were gone. I staggered to the side of the building and leaned against it, drawing in deep breaths to stop my limbs from shaking.

I had no idea who I'd heard. The anger had distorted their voices. Nor did I know when this happened—if it was past or in the future. Had the couple come from the studio or were they just people on the street—perhaps from one of the nearby restaurants?

I got myself under control and made my way back to the car. Once behind the wheel I paused. I should go to Bobby Jack with this, but for the first time in three years, didn't want to tell him. I wanted to tell Reed. Bobby Jack was no longer impartial. Reed could help me interpret this with a detached mind.

****

When I arrived back at Reed's, I turned on my laptop and found Brannon had e-mailed me the report on Mike Young's murder, including the forensics information.

According to the coroner, Young has been struck first in the right temple. Defensive bruising on his right arm and wrist indicated he'd seen the blow coming.

Like maybe Mike had thought he was alone, and turned when he realized he wasn't?

I read on. Blood spatter had indicated he'd staggered several feet before collapsing. Time of death was placed as anywhere between ten in the evening and two in the morning. This was nothing I didn't already know. However, the report did supply the name of Young's next of kin—a brother, James Young of Chicago. According to the notes, he'd been contacted and would be in town sometime this week to make funeral arrangements.

It struck me as odd. His brother is murdered and he doesn't come immediately? Why not?

Puzzled, I called the police station and asked for Brannon.

"Hi, it's Sasha," I said when he answered. I expressed my confusion.

"Struck me as odd, too, so I asked about their

relationship. Seems they hadn't spoken in close to five years. The brother is married with three kids. One of them got caught shoplifting and had to do community service washing police cars on a Saturday morning and taking a tour of the jail with the parents to show the kid how crime doesn't pay. According to the brother, Young made some nasty comments about their child-raising skills. He and his wife took exception to the remarks. The exchange became heated. The upshot was neither of them made an effort to forgive and forget."

"How old was the kid?"

"Ten or so. The brother told us his son hasn't shown any desire to enter the criminal world since then."

"Is this brother the only relative?"

"As far as we know. Young's will—dated eight years ago—listed the brother as beneficiary. In fact, he's due to arrive on Saturday."

I thanked Brannon for the information and hung up.

Reed came home a couple of hours later with a grocery bag containing two steakhouse-cut t-bones, two large potatoes, a bag of lettuce, salad fixings, a container of sour cream, and most important, an expensive bottle of cabernet.

"Wow, that's a lot of food," I said as he laid the purchases on the counter.

"I'm a growing boy," he replied with a grin before leaning down to kiss me. "Plus I'm frustrated. I didn't get much from the interviews with the Margie Hollis case, although one neighbor did say she heard a lot of shouting from time to time. Just because the Hollises argued, doesn't mean he killed her."

"If I remember right, he had an alibi. You'll find who did it. Just wish I hadn't seen the crime through the eyes of the killer." I reached up and kissed his cheek. "Now start that grill. I'm hungry."

It wasn't until after polishing off a really fine dinner that I told Reed about my vision today at Charlie's studio.

"You heard the conversation? Can you identify the voices?"

I heaved a huge, frustrated sigh. "No. The voices rattled around in my head and had an echo quality. Hell, for all I know, they have nothing to do with Charlie's studio. It could have been a couple out to eat at one of the nearby restaurants."

"Have you ever had multiple visions before? I mean, this dream had three distinct scenes to it, which may or may not be connected. And then there's the vision you had about Mike Young's death."

I bit my lip. "I think the sensible thing to do is concentrate on Young's murder." I told him about my conversation with Brannon.

He hesitated. "I heard a rumor today that four cops from the Fourteenth were arrested last night—Steve Winslett was one."

"Do you think he killed Young?"

"He or one of the other guys now calling jail home. It's gonna be tough to unravel this. They've already lawyered up and shut up. Sooner or later someone will cut a deal and the floodgates will open."

"Yet the evidence—and my dream—suggest Mike let the killer in. Would he do that with someone he knew was pissed off at him?" I asked remembering his confrontation with Winslett in the police station.

"He'd just had an argument with Jill. Could be he was still angry and opened the door before thinking to check who was outside. Then before he could slam it, the killer shoved his way inside."

I swirled the remains of the deep red wine in my glass before gulping it down.

"I read the coroner's report. The first blow was struck from the right and he had defensive wounds on his right arm and wrist—as if he'd turned partially away. Would he have turned his back on someone who'd just muscled his way into the house?"

Reed frowned. "Could be they had words, but Young wasn't afraid. Maybe the person turned as though to leave, changed his mind, and came back. Young had also turned and headed for the family room, thinking it was all over."

"So the guy grabs the eight iron, kills him, and then proceeds to trash the house." I tugged on my earlobe. "I suppose it could have happened that way. But I just can't see Mike Young being so careless."

"Well, he wouldn't have been afraid of Jill. And according to you, she was royally pissed."

Reed turned on the TV while I sat back and thought. No, he wouldn't have been afraid of Jill. I hadn't noticed when inside the house if there had been blood spatter anywhere except the family room. There was just too much of it. What if the two had argued and Mike had told her to get out, and then turned. She could have grabbed the golf club and followed. And Jill was smart enough to know how to conceal the evidence.

Then another thought came to mind. Conceal evidence. *Oh my God, what if Jill had concealed evidence?* Suppose someone from the Fourteenth had

271

killed Mike, and then called Jill to help cover it up? If she was dirty like her partner insinuated, then she could be an accessory.

A snippet of information tossed around the conference room at the police station the day after Mike Young's death came to mind. Coupling it with Lisa's remarks about Young harassing her, led me to a different conclusion.

Jill had mentioned to Charlie that morning that she didn't appreciate him keeping her sister out until the wee hours of the morning. The time of death had been narrowed down to between ten at night and two in the morning. And Lisa had told me she'd informed Charlie of Mike's constant calling.

Suppose Charlie had gone to Mike's after dropping Lisa off from their date? Suppose *he* and Mike argued. I could just hear Young making insulting comments to Charlie, and not fearing the artist, had turned away in contempt. Suppose *Charlie* was the person enraged. *Suppose Charlie grabbed the eight iron from the golf bag.*

Or what if Young had called Lisa after she returned to Jill's? What if, during a previous call, she agreed to meet him at his place after her date with Charlie? What if he came on to her, she rebuffed him, and he tried to force himself on her? What if Lisa grabbed the closest thing to defend herself? What if *Lisa* killed Mike Young?

She could easily have been lying about how she considered him harassing. And Jill would have helped cover up for her sister in a heartbeat.

272

Chapter Nineteen

I told Reed my suppositions about Lisa killing Mike, and Jill covering it up.

He shook his head. "If that was the case, then Jill would have called it in and Lisa would have said it was self-defense. Plus you're forgetting all the damage. That's inconsistent with this theory."

"Not if Jill panicked and covered up. She could have done it to throw everyone off the track. And even if she didn't panic, she'd have wanted to keep her sister's name out of it," I argued.

"I'll ask Brannon if he has Young's cell phone records yet. Those will show who he called and who called him."

I sat back and sighed. Jill would have anticipated pulling phone records immediately. She was too good a cop not to. Still, I didn't abandon my theory completely. Then another thought crossed my mind. *What if the voices I heard this morning were Young and Jill the night of the murder?*

And then there was Charlie. According to Lisa, she'd told him Mike had been harassing her. Could he have dropped her off and gone to Young's to tell him to knock it off? And could things have escalated into more than just a warning? Mild-mannered Charlie Kendall as a killer? I didn't see it, but Lisa had told me he'd been calling her constantly, too. I presented this theory to

Reed.

"You have a lot of supposes and what ifs in this. Young calling Lisa will show up. We'll have to see if she called him. As for Charlie, I don't know. Maybe, maybe not."

I was about to get another glass of wine when my phone rang. I glanced at the caller ID and groaned.

"What?" Reed asked.

"It's Schenk—again."

He didn't hesitate, but rose, snatched my phone off the coffee table, and answered.

"Hello?…yes, this is Sasha's phone…no she's not available at the moment…it doesn't matter who I am…no, I will not pass along a message. I believe she's already reported you for harassing calls and told you she's no longer interested in your crackpot suggestions."

Reed's voice was like ice and his face looked carved in granite. Clearly, my former shrink would get nowhere fast with him.

"Buddy, I have another suggestion for you, complete with instructions on how far you can cram it up your ass…take my advice. Do not call Sasha again. If you do, she'll report you to whatever professional organization that governs the rules you shrinks operate under. I don't think you really want that now, do you?… No there's been no misunderstanding. Do not call again."

He hung up, sat on the sofa and tossed my phone next to me. "There. Problem solved."

I had to laugh. "I bet Schenk is sweating bullets as to whether or not I've already contacted the American Psychiatrists Association. Linnie suggested I do so, but

I haven't gotten around to it yet."

"Do it tomorrow. This guy is a pain in the ass. If he's been this obnoxious with you imagine how many other patients he's victimized."

He had a point. I recalled my fear when he'd shown up at my house. He had been mad enough to kill, but looking back on it, he'd have never followed through. He was too much of a weenie.

Reed had leaped in and shut Schenk down in no uncertain words. A wave of contentment washed over me leaving a warm sense that he cared. But then, I'd always known Reed cared—and cared deeply. No wonder I loved him so much.

I slid closer cuddling next to him. "Are you going to Charlie's class tomorrow night?"

He slung his arm across my shoulder and hugged me tighter. "Hadn't planned on it. Why? Are you going?"

"I thought I would. After Lisa's comments about Charlie, something tells me I need to go if for no other reason than to set my mind at ease about him being a possible killer. It's probably okay, but for some reason his former model, Celine, bothers me."

"How?"

"I don't know. Maybe it's just my senses on overload. She was a blonde, but now she's not, but she may be again."

He frowned. "If you feel that unsettled, I may as well go, too, just to make sure something doesn't happen. Is Jill going?"

"Not to my knowledge. She and Lisa are on the outs. I have the feeling Jill is backing off."

"You told me that not only did Young call Lisa

numerous times, but that Charlie is also a regular phone addict."

"And Lisa is not happy about it. She likes Charlie, but said he bored her to tears. Young just pissed her off. But today at the gallery, Celine wasn't having real pleasant thoughts about Lisa or Charlie for that matter."

"At least Keith is on the job."

"Or one of his associates." I yawned as my phone rang again.

"That had better not be Schenk," Reed said with a dark look.

I picked up the cell and glanced at caller ID. "It's Jill. Hi, Jill, what's up?"

"Sorry to be calling you so late, but I wanted to thank you for talking with Lisa. We had a long heart-to-heart last night after she got home. I'm furious with Charlie for letting it slip about the drawing, but it did open an avenue of discussion. She understands my anxiety now, and although she still insists she's not in danger, promised she'll be careful when out on her own."

"That's good to hear. I'm glad I could be of some help." I paused selecting my words carefully. "I also saw Keith Simmons at the restaurant. How's that going?"

"Good. He gave me a report today. Lisa went straight to dinner with you and came right home. He also has an operative keeping tabs on her when she jogs."

"Is she going to continue modeling for Charlie?"

"For a while. I'm not too happy about that, but I didn't say anything. I promised I wouldn't come to any more classes. She in turn promised she'd have someone walk her to her car after it was over. Keith is working on having someone join the class without raising suspicion."

"I take it Lisa has no idea about this bodyguard thing."

"Good God, no! She'd have my head on a platter."

"Keith is discreet. Even if she's keeping her eyes open for potential trouble, she might not notice him or his people."

"Lisa's idea of keeping her eyes open and mine are two different things," Jill said in a dry tone. "The good news is we spent some quality time together today at the mall."

"Where's Lisa now?"

"On Beale Street with some people she met jogging. I called Keith and he said his guy is one of the group. Can't say I'm not nervous, but I do feel better."

"How's everything else?"

"As good as can be expected. I'm due to give testimony at an Internal Affairs hearing tomorrow. Won't be a fun day."

"Did you ever meet Mike's brother?" I asked remembering Brannon's comments on how long it was taking for the next of kin to show up.

"Once—and that wasn't pleasant either. All he and Mike did was argue."

"About what?"

"Money. The brother has a son who is starting college next year. I guess he and his wife are kinda short of cash and asked for a loan. Mike refused and said something about not throwing good money after bad—whatever that meant."

"Sounds like it wasn't the first time the brother

asked for money. Also sounds like the previous loans weren't repaid. Did they actually have the bad taste to argue in front of you?"

Jill hesitated. "I'm not proud of this, but when his brother arrived at the station, Mike and I were in the conference room going over a couple of cases. Mike introduced us and when the brother said, 'We have to talk,' I excused myself and left the room. I didn't, however, close the door all the way. I eavesdropped. I was looking for any reason I could find to facilitate my transfer, and since the two of them were glaring at each other, I listened. The shouting began within seconds. Mike called him a fool and his brother called him a skinflint. I only stood there for a minute or so, and then left."

"Wow. No wonder the brother is taking his time coming to deal with the funeral arrangements." Then her comment about her transfer hit home. "When did this all happen?"

"Two weeks ago. As far as I know, this guy is Mike's only relative, so I guess he'll be getting his money after all—assuming Mike refused the request."

"I'd hate for my last words spoken to a family member to be in anger. What a shame."

"I suppose. Look, Sasha, I've kept you long enough. Just wanted to say thanks and I'll be in touch."

"Right. Keep me posted on what's going on. Seems like heads are rolling fast at the Fourteenth."

"You can say that again. I just hope one of them isn't mine. I'll call you soon."

I disconnected and relayed the conversation to Reed.

"You know, Mike would certainly let his brother

into the house and turn his back."

Reed nodded. "And the brother is the only living relative."

"According to Brannon, the brother said he and Mike hadn't seen each other in five years. Yet Jill just told me she saw them together two weeks ago. I wonder if the brother hopped a flight from wherever it is he lives, rented a car, and came to the house that night."

"It sure needs checking. I've got to let Brannon know this."

While Reed made his call, I had a hunch that even though another suspect had come to light, Mike Young's killer had no familial ties.

****

The next morning, Reed was flipping pancakes while I sat sipping my first cup of coffee when his phone rang.

He answered and listened for a few seconds before a grin split his face.

"No kidding? That's great. Details, I need details...how's Linnie?... Of course, we'll be down. Is noon too soon?" He laughed. "See you then."

"The baby?" I asked as he hung up.

"A bouncing baby boy, eight pounds, twelve ounces born at five-seventeen this morning. Mother and son are doing fine."

"Whoopee!" I stood and danced around the kitchen before hugging Reed. "You're an uncle and I'm...well I'm not sure what I am, but this makes my day."

"Mine, too. My younger brother in Hernando has two boys and a girl. Now, Bill has something to brag about. He suggested we come down later. Linnie's anxious to see you."

"I'm anxious to see her and the baby."

"Let's eat and go." He turned back to the stove.

Now, Bill has something to brag about. When would it be Reed's turn?

We ate, dumped our dishes into the dishwasher, showered, dressed, and jumped in the car. In the back seat were several packages of baby gifts I'd bought over the past few months.

"Did Bill give you any clue as to what they've named him?" I asked as we swung onto Interstate 55 and headed south.

"Nope, but I can assure you Linnie wouldn't agree to Bruno, although at almost nine pounds, middle linebacker isn't off the table."

I had to laugh. "Knowing your brother, he probably has him already enrolled at Ole Miss."

"I wouldn't be surprised."

"How did you end up with the name Reed?"

"That was my mother's maiden name. How did you come by Sasha?"

"I'm not sure, but I think it was the name of a character in a book my mother was reading at the time. I'll bet Linnie has been scouring books and the Internet for names for months."

The drive took less than an hour and we pulled into the hospital parking lot a little after noon. After signing in and receiving our visitors' badges, we hustled up to the maternity ward. The nurse at the desk directed us to Linnie's room. Bill, on the phone, waved us in when I opened the door.

"Yeah, yeah, he's perfect. All the right number of fingers, toes, and whatever else. Even has some dark hair...well, he looks like me, of course!"

A derisive snort from my left had me swinging my gaze to Linnie. Her grin said it all. She looked fabulous. Her hair was held back with a headband and she wore a pink, ruffled bed jacket.

I rushed over and hugged her. "Congratulations! How are you feeling?"

"Great, now that it's over. I not only talked to God in those last few minutes, but threatened to kill my husband in the bargain. I'm told that my mind will forget the pain soon. Better be true or else he's doomed to remain an only child."

I laughed and recalled Bill's words. "So where is this perfect specimen?"

Linnie threw back the covers and inched to the side of the bed. Her floor length nightgown matched her bed jacket. Moving slowly, she slipped her feet into a pair of hospital supplied slippers. Bill ended his call and rushed to help her.

"Are you supposed to be up?" he asked in an anxious tone.

"No one said anything about staying in bed," she replied.

"I'll take them down to the nursery. You lie here and recuperate."

"I had a baby, not pneumonia. Besides, the quicker I get to moving, the faster I'll be able to go home and become a real mother."

With Bill on one side of his wife and Reed on the other, we made our way down the hallway and around the corner. Bill held up a card at the window. The nurse on duty nodded and wheeled a small bassinet over to it.

"Reed, Sasha, meet our son, Everett Anderson McIntyre," Bill announced.

"Everett," Reed said in a soft voice. "After Dad. He'd be so proud."

"We'll probably call him Andy," Linnie added.

Bill made cooing noises and silly faces at his son through the glass. The baby waved his arms and began to cry. Even with his little face all screwed up, he was gorgeous.

"So tiny," I murmured.

"I know, every time I hold him, I hope I don't drop the poor kid," Linnie said.

"Practice, practice, practice," Reed answered with a grin.

We spent the next couple of minutes admiring, cooing, and taking photos with our cells before Linnie declared she'd had enough exercise for the time being. We helped her back to the room and into the bed. When she was settled, I gave her the packages where she ooed and ahhed over everything.

Reed glanced at his watch. "I suggest we let the new parents get on with things and head back home. Are we still going to that class tonight?"

"What class?" Linnie asked, fingering a Winnie-the-Pooh bib.

I explained some about Lisa and my visions along with my doubts.

Linnie frowned. "So you're kind of keeping an eye on her at this artist's gallery?"

"For the time being, but I'm not sure I have to do so much longer. Her sister has hired Keith Simmons to take over. Remember Keith?"

"The guy who was keeping an eye on you when Jeff Hammond was running amuck?"

"That's the one. He'll do a good job until Lisa

decides to go home to St. Louis."

"You haven't mentioned this parapsychologist lately. What's going on with that?"

"He's only an occasional pain in the ass."

"He called last night, but I answered and told him what he could do with himself. I think he got the message," Reed told her.

"Have you called the medical association yet about him?" she demanded.

I shrugged. "Not yet. I may not. Like Reed said, he got the message."

"Do it," Linnie ordered. "It's guys like him that give the rest of us a bad name."

"I will." I gathered up my purse, leaned over to kiss her cheek, kissed Bill, and looked at Reed. "I'm ready when you are."

We kept the conversation light on the drive home before stopping for a late lunch at a restaurant in Germantown. I fiddled with the napkin and silverware after we gave our order.

"You're looking kind of glum," Reed said. "What's wrong?"

"Nothing. Everything. I don't know." I heaved a sigh. "I guess it was just seeing Linnie and Bill. Their lives are complete, while mine is…is…"

"Complicated?" he finished.

I shook my head. "No, unhappy. For the first time in years I'm on my own, psychically speaking. I no longer have a shrink. I'm not sure how to react to that. I'm used to a whole army of shrinks—both good and bad. I have the feeling I won't be able to cope."

He reached across the table to hold my hands. "You've had Linnie helping you. She's the best.

Silberstein was all right, but Schenk was bottom of the barrel. Maybe it's time to try coping on your own for a while. Forget about talking to a professional and talk to a friend. Talk to me."

"I'm scared. Psychiatrists have been a part of my life for so long, I'm almost afraid to let go."

He released my hands and leaned back, taking a sip from his glass of iced tea.

I sneaked into his mind. He was hurt and disappointed I hadn't expanded on his suggestion of talking to him.

"Maybe you're right. Maybe I do need to talk to someone who isn't involved with the psychic world. Perhaps talking to you is the best medicine."

He smiled as I sensed relief flood through him. "I'm here anytime you need me."

"In that case, I think I'll confess something. I didn't tell you quite the truth the other day."

"About what?" he asked with a frown.

"About when Schenk came to my house. He was worse than angry. He was incensed to the point of irrationality. He forced his way in after I told him to get out. I slipped into his mind. His exact thoughts were, 'I'm going to kill the bitch.' "

Reed's frown turned into a scowl and I sensed his anger rising like an out-of-control fire.

"Why that no-good…"

I raised my hand. "I got mad in return, not to mention scared. This time I did more than move a screwdriver. I moved him. I gathered my emotions and shoved. He flew across the floor. By the time he landed on his ass, he wasn't angry anymore, but terrified. I told him to get out or I'd send him into orbit. He left."

"A part of me wants to laugh at the image, but you need to report this son of a bitch. He's dangerous." His anger had calmed but not by much.

"I know."

"So do it."

"I will, I promise, but to be honest, I don't think he'll bother me again."

"It's not just you, it's what he might do to others."

Our food arrived cutting off further conversation along this line. I changed the subject to Linnie and the baby. Reed's phone rang as we were leaving the restaurant.

"McIntyre here...oh, really. Is he coming in?... Good. I can be there in fifteen or twenty minutes." He hung up. "There's a new witness coming in to give a statement about one of my cases. Do you mind going to Charlie's tonight alone?"

"No, that's fine. Is it the Margie Hollis case?" I still held out hope that one would be solved.

He shook his head. "No, this is one from over six years ago. Are you sure you'll be all right?"

I stood on tiptoe and kissed his chin. "I'll be fine. You go solve your case."

He pulled me close and did more than kiss my chin. "I'll be home as soon as possible. Maybe we can talk some more."

"I'd like that."

He dropped me off at the house before heading downtown. I still had several hours until leaving for the studio, so made the most of it by doing a load of laundry. I was folding the clothes when my phone rang. It was Jill.

"Am I disturbing you?"

"Not at all. What's up?"

"Are you going to Charlie's tonight?"

"I planned on it."

"When I came home from the station this afternoon, Lisa was not in the best of moods. I think she and Charlie had an argument. I was hoping you'd go as my stand in—just to make sure she's all right."

"What about Keith Simmons? Hasn't he got someone covering?"

"He said he does, but Lisa knows and likes you. If she had any problems, she wouldn't turn to a new student in the class. You don't mind, do you?"

I heard the anxiety in her voice, but couldn't slip into her mind. A cell phone wasn't a good conduit for psychic intrusions.

"Of course not."

Jill heaved a sigh. "Thanks, Sasha."

"How did it go at Internal Affairs?"

"Lots of questions about Mike and his dealing with fellow officers at the precinct. Then I had to talk to Detective Brannon again about the murder. I'm not sure he believes me. I swear to God, I didn't kill him."

"These things have a way of working out. Brannon's good. He'll find whoever killed Mike."

"I hope so. I'll let you go for now. Call me if something happens."

"Will do." I disconnected and sighed tempted to call Brannon. I dismissed that thought immediately. He wouldn't or couldn't say anything at this point in time.

Charlie's class wasn't due to begin for over an hour, but maybe I could catch him in and talk to him. If he and Lisa had argued I needed to get some vibes. I just hoped they were the right vibes.

All in all, I was getting tired of snooping in people's minds.

Chapter Twenty

I arrived at the gallery forty-five minutes before class. To kill some time, I walked up the street gazing into windows of boutiques and trying to formulate what I'd say to Charlie.

Heading back to the gallery, I stepped off the curb to cross a street. From out of nowhere, a car roared toward me. I froze.

"Lady, look out!" a man shouted. He grabbed my arm and slung me back to the sidewalk where I clutched at a parking meter. The car raced by, blew the stop sign, and disappeared.

"Are you okay?" the man asked.

Gasping for breath, I nodded. "Yeah...yeah, I think so. Thanks."

"You wanna call the cops?"

I shook my head. "Car's gone. I can't ID the make or model and didn't get a look at the driver. How about you?"

"Naw, I just saw it coming and you in its path. If I hadn't grabbed you, you'd be splattered all over the pavement. You sure you're all right? Damned asshole drivers. Probably came out of a nearby bar sloshed to the gills."

His use of imagery was less than appealing. I pulled myself upright and took a deep breath. My legs wobbled slightly and my heart pounded away at ramming speed, but I was unhurt.

"Probably. Lesson number one—don't jaywalk. Thanks again."

"Can I help you to your car?"

"No, that's all right. I'm just going to a place a couple of blocks away. I'll be fine. Really."

The man nodded and went on his way. I gathered my wits about me, made my way to the corner, and walked slowly to the gallery.

Entering the door, I gazed around. A young man with long hair, lots of gold jewelry, and a shirt open almost to his navel looked up from behind the counter.

"May I help you?"

"Uh, no, that's all right. I'm here a bit early for the class, so thought I'd look around. Where's Celine?"

"Oh, she doesn't work here anymore."

"Really? I was just in the other day. She seemed to like her job. Why did she quit?" I probed.

"I have no idea if she did. All I know is that Charlie called me this morning, told me she no longer worked for him, and asked me to cover for her. I'm Anton. If you need anything, just let me know."

I slipped into his mind. He really didn't know why Celine wasn't here. I couldn't imagine Celine not showing up to class, if for no other reason than to glare at Charlie and Lisa.

Charlie walked into the gallery from the studio.

"Sasha, you're here early."

"Yes, had some time on my hands and thought I'd look around. You have such beautiful pieces."

He smiled. "Glad you like them. Anton, the truck from the artist's supply place is out back with a delivery. Would you take care of it?"

"Are all of these yours?" I asked as his assistant exited the room.

"Some. Others are on consignment. Let me show you around."

As we walked from piece to piece, I searched for a way to question him.

"Where's Celine?"

"I fired her last night."

I stopped to stare. "Fired her? Why? I was in the other day and she seemed nice."

"Celine had a problem letting go. She demanded I boot Lisa from modeling. I told her I'd use whatever model I wanted. She got angry and said a few nasty things. I don't need a jealous former model making trouble."

My thoughts ran back to the conversation that had rattled around in my head. Could it have been Charlie and Celine?

"Is Lisa posing tonight?"

"As far as I know. Now, here's a painting that's right up your alley."

I had no problem slipping into his mind. He was not a happy camper. He was angry with Lisa and couldn't understand why she didn't want to pose for him anymore.

"I understand Lisa may be going home soon," I ventured.

"I want her to stay. She's a perfect model. I can't see how St. Louis has anything to offer."

I probed deeper into his psyche. I had a brief vision of him on a path in the woods. On my God! The jogging trail? Could the man I saw stalking Lisa have been Charlie?

"I take it you find Lisa attractive from a personal point of view, too."

"Yes, I do. I've tried to talk to her several times, but she won't take me seriously."

I made a wild guess. "Like when you followed her on the jogging path?"

"She didn't even pay any attention to me. I ran out of breath before I could catch up and say anything." He shot me a sharp look. "How do you know about that?"

I laid my hand on his arm and lied. "Lisa told me. She saw you, but didn't want to be disturbed while jogging. It's her form of relaxation."

"I see. Well, I'll talk to her again tonight. Maybe she'll see things my way. If you'll excuse me, I have to get the studio set up for the class. Come on back when you're done browsing."

He left the room abruptly, suspecting I'd been in his head. He didn't like it.

So Charlie was the man in my first vision. And here I had referred to him as harmless only a few days ago—and that I'd thought of him in a non-sexual way. Oh, boy, how wrong could I be? What about the mall? Had he also followed her there? If so, that didn't bode well for the final, more troubling scene. I'd have to make sure Lisa wasn't alone for even an instant tonight. I just hoped Keith's operative was actually in the class.

A couple of people carrying sketchpads entered and walked through to the studio. I followed. Charlie supplied things like sketchpads and easels, both the tabletop and floor variety, for amateurs like me. I selected a tabletop model along with a pad of paper and set up near the front of the room.

More students arrived—none of them Celine. I

kept an eye out for her and anyone new. So far, I noticed two people I hadn't seen the last time, but then this was only my second appearance, so how would I know? There was only one way. I slipped into their minds and quickly identified Keith's operative—a woman at a floor easel near the end of my table. She looked young, no more than twenty-five, and would arouse no suspicion with Charlie, Lisa, or anybody else.

Charlie reentered the room and greeted his students all the while checking the clock on the wall. It was almost seven and still no Lisa. I was ready to write her off as a no-show when she walked through the door.

"Thank goodness. I was beginning to think you weren't coming," Charlie said to her as she brushed past him toward the back changing room.

"Traffic," she replied in a clipped tone.

"You're here now. That's all that matters. Your clothing and props are on the table."

Lisa nodded and entered the small room closing the door behind her. Meanwhile, Charlie distributed boxes to a dozen or so attendees. There was still no sign of Celine.

"Tonight, as you can see, we will be working in that grade-school medium of colored pencils. Don't laugh. It's a valid form of art and can be very effective." He finished and returned to the small modeling platform. A chaise lounge sat in the middle of it. "I see we have a couple of new students tonight. Welcome. Why don't you introduce yourselves to the rest of the class?"

They did as requested, with the operative giving the name Connie.

"Thank you for coming. I hope you learn

something and will return," Charlie commented casting a glance at the clock, and then at the closed dressing room door.

Lisa finally appeared and her expression was not happy. She was dressed in a red satin and lace negligee. The plunging neckline left little to the imagination. The feathered slippers on her feet had four-inch high heels. Her hair was pulled back into a ponytail.

Charlie slipped behind her, pulled the hair from its holder, and fluffed it around her shoulders, then indicated the chaise. She reclined with a glare at the artist who immediately began posing her. Both arms were flung over her head. He then twisted her lower body with the fabric pulled aside to expose the long lines of her legs.

Lisa had every right to be angry. The whole effect was like something out of a whorehouse.

"I think we'll entitle tonight's exercise, 'Petulant Woman Waiting for Her Lover.' That seems appropriate, doesn't it?" He said it with a smile, but his eyes showed massive irritation.

I didn't hesitate, but entered his mind. He was disappointed Lisa didn't smile or even pretend to enjoy herself. He also sensed that tonight was her last time posing and no amount of begging would change her mind. That highly irritated him. He was going to talk to Lisa after class.

My thoughts centered on how to stay around after class without arousing suspicion. I cast a quick look toward Connie. Would she also linger? Maybe I could start a conversation and delay both our departures.

Charlie finally stopped fussing with arranging the satin negligee around Lisa's legs and turned to us.

"I want to see the shadows tonight. Shadows give depth to the material and to the model. Make her come alive on paper for me."

I glanced frequently toward the door, but Celine was nowhere to be seen. Maybe she wasn't coming.

I didn't even attempt to make an interesting drawing. Instead I slid into Lisa's mind. She was furious with Charlie and considered the costume totally inappropriate, rightfully so. His hands had once again brushed her breasts and thighs as he'd arranged the folds of the fabric, but this time he'd made eye contact with her. She knew it was no accident. As of now, all she wanted was the next two hours to be over. The only reason she'd come was because she had promised to show up.

"Very stiff, Sasha. Try to blend the darker colors into the lighter ones more gradually. Be subtle about it."

"I'm afraid I'm not very good at this."

"You'll get the hang of it soon. Practice makes perfect as the old cliché says." He may have chuckled at his comment, but his mind agreed with me.

It was a long two hours. Finally, he strode to the platform.

"That's it for tonight, ladies and gentlemen. Thank you all for coming. Just leave your pencils and pads on the tables."

Lisa broke her pose and stretched what must have been cramped muscles.

The students began filing out of the studio. I turned to introduce myself to Connie, but she was halfway out the door. Then it dawned on me that she was likely heading to her car so she could follow Lisa home.

Charlie spoke to his model with a scowl on his face. "Lisa, I'd like a word with you before you leave."

Lisa nodded and rose from the chaise.

"Goodnight, Sasha. Hope to see you next Thursday. Now, if you'll excuse me, I have to talk to Lisa for a moment." He practically shoved me through the studio door.

I looked over my shoulder. Lisa had entered the dressing room. Charlie cleaned up the tables and put the easels away.

I dawdled as the last of the students left the gallery, and then turned back to the studio. The lights were still on. I heard voices coming from the back room. Not wanting to be caught eavesdropping, I wedged my body between the wall and a large supply cabinet near the corner. By leaning forward, I could just see the door to the back room and the one heading into the gallery from the studio. I heaved a deep breath and listened.

"All right, what's going on with you?" he demanded in a loud voice.

"Charlie, I won't be returning to pose for you. You'll have to find someone else, and that includes the sculpture thing."

"Lisa, you can't mean that," Charlie replied. "I have great plans for you—for us—in the art world. I can make you famous."

"Charlie, you're a nice guy, but frankly, your attention is making me uncomfortable."

"Uncomfortable? I'm an artist. I need a muse."

"Are you kidding? That's the hokiest thing I've ever heard, and to be honest, as a pick-up line, it sucks. Besides, I'm an actress. *That* is my career—not being somebody's muse."

"I don't understand. I thought we had an agreement that you'd pose for me. I had plans for us," Charlie repeated in an astonished tone.

"I'm sorry, but I don't need to be immortalized in stone or anything else. Please, don't be mad, but I don't need to be a muse, or your lover either. It's just not in the cards."

"Why not?"

Lisa sighed. "Charlie, don't make me go into details."

"But I want details."

"We had one kiss that wasn't all that electrifying and to be brutal, you're way too old for me."

"Old?" His voice rose several octaves.

"I can see by the look on your face that possibility never occurred to you. I'm sorry if this hurts your feelings, but that's the way it is. Now, if you'll excuse me, I want to get dressed and go home."

"But you can't do this to me. You just can't."

His begging bordered on pathetic. And then it dawned on me that his words echoed those of Schenk. I shivered.

Lisa sighed. "Charlie, I'm sorry, really sorry, now I want to get dressed."

A long moment of silence ensued before he replied, "Very well. I need some air. I'll be back shortly to lock up."

I was leaning halfway around the cabinet, but now scrunched back as far as possible. Footsteps hurried from the back room, through the studio, and into the gallery. Then the little bell above the entrance tinkled signaling his exit. The sounds of someone hurrying to dress came from the small room. I tapped into Lisa enough to know she was relieved this whole thing was over.

I had no idea what to do next. Leaving sounded like the best bet. If Lisa or Charlie discovered me, they'd be furious and I'd be embarrassed. My suspicions about the artist dwindled. I'd tapped into his emotions enough to know he'd been hurt, but not angry. Frustrated, yes, but at no point did I get he planned to harm Lisa.

I slid from my hiding place when the bell tinkled again. Charlie already? I crammed myself back into my corner. Light footsteps this time crossed the floor of the gallery and the studio toward the dressing room. I sensed fury and hatred immediately.

"We need to talk," a woman's voice demanded as the door opened. Celine.

"No, we don't," Lisa replied.

"If you think I'm going to stand around with my thumb up my ass while you screw my man, you're crazy!"

"Look lady, I have never had any interest in Charlie Kendall," Lisa said. "So knock it off. He asked me to pose and I agreed, but as of tomorrow, I am going back to St. Louis."

"So you say. I'm the one who inspires him."

"Yeah, well if that's the case, how come he's been sniffing after me for the last week or so? I have the feeling Charlie finds a lot of muses. I'm this week's. You were last month's, and no amount of hair color is going to bring him back, so live with it and get out of my way!"

The footsteps this time were strong and quick. I peeked around the corner of the cabinet just in time to see Lisa enter the gallery. The bell told me she'd also left. Celine followed. She was now a blonde. Rage, jealousy, and hate filled her to capacity. She was on the edge of losing it. She paused a few steps into the studio. I pulled back, but she wasn't even thinking of looking in my direction.

"Bitch," she sputtered out loud into the empty room. "I don't believe you for an instant. He's mine and by God, he's going to stay mine."

I dared a small peek into the room. Celine reached into the pocket of her brown leather jacket and pulled something out. She held it in the palm of her hand as she stared into the empty gallery.

"No, you little whore, you are not going to screw me."

A small clicking sound followed by a louder noise made me catch my breath. A long blade appeared from the object she held. Pushing the point of the switchblade against one of the tables, she closed it and dropped it back into her pocket.

In a flash, I remembered my last vision of the blonde victim on the street. The attacker had worn a brown leather jacket with a small tear near the right elbow. I squinted at Celine, but couldn't see well enough to make a determination. It didn't matter. She was wearing a brown leather jacket, had a knife, and I knew she had murder on her mind.

What the hell do I do? I can't just let her follow Lisa and fulfill my vision. And whipping out my cell phone wasn't an option either. Besides, I'd turned it off during class.

Knowing Reed would be furious with me, I did the only thing I could. I stepped from behind the cabinet and into full view.

"Don't do it, Celine."

Her head whipped around as her hand snaked back into the jacket pocket.

"What the hell are you doing here?" she demanded in a high-pitched voice.

"It doesn't matter. Don't do it." I took several steps toward her.

Quick as a flash, she removed the knife and snapped it open. "She's not going to get away with it."

I licked my lips and prayed Charlie would come back like he said.

"She's telling you the truth. She has no interest in Charlie."

"No, lady. Everyone wants Charlie. I'm the one who keeps him going. *I'm* the one he can't do without."

I still didn't have a plan. Celine's mind was tumbling with jealousy and rage. Emotions swirled and crested like a raging river. Surely, by now Lisa had managed to make it to her car. Did I dare pull out of Celine's mind to enter Lisa's? I had no choice but to confirm if Jill's sister was safe and on her way home.

I exited Celine's head and entered Lisa's. She was standing on the sidewalk talking on the phone. Damn!

Lisa, get in the goddamned car and take off! Now!

I'm not sure if I actually communicated with her, but she ended the conversation and walked away. I hoped Keith's operative was on the ball and about to follow her home. The whole incident lasted less than five seconds.

I wasted no more time with Lisa, but returned to the problem in front of me.

"Celine, put the knife down. Get a hold of

yourself."

"No. You're a friend of hers. You kept me talking while she got away."

Her anger was now directed at me. In her mind, she charged. An instant later the actions in her head became reality.

I gathered my strength and mentally pushed her hard just like I had with Schenk a few days ago. She staggered back against a table. Her jaw dropped in surprise. She thrust herself away from the table and came at me again, the knife held in front of her. This time I sent her literally flying, her feet just off the floor. She once again crashed into the table and fell. With her mind a mass of confusion, she scrambled upright and stared with wide eyes.

"What the hell just happened?" Celine asked in a scared tone.

"Put the knife down. Now."

Before she could comply, I made sure of it by giving her wrist one hell of a mental karate chop. The knife hit the floor. I used telekinesis to kick it under a table. At the same moment, the bell above the outside door rang. A few seconds later, Charlie entered the room. He wore the same long-sleeved flannel shirt he had earlier in the evening.

"What's going on here?"

"Ask her." Celine said in a shaky voice. "She's not normal."

Charlie looked at me, and then back to Celine. "No, she's not what you and I call normal. She's special. What are you doing here, Celine?"

"You can't be interested in that little bitch. I'm the one you want," she declared. Her gaze had a pleading look.

"Sasha, what's going on?"

I gave him the details of the past few minutes. He turned back to his former model and gallery assistant.

"Celine, after my last divorce, I faced the fact that I had no capabilities regarding monogamous or lasting relationships with women. Never did. I drift like a leaf in a stream getting caught occasionally on the bank before moving on. I like you, maybe even loved you for a while. Who knows, perhaps I'll come back." He bent over to retrieve the knife from under the table, pushed the blade back in, and slipped it into his pocket. "Now, why don't I see you home?"

"To spend the night?" Celine asked in a low tone.

"We'll talk, okay?" Charlie turned to me. "Sasha, thank you for what you did. You outfoxed your vision. Why don't you leave? I've got this under control."

I gazed from him to Celine. Charlie was calm and determined to see no harm came to the volatile woman in front of him. Even Celine's head had cleared of the hate and rage. Now, she just hoped her lover would come back and that all would be well. From what I gleaned of Charlie's emotions, that was a possibility.

"Goodnight, Charlie. Take care."

I left the room, and then paused at the gallery entrance to look back. Charlie had his arm around Celine's shoulders, his lips caressing her temple. I pushed open the door, the bell tinkling as if all were right in the world. For all I knew, it was.

I rushed around the corner and gazed up the street. Only a couple of cars remained at the curb. Lisa's was not one of them. I heaved a sigh of relief. I had beaten my vision.

Chapter Twenty-One

Dog dead tired and barely able to walk, I stumbled into the house. Reed was sitting in his chair watching TV, but one look at me had him clicking the set off and leaping to his feet.

"Sasha, what's wrong?"

I rushed into his arms. They folded around me like a warm, welcoming cocoon. He steered me toward the sofa and I collapsed into the corner. He then sat next to me.

"Sasha?"

"Oh, God, Reed, it was awful." I bit back a sob and told him what had happened.

"So your vision wasn't a man, but a woman? Wonder why none of us picked up on that."

"It also proves those scenes were not necessarily connected, except for Charlie following Lisa to the park." I sat upright and wiped the remnants of moisture from my cheeks with the back of my hand.

Reed frowned. "I hope Charlie's all right. If this Celine had murder on her mind, how safe is he?"

"She adores him and I think in his own way, he feels the same. To be honest, in the last few days, I've seen Charlie Kendall in a whole new light."

"How so?"

"I always thought of him as just being there to help with my visions—drawing what I saw or dreamed. He was a non-threatening entity. But now I know he is basically a womanizer. He flits from one model to another. When he's tired of one, he moves on to another. And he has incredibly strong emotions involving them—a lust type of thing."

"I never suspected that kind of emotion from him."

"He was also shallow—selfish *and* shallow. It's all about him. Until a couple of weeks ago, I'd never bothered to tap into his mind. That day he drew the picture of Lisa, I was surprised that with all the turmoil among Jill, Mike, and the rest of us, his only thoughts were how he wanted to sculpt her. I should have delved deeper, but didn't."

Reed tucked an errant strand of hair behind my ear. "If I remember that day correctly, the emotions flying around were intense. It's no wonder you didn't tune into Charlie. Charlie Kendall is one of those people you see but don't see, if you get my drift. He blends in."

"Exactly. I didn't even do it that first night at the studio. I knew there was tension, but it was between Jill and Lisa. And then Celine came in. A lot of other people thought a lot of nasty things about her. I totally missed Charlie's reactions."

"Which tells me, you can't be right all the time."

"Looking back on it, I wonder if some of those thoughts were his."

Reed rose. "Would you like a glass of wine or some tea?"

"Wine—a big glass."

As he left the room, I had to admit he was right. I'd thought the same thing a few days ago. Visions, conversations, emotions all swirled and rushed through my mind until I was so confused I questioned my own conclusions. Not every weird dream was sinister. I blamed Schenk for some of it, but if I looked deep, I was the one who allowed this to happen. Sometimes, I was my own worst enemy.

Reed returned with two glasses of white wine. I stood, shed my jacket, and resumed my seat, taking a healthy gulp. I told him about my near miss with the car.

"You should have called the police," he said with a frown.

"I suppose, but it's too late now. I'm sorry, I didn't even ask how your night went. Did you get a statement from your witness?"

He nodded. "It gives us another avenue to pursue. I also had a talk with Brannon. He said Young's brother is in town. He admits to having been here a few weeks ago, but has an alibi for the night of the murder. He claims to have been at home with his wife in Chicago."

"Or so he says, but I guess there'd be a record if he hopped a plane and came down."

"He could have driven. It's only nine hours—less if he kept the pedal to the metal. I'm sure credit card receipts will be pulled. He'd have to fill up with gas sometime."

"Unless he had murder on his mind and paid cash. What else did Brannon have to say?" I asked.

"He said that Steve Winslett, the cop under arrest, admits he was at the house that night. Claims he and Young argued, but that Mike was alive when he left at eleven."

"Definitely after Jill. The neighbor said he heard a car pealing out around one-thirty. I wonder if anybody else from that precinct paid Mike a visit later."

"Winslett could have returned—or Jill."

I shook my head. "I still can't believe that Mike Young, asshole that he was, would turn his back on Winslett when he'd just had an argument with the guy. Doesn't make sense."

"The only thing I can think of is that he tossed Winslett out, but Winslett reentered the house, grabbed the golf club and nailed him."

I sipped more wine. "Do you think Jill will be reinstated?"

"I think if she asks for a transfer, it'll be granted in record time. If she doesn't, she'll be sitting at a desk forever, bored out of her skull."

"Bored enough to quit?"

"Possibly. That would solve the department's problem without them having to fire her. Firing her could lead to union intervention. On the other hand, who knows? She might get a promotion out of all of this. A lot of people higher up the food chain in that precinct will be transferred or take an early retirement. It smells big time."

I was about to comment when my phone rang. I fished around in my purse, found it, and glanced at the caller ID.

"Hi, Jill."

"Hi, Sasha. Lisa came home a while ago and seemed a little rattled. Said she'd told Charlie she wasn't going to pose anymore, and then had an argument with some woman. But what really creeped her out was the voice."

I held my breath. "Voice?"

"Yeah, said she had left the gallery and was talking on the phone to the director who's doing the next play

305

at her theater company when she suddenly heard this voice say to hang up and go home. She looked around and was all alone, but ended the call and raced to the car. Said she'd never been so scared in her life. Were you there? Did you see anything?"

I wasn't sure what she meant by "see," but took it literally and decided to tell her about tonight's events.

"So this Celine was the threat to my sister? Not some guy?"

"Yes. When I left the studio, Charlie had things under control. He admitted earlier that he'd followed Lisa to the park one day, but he couldn't keep up. I think we can put this one to bed. Your sister's safe and likely to remain that way."

A huge sigh sounded in my ear. "Thank God. That's one problem solved. I'm so glad you were there to help. You may have saved Lisa's life. She's going home in a couple of days. I may go with her for a change of scenery. I still don't know about my status, but can only hope things will work out."

"I hope so, too. Tell Lisa goodbye, and I hope you have a nice trip. Maybe get a new perspective on things."

"Maybe, and thanks for all you've done."

I hung up and relayed the conversation to Reed. "If she's been cleared to leave town, then I'd have to say she's no longer a suspect in Young's murder."

He shrugged. "Possibly, but she may not have said anything to the cops about going to St. Louis. She's still a suspect, but they don't have anything concrete against her right now."

I finished my wine. "Well, if nothing else, I can put those scenes of blondes out of my mind."

"But you still have that dream about Young's death to contend with."

"And that's the one I'll concentrate on starting tomorrow. Come on, let's go to bed."

An hour later after making sweet love I was still awake. Reed was right. I needed to see deeper into the nightmare of Mike's murder. I'd banished one mental killer tonight. The problem was I had a real one still out there.

****

I awoke shivering, the images from my dream still jumbled in my mind. I glanced at the clock on the nightstand—five forty. I eased out of bed keeping a close eye on Reed. He slept on.

Padding down the hall, I entered the office and turned on my laptop. I needed to record this latest vision immediately before the clarity blurred. Not that it was all that clear to begin with, but I had to get it down.

I typed in a stream of consciousness mode not bothering with punctuation or proper spelling. I'd fix it later.

"A nightmare?" Reed asked from the doorway.

I should have known he'd be here. He was a light sleeper.

"Not in the usual sense, but weird all the same."

"I'll make some coffee while you finish."

I nodded and continued my remembrances. Finished, I wandered into the kitchen just as Reed was pouring the tantalizing brew into the mugs. We sat at the table, him in his jeans and a T-shirt, and me in my T-shirt.

"Wanna talk about it?"

I nodded. "It was a jumble of stuff. First, I dreamed

Mike was here in the house. He kept trying to grab me and seemed to be angry."

"He always seemed angry."

"I once heard it said that if you dream of those who have died, it's them trying to contact you, much the same way Kathy Watson did with me about Jeff Hammond. I had the distinct impression Mike wanted to tell me something."

He sipped his coffee. "Like who killed him?"

"I think so. At any rate, I was scared and he could never catch up to me. Then the images changed and he was in his house messing with his golf clubs—you know, taking them out one by one and inspecting them. Does that sound like something a golfer would do?"

"I have no idea. I don't play. Go on. What happened next?"

I heaved a sigh and blew on the hot liquid before taking a sip.

"The images vanished, but I heard him talking—similar to the conversation of the other day—only this time I didn't hear a second party. Mike said, 'You again? I thought I told you to get lost.' Then there was a pause as though the other person were saying something. Then he continued. 'You are one hot mess, you know that? Totally out of control. So go home and quit accusing me of causing all your problems. You brought them on yourself.' Finally, there's this long pause until he had enough. I don't actually see what happens, but I can hear someone stumble as if Mike has shoved or is shoving him or her toward the door or something." I took another sip of coffee. "This is all so confusing."

"Take your time."

I shivered. "The next thing I heard were footsteps and Mike—at least I think it's Mike—screaming 'No!' Then he groaned several times. That's it. Any ideas?"

Reed's brow furrowed. "The 'you again' comment suggests it was someone who'd been there recently."

"Like Jill, Winslett or someone else from the Fourteenth—or his brother."

"Possibly. The 'out of control' part could also refer to them as could the 'bringing the problem on yourself' words. Winslett or someone from the Fourteenth for their criminal activities or Jill for her obsession with her sister."

"And why can't I hear the second person? I did the other day."

He shrugged. "The overload thing again? How long are the pauses between what Young says?"

"The first two or three aren't long, but the last one where he's like scuffling with someone is much longer. I have the impression the 'No!' is shortly after. It's obviously when he was attacked."

"Anything more on the original dream? You said something about lights and trumpets and seeing things through a waterfall."

"No, nothing. I wish I could be hypnotized. That might help, but the only person I trust to do that just had a baby."

"Schenk didn't do it?"

"He tried a couple of times, but said he didn't get anything useful. Accused me of deliberately blocking him. Looking back on it, I think he was right. Subconsciously, I didn't want to tell him. Why don't I lie down and try to bring up the death dream again?"

"Use the spare room. I'll shower and get dressed

309

then call Brannon to meet us at the station."

"Can't hurt to try."

I closed the door to the spare room and settled in on the bed. I let my mind drift over the images and sounds. An hour later, I gave up and joined Reed in the living room.

"I'm trying too hard. Nothing's coming through."

"I talked to Brannon and told him about the dream and the voices. He'll see us around ten or ten-thirty."

As I showered, I couldn't shake the feeling that everything was coming to a head. I kept my fingers crossed that perhaps re-reading the police report and anything new Brannon had might help.

****

Brannon met us in the conference room at the station. I told him about the dream and our conclusions. But he had news of his own.

"I think we're coming close to making a breakthrough in the Fourteenth," Brannon said. "The corruption case has been in the DA's hands since the arrests, but I heard from ADA Bob Hutchins this morning that one of the guys they have locked up wants to meet. Perhaps to cut a deal. Looks hopeful we might be able to put the murder to bed, too."

"How about what Sasha saw and heard last night? Did it help?" Reed asked.

"Not much. We already know pretty much how it happened. I think I'm going to get who in a short while. Shame you couldn't hear and identify the second voice."

The door opened and Bobby Jack walked in. His eyes were only slightly bloodshot, but his demeanor was upbeat. "Good morning, all. Sorry I'm late. What's the latest?"

Brannon glanced at his watch and frowned at Bobby Jack. "I'll let Reed and Sasha bring you up to date. It's not much as far as the Young case goes. I have to get back to work. A new case landed on my desk this morning. A young woman was found in an alley on the north side. You catch anything on that, Sasha?"

I shook my head. "No, sorry."

"Oh well, I'll talk to you later."

He left and closed the door behind him. Bobby Jack glared for a moment, and then rubbed his hands together.

"Okay, Sasha, let's go into this blonde woman in danger again."

"Uh, that kind of solved itself last night," I said giving him the details.

"No, no that can't be right. They must be connected. And why didn't you contact me?" His voice rose and I sensed desperation.

"Trust me, they aren't, and I figured I'd tell you today. Charlie admits to having followed Lisa to the park one day, and the person in the brown leather jacket was his assistant and former model, Celine."

"But what about the mall? You saw a man stalking a blonde woman in the parking lot."

I hated the pleading tone, but decided to tell him the hard truth.

"It was just that. A man looking at a woman. The dreams were precognitive and I was off on the jogging trail being dangerous. Charlie would never have hurt Lisa or anyone for that matter."

"The real danger was from Celine, and Sasha prevented that from happening. Charlie helped," Reed said.

"What we should be focusing on is Mike Young's murder," I added. "The killer's still out there."

Bobby Jack waved his hand in irritation. He was peeved as hell with me.

"I don't give a rat's ass about Young. He got what he deserved. Besides, we aren't in the loop on that one—at least I'm not."

Before I could reply, the door opened and a uniformed officer poked his head in. "Detective Beauregard, Lieutenant Sims wants to see you."

"Right now?" he snapped.

"That's what she said."

Bobby Jack muttered something under his breath and stalked out.

"I can't believe this," I commented to Reed. "He acted like what happened last night was a figment of my imagination."

"What I can't believe is his dismissal of a cop's murder. You'd think that would be his priority now."

"He's madder than hell that Brannon isn't sharing and that I'm working with *him*. I can tell you that right now, he is not a happy camper. In fact, the vibes this morning are strong."

"Strong how?"

"Damned strong. And getting stronger. I just can't"—I verbally stumbled searching for the right words—"separate them into any kind of logical order."

The door opened again and Charlie entered.

"How's Celine?" I asked immediately.

He shrugged. "All right. I stayed at her place last night. She'd calmed down and said she was sorry for everything."

"Charlie, that woman has real mental issues."

"I know. Maybe I do, too. I've rehired her as the manager of the gallery and will be using her as a model again. She really is one of the best I've ever had. We'll see."

"What brings you down here?" Reed asked.

"I got a phone call about half an hour ago telling me to come clean out my locker. I am officially no longer working as a sketch artist. Hello, computers. Seems one of the techno guys also does sketches. Two for one. Just thought I'd drop by on the off chance you were here and say goodbye. I take it neither of you will be returning to class."

Reed and I both shook our heads. "No, I stink at it anyway," I confirmed.

"Good luck, Charlie. Hope everything works out or you," Reed said.

Charlie nodded and left.

"Wow, he's taking Celine back. I hope I don't have a nightmare about him getting stabbed by that lunatic."

"He's a big boy. And if you do, you can always call it in to Brannon."

I shot a quick look at him. Brannon? Not Bobby Jack? I tried to probe his mind, but was shut out. I sensed he knew something I didn't. I wasn't surprised. With all the psychic shit swirling, I wasn't processing everything. Maybe he suspected Brannon would be my new contact since Bobby Jack was going into rehab.

The door once again opened and the object of my thoughts walked in, his step slow and his expression grim. He staggered to a chair and plopped down hard.

"It's over. I'm out. You're out. We're no long useful."

I looked at Reed who nodded. "When I talked to Brannon this morning, he told me the axe was going to fall on the psychic experiment."

In a way, I was relieved. "Look at it this way, now you can go get the help you need."

"A couple of cold cases and they pull the plug. It's not fair." He banged his fist on the table. "It's not fair!"

I jumped at the rage flowing through his mind.

"Bobby Jack, go to the rehab center. When you return, you'll be back on the job. It'll just be in a different department."

He glared at me. "I've got three years until retirement. Know what Sims told me? She said I'd be on a desk, shuffling papers until then. I'm being let go."

"Then you'll find something else to do. It happens all the time. Besides, it'll give you a chance to put things right with your family," Reed told him.

"Oh yeah, Cindy doesn't care. I talked to her last night. She gave me an ultimatum—either I'm in rehab by tomorrow night or she's leaving."

"Cindy cares or she wouldn't have given an ultimatum," I said in a soothing tone. His anger levels were escalating.

"If she didn't care she'd have left already," Reed added.

"What the hell do you two know? You don't care either."

I sat back feeling helpless. All of that psychic energy swirled around him—dark and foreboding.

Then it happened. Just like old times. The feeling of being filled like a water glass came over me. The edges of my vision blurred. Reed caught on immediately.

314

"Sasha?" He sat beside me and held my hand.

I went under. I came back to reality having no idea how long I'd been out.

"Reed? What happened?"

"You zoned out and started babbling about the lights, the noises, Mike, the golf club, but nothing made a lot of sense."

Bobby Jack stared. "So what did you see?"

"It was basically the same as the first time, only now, the bright lights and trumpets are louder and fade quickly. I'm not even sure they're trumpets. I hear raised voices and sense lots of rage. I may be ready to see more, but I'm just not there yet."

My former boss rose. "Now you see this. Why not yesterday, the day before, or last week when it could have done some good?"

As he stalked from the room Reed came over and gathered me into his arms. "Son of a bitch."

I drew in a ragged breath. "Don't be too hard on him. He's devastated by everything that's happened."

"Let's get out of here," he muttered. "I'll take the rest of the day off. We'll have lunch at that little restaurant over in Somerville you like so much, and then head back home. I've been meaning to clean up the garage from months. Today will be a good time to do it."

I agreed to please him, understanding full well he didn't want me to be alone. The old familiar guilt at not being able to solve all problems surfaced. God knows Bobby Jack believed I could have done more.

Chapter Twenty-Two

Oddly enough, the afternoon passed quickly while I stayed inside watching old Fred Astaire and Ginger Rogers movies. Occasionally, I heard bangs and thuds coming from the garage. I blessed Reed for giving me some space, yet being nearby in case I needed him.

In spite of the sense of peace his presence gave me, my nerves hummed, sending a tingling sensation throughout my body. I hated the *Star Wars* term "a disturbance in the force," but that's exactly what it was. The psychic air crackled with electricity. I could almost smell the ozone. Something was about to happen. Something bad. I sensed a combination of fear, anger, and sorrow.

Top Hat ended. I switched the channel to the news and wandered into the kitchen. A few minutes later, I poked my head into the garage.

"We have frozen meatballs in the freezer, bottled sauce in the pantry, a box of spaghetti, and bagged lettuce in the fridge."

Reed grinned and wiped his arm across his forehead. "Sounds like dinner to me. How are you feeling?"

"Better. I'm just sorry for Bobby Jack. He's really floundering at the moment."

"Honey, it's his problem. You can't do a thing about it."

"I know, but it just hurts to see a friend in pain."

He smiled. "Why don't you get dinner started? I'll be in shortly to shower and help."

I opened the sauce, dumped it into a pan, shook some garlic powder and oregano to the mix, and then added the meatballs. Not exactly gourmet, but it would do. I was cutting up tomatoes for a salad when a loud pounding on the front door startled me. Hurrying to answer, I looked through the sidelight and saw Bobby Jack on the stoop.

He pushed his way in as I opened the door. He was a mess. His clothes were rumpled and his hair stood on end. I didn't need to see his bloodshot eyes to tell me he was drop-dead drunk. He smelled like a distillery.

I closed the door and turned to face him.

"Oh my God, what have you done to yourself? Did you *drive*? Good heavens, let me call a cab."

He glared at me with his lips set in a thin line and his nostrils flaring. He swayed on his feet. I felt the anger filling him—anger and hatred. Fear darted through me.

"Bobby Jack?"

"You're as much to blame as the rest of them," he slurred.

"What?"

"If you'd tried harder to solve the Margie Hollis and Rafe Quillen murders, we'd still be in business. But no, you slacked off."

I slipped into his head, but his thoughts were swimming in an alcoholic haze. I sidled past him with the intent to get Reed. Maybe he could talk some sense into my former boss.

"Don't you dare walk away from me! Everybody

walks away—Lieutenant Simms, Cindy, Young, and now you. Well, I'm done being the nice guy. I'm done, do you hear me?" His voice escalated into a scream.

It was easy to read his enraged emotions, but I also caught a glimpse of him behind the wheel of a car, the accelerator floored as it roared down the street toward me stepping off the curb.

Truly frightened now, I turned just in time to see him fumbled under his jacket. A second later, I stared at the business end of a Glock. The haze in his mind turned red.

"Bobby Jack! What are you doing?" I backed toward the kitchen no longer merely frightened, but downright terrified. At the same moment, the door to the garage slammed.

"Hey, dinner smells good. Let me get—" He stopped in the doorway and gazed at the scene in front of him. "What the hell?"

The gun wavered from me to Reed. Bobby Jack fired. The bullet missed Reed's head by inches as he reeled backward. I screamed and hit the floor.

Another shot blasted into the room. The picture window behind me shattered. I no longer saw Reed. Was he on the floor like me or going for his gun in its holster hanging on the coat rack in the mudroom? I didn't stop to think. I had to do something.

Gathering my forces, I rose and mentally shoved Bobby Jack as hard as I could. He flew across the foyer, his feet a good foot off the floor, and slammed into the wall. The gun discharged a third time. I had no idea where the bullet went. Bobby Jack had regained his feet. I shoved again. He staggered back and stared at me with a horrified expression.

"Oh, my God," he cried. "What the hell have I done?"

He fumbled to open the door and ran into the night. I mentally slammed it after him and locked it.

This all took no more than a few seconds. Reed appeared with his gun.

"Are you all right?" he asked in a gasping tone, his frightened gaze following me as I pulled myself to my feet. "Where is he?"

"I'm fine. He went out the front door."

"Call nine-one-one."

I stumbled toward the kitchen as Reed passed me on his way to the front door. I never made it. I collapsed onto the floor as the vision enveloped me, and this time I saw the truth. The pieces I'd fumbled to put together the night of Mike Young's murder now slipped into place. I viewed everything and a whole lot more.

Outside, another shot echoed into the night.

****

I regained consciousness lying on the sofa, blinking my eyes to get rid of the disorientation that always followed a vision. Reed knelt beside me. One hand held mine while the other stroked my cheek. Bright blue, red, and white lights flashed through the front windows.

"Sasha? Thank God. For a moment there, I thought he'd shot you after all."

"No, it was the vision. The one from the night of Mike's murder." The fog lifted and I sobbed. "Bobby Jack killed Mike Young."

Brannon had entered the room through the open front door and now stood at the end of the sofa. A lot of people came and went. "You okay? What did you see?"

he asked.

"I viewed the action through the eyes of the killer again. The flashing lights and what sounded like trumpets were car headlights and horns blaring. The driver was jerking the steering wheel. I knew instantly the driver was Bobby Jack and that he was drunk. The rain was coming down hard. The wipers had a hard time keeping up. That's why things were blurred in the first dream. That and the fact his eyes had a hard time focusing. Then he arrived at Mike's. Mike let him in. I think Bobby Jack may have been there earlier in the evening. Could I have some water?"

Reed headed for the kitchen and returned with a bottle. I took a long swallow and tried to gather my thoughts.

"I had heard Mike's part of the conversation earlier this morning in a dream, but the upshot was, Bobby Jack came back to rail against Mike's attitude and how unfair the whole thing was. They argued and he called Mike some very nasty names. Mike finally had enough and threw him out, only he didn't lock it. Bobby Jack came back in a few seconds later."

I shuddered and drank more. "God, this is so hard."

"Take your time, Sasha," Reed said.

I inhaled a deep breath. "Mike was almost in the family room when Bobby Jack barged in. He grabbed a club out of the golf bag. This time I saw it all. He hit Mike again and again, then smashed everything he could find in the room. When it was over, he just left. I may have heard him in my dream this morning, but my mind refused to acknowledge it. At that time I couldn't accept the truth."

The same thing had happened three years ago when

Linnie had been attacked.

"Is that all?" Brannon asked.

I shook my head and swallowed a sob. "I saw Bobby Jack looking at his gun, then he put it under his chin. He's dead, isn't he?"

Reed pulled me into his arms. "Yeah. Killed himself in his car."

"We found his cell clutched in his hand. He'd pulled up a photo of his family," Brannon said.

I choked on another sob. "He was drunk and enraged, but I'm not sure if he remembered what he'd done—at least not right away. Did you seriously suspect him?"

"He was right up there on the list. His fingerprints were all over the file folders we found at Young's, not to mention the doorknob, door, and walls of the foyer."

Reed shook his head. "I was sure it was someone from his old precinct—or his partner. I guess we all hoped that. I think he remembered but didn't want to believe. His drinking accelerated after that."

"Could be," Brannon said. "Do you feel well enough to come down to the station for a formal statement?"

I nodded. Reed helped me to my feet and led me from the house. Bobby Jack's car was at the curb surrounded by forensics and photographers. I averted my head and got into Reed's car where I told him Bobby Jack also had tried to run me down. "In the hubbub that went on, I'd never told him about my dream the night of Mike's death. When I finally did he was both surprised and scared. Urged me to forget about it and concentrate on the park and mall viewings."

He sighed and nodded. "He knew you'd put it all together eventually, so must have followed you, and waited for his chance. He was probably drunk."

I shook my head and wondered how long Bobby Jack had been stalking me. "I'm not so sure about that. I think he was stone-cold sober for a change. He must have followed me from my house to the studio."

I couldn't contain my tears. Of all the dreams, of all the visions I'd had over the past three years, this was the worst. I wondered if I could ever live with them again. The drive downtown was silent, except for my sobs.

****

Four hours later, we pulled back into the driveway. All the police cars and paramedics had left. Bobby Jack's car was also gone.

Once inside the house, Reed hugged me close and kissed the top of my head. "You have no idea how scared I was when I heard that second shot and the window shatter. And then came a third shot. I almost couldn't get the gun out of the holster."

"It seemed to take forever for you to come back."

"Why did he leave? With a little concentration, he could have finished off both of us."

"I did to him what I'd done to Schenk and Celine." I gave him the details. "I think it sobered him up enough to realize it was all over."

"Thank God for telekinesis. Never thought I'd say that."

I started to laugh, and then sniffed. "What's that God awful smell?"

"I think I know." We walked into the kitchen. The meatballs and sauce were a blackened mess. "Looks like one of the officers turned off the burner and moved what was left of dinner off to the side. Are you hungry?"

"Oddly enough, I am."

"Pizza?"

"Why not? I'll pour the Chianti while you phone it in."

I managed to choke down two slices and three glasses of wine. It had been that kind of a night. Now, other things crowded my mind—like the rest of my life. We entered the living room where I turned to face him.

"So it's all over. What about us?" I asked. "What's going to happen to us?"

"What do you want to happen?"

I looked him in the eye. "I want another chance. I never stopped loving you."

He ran a finger down my cheek. "I'm not complete without you."

He let me in to probe. He was still concerned about my abilities.

"I don't think I need a parapsychologist anymore. I'll find a regular shrink to keep my head on straight, but from now on you'll be my sounding board, provided you can take what I might see or dream."

He pulled me into his arms and kissed me hard. "I can handle it. I've also decided that the cold case department isn't so bad after all. I'm never going to get back to what I had before. Who knows? I might even consider going into the private investigation field when I retire. Maybe your abilities will come in handy."

"You mean like getting back to the basics with dreams and visions? I'm all for that. I'll forget about all the telekinesis, dual consciousness, reincarnation, and astral projection stuff. Psychic abilities are like any other talent. The more you use them, the more they improve. Don't develop them and they may weaken or disappear completely."

"Oh, I don't know. Substitute the TV remote for the telekinetic screwdriver and I'm cool with that."

I had to laugh. "So now what?"

"How about we actually get married?"

I stood on tiptoe and kissed his chin. "I thought you'd never ask."

He chuckled and kissed me again. Finally, we would both be happy.

Epilogue

Reed and I were married two weeks later in a little church in Gladden, Mississippi, with Bill, Linnie, and of course, baby Andy beside us. I wore a simple sleek, white, satin floor-length dress.

"I love it," Linnie declared. "It looks like a nightgown. You are obviously ready for the wedding night."

Reed looked sexy as hell in a navy blue suit with a light blue silk shirt that matched the color of his eyes. Later that afternoon, we hopped a flight to St. Kitts.

The fallout from Bobby Jack's suicide was immediate. Any hope of keeping the gruesome details quiet like in the Jeff Hammond case was impossible. Too many people had seen the aftermath. I heard that his wife and children left town as soon as the funeral was over. I had the feeling they would not return.

Brannon told us they'd found blood on the passenger seat and floorboards of Bobby Jack's car. DNA showed it matched that of Mike Young. The murder weapon was never recovered. He'd probably tossed it into a creek or a vacant lot after he'd left Mike's house.

Jill had called me the next morning. "Bobby Jack killed Mike? I never had a clue. I'm sorry for you. I know you two were close."

"Too close as it turned out. I totally missed

everything between him and Mike. At least, you're exonerated."

She sighed. "Yes, but my career in Memphis is over. Just too much baggage. I turned in my resignation. I'm leaving tomorrow for St. Louis with Lisa. Maybe I can find a job with one of the smaller municipal police departments there."

I wished her luck. She said she'd keep in touch, but I doubted it.

It's been almost three months now and while I have had some very strange dreams, none were homicidal. The next time I have one, I'll contact the police, give them my vision, and let them deal with it.

Settling in to married life was easier than I expected. I can't wait until Reed gets home tonight so I can give him the good news. I'm pregnant and happier than I ever thought I'd be.

And that's what it's all about.

A word from the author...

I was born in Indianapolis, Indiana, but lived for many years in Memphis, Tennessee, which I now consider home. I have two adult children and seven grandchildren. After many years of living in Ft. Lauderdale, Florida, my husband and I have moved back to Memphis.

I belong to Romance Writers of America and River City Romance Writers. I'm also a member of Mystery Writers of America along with the Florida chapter of that organization.

I love writing and hope readers enjoy the journey along with me.

Thank you for purchasing
this publication of The Wild Rose Press, Inc.

If you enjoyed the story, we would appreciate your
letting others know by leaving a review.

For other wonderful stories,
please visit our on-line bookstore at
www.thewildrosepress.com.

For questions or more information
contact us at
info@thewildrosepress.com.

The Wild Rose Press, Inc.
www.thewildrosepress.com

Stay current with The Wild Rose Press, Inc.

Like us on Facebook

https://www.facebook.com/TheWildRosePress

And Follow us on Twitter
https://twitter.com/WildRosePress